Solomon's Seal

Matthew R. Hellman

BEACON
PUBLISHING GROUP

For information, or to order additional copies,
please contact:

Beacon Publishing Group
P.O. Box 41573, Charleston, S.C., 29423.
800.817.8480 / beaconpublishinggroup.com

Publisher's catalog available by request.

ISBN-13: 978-1-949472-50-9

ISBN-10: 1-949472-50-7

Published in 2019. New York, NY 10001

First Edition. Printed in the USA.

CHAPTER ONE

Mitch Stackwell stared down at the body of his friend and colleague. Roy's face and neck were unrecognizable – nearly unrecognizable as human. At least Mitch wouldn't have to break the news to a worried wife and family, but it didn't make it any less painful. He knew he would have to find whoever was responsible and put an end to this before... He took a deep breath and closed his eyes, only opening them when he knew they'd remain tear-less.

Mitch nodded to the local deacon, who lowered the coffin lid. He watched as the broken body of a man, whom he'd believed to be invincible, was wheeled away. The scent of incense, spicy and tart, hung in the vacated space.

"Are you going to be all right, Mitch?"

"Yes, your Excellency," he answered. He turned to face the other three men in the chamber. The bishop, still holding the smoking thurible, gave him a sad smile, typical of clergy trying to comfort the grieving.

To the bishop's left was Ben, whose glassy

eyes emphasized his youthful appearance. On the right, olive-skinned Reginald, looking slightly more experienced than Ben, fixed Mitch with a concerned stare.

"Can you do this alone?" Reginald asked, his English accent belying his Persian appearance.

Everything is possible with God. He'd told himself that so many times before, even offered it to doubters. But now the words were stuck in his throat. He closed his eyes and nodded.

An electronic jingling echoed off the stone and wood walls. Ben dug into a satchel near his feet and pulled out a small programmable tablet. Reginald stepped to his side and the two men peered at the device with undivided attention. Ben sucked in a deep breath before looking up. Reginald's eyes were already fixed on Mitch. "We've got another one."

"What in hell is Fang barking at?" Colin Hampton asked. He came out of his den, walking to the kitchen where he could look into the back yard and see what all the commotion was about. The dog's constant *Hoowruf, Hoowruf, Hoowruf,* had finally struck Colin's last nerve.

"I dunno," Julie answered. She peered through the kitchen window.

"If he doesn't shut up, he's going to wake the baby." He smirked at his wife.

"Too late for that," she said. "He's been

kicking a lot already. Maybe he's trying to break out." She smiled at Colin as she caressed her abdomen.

Colin gave Julie's belly a pat, stepped to the patio door and stared out at the family dog. Fang, a German Shepherd mix, was facing the edge of the hundreds of acres of New York forest that butted up against the Hampton's three-acre plot of land. Fang was low to the ground, ears laid back, tail curved between his hind legs. The barking was fierce – uncharacteristically so.

"Looks like he's locked on to something out there," Colin said.

"He's been acting weird all day," Julie said.

Hoowruf, Hoowruf, Hoowruf.

"Wonder what's got him going?" Colin scoured the tree line, but along the edge of the yard, the branches grew low and were heavily laden with leaves, forming an impenetrable wall to the vast wildlife preserve. From this distance he couldn't see past the reds, oranges and yellows of the fall foliage that wavered in the October breeze. But the dog made it clear. There was something out there.

A rapid concussion of thump-thump-thumps forewarned of incoming joy. Like a tiny linebacker, Claire, the Hampton's six-year-old daughter, charged into the kitchen, golden hair aflutter in her wake, smacking into her dad and wrapping her arms around his thighs. "Daddy, why is Fang still barking?" she asked, looking through the glass patio door. "Is there a monster?"

"I dunno," Colin laughed. "If there is, Daddy will take his sword and go scare it off." He drew the imaginary sword he wielded when he defended Princess Claire from make-believe backyard villains. Sliding the door open, he burst forth, chest puffed out, shoulders back and sword held high. He surveyed the yard briefly before marching down the four stairs that deposited him onto the field of battle.

Hoowruf, Hoowruf, Hoowruf.

The autumn sun was approaching the western horizon, peeking below the scattered clouds that were the last remnants of what had been an overcast Saturday. Its orange rays dropped shadows across the yard, stretching out a huge skeletal hand that enveloped the home, strangling it. Colin shook himself, wondering where such a morbid thought had originated. Too much T.V.

Hoowruf, Hoowruf, Hoowruf.

The damned dog wouldn't shut up. Colin started forward, determined to at least drag Fang back inside so he'd be quiet. He still couldn't see what Fang was barking at. Probably just an animal too stupid to run away, cowering just beyond the wall of leaves. So why wasn't Fang charging head-long into the brush in pursuit?

He had cut the distance between himself and Fang in half when, despite the warm front that choked the upstate region, his skin pinged with goose pimples. The hairs on the back of his neck stood erect, stopping him in his tracks. An image thrust itself into his consciousness: a flash of crimson lightning, a memory of the storm early that morning. He had awakened at the clap of wall-shuddering thunder and seen the red strobe of light that accompanied the next, and final, boom. At the time, he didn't know if he was awake, dreaming, or a little of both. He felt the same way now, like he was walking with one foot in a nightmare and the other in the waking world. Though he stood beneath a mostly clear sky, it seemed a scarlet bolt could strike him at any moment.

Grrrraaff, Grrrraaff.

Fang's racket yanked him back to himself. He could sense the dog's lips pulling back to reveal long, deadly teeth; a motivating deterrent to all but the very dumb, or the very strong. Seeing the shepherd's ferocity, he wished he had a real sword. Better yet, a gun. Fang's front feet were splayed outward, his chest near the ground and hind quarters held high. Colin made his way closer, keeping a careful watch on the shadowy tree-line.

"What is it, boy?" he said, though his voice was so weak he could hardly hear it himself.

He focused on the twitching leaves that were now only twenty feet away. Like he had switched to a black and white channel on television, the kaleidoscopic array lost its brilliance. The forest in front of him was suddenly painted in shades of gray.

He looked to either side and saw the colorful world he expected. Turning forward again, he saw the colorlessness flow closer, the green grass changing to a bleak, ash color. The darkness moved faster, enveloping Fang and silencing the barking. Colin stepped backward and snapped his arms up, as if he could defend himself from a physical blow. The shadowy wash flew towards him, too fast for him to flee. When he saw the tips of his shoes go dark, horror crashed over him like a tidal wave, driving him to one knee. He regained his feet, wanting to run, but his legs were spongy and weak. He was standing knee-deep in trepidation that seemed to be rising flood waters, threatening to drown him in terror.

A tinkling, innocent voice broke through his dismay. "Hey daddy! Did you get it?" Claire came running down the deck steps.

Dread filled his soul and he spun around. "Get back in the house," he snapped. Claire's eyes widened and her mouth sucked into a pout. "Now!" She scampered back into the house. When he turned back to the forest, Fang was gone.

The undulating wall of leaves shivered in the breeze, the colors once again vibrant, the television switched back to living color. There was no sign of Fang. No barking. No sounds of fleeing prey or Fang in a battle to the death with another animal.

"What the hell is going on?" All he knew is

he didn't want to go into that forest after the dog. He frowned and wiped a sheen of sweat from his forehead. "What? Are you afraid of shadows now?" He dried his palms on his pants. "This is stupid." He took a slow step forward, having to tear his foot from fear that was ankle-deep, sucking mud. Step by sucking step he moved forward, trying to peer into the forest.

Then the smell hit him. It was retched and strong, like diseased, rotting fish left out in the sun. He stood there staring, looking at the ground through a break in the leaves. Was something there?

He took two steps forward and saw it. A deer, lying on its side. A huge chunk had been torn from its neck, ragged bits of flesh dangling from where teeth or claws had ravaged it. Blood pulsed from the wound, flowing out to pool on the forest floor. He could see one eye, wide and filled with fear. Its front leg twitched in a feeble attempt to raise its body. It wasn't dead yet. A wound like that should kill the animal in no more than four minutes. Colin's breath quickened. He scoured the forest, looking for the predator that had done this.

Where was it? What was it?

He saw another section where the leaves were spread apart enough for him to look through, into the forest beyond. The opening was complete darkness.

The darkness moved.

In full panic, he spun away from the trees

and sprinted toward the house. He burst through the patio doorway. Julie and Claire were staring at him.

"Daddy! Where's Fang? Did he run away? You have to go find him." Her right eye started to blink as the tears fought for release. Funny. It was always just that one beautiful blue eye that gave her away, twitching, moments before her cheeks were moist with her sorrow.

His heart still thundered from the fear and flight. But as he looked down at Claire, he smiled, a broad, confident smile. "Yeah. I'll go find Fang. You head upstairs and get ready for bed." Colin gave her a hug and she trotted off and up the stairs.

"What's wrong?" Julie asked.

"Dead deer just inside the trees," he said.

"I saw you yell at Claire."

"Something just killed it. Still bleeding." Colin looked out into the yard and shrugged. "Now Fang took off."

"You think Fang killed it?" She looked into the yard.

"No. I think he was barking at whatever did kill it."

"You think it's still out there?"

"It can't be far."

"What do you think it is?" Julie asked.

"I dunno. Deer had part of its throat torn out. I could see that much." He faced his wife. "I saw something move. Something black. And it was close." He didn't mention the wave of gray or fear he'd felt. His fleeing back into the safety of the house was less than flattering.

"Bear?" Julie frowned. "No. Black bears don't eat deer."

"No. And they don't smell like whatever is out there."

Julie raised her eyes to the ceiling in the direction of Claire's bedroom. "You gonna go look for Fang?"

Colin nodded.

"Maybe you should ask Tim to go with you."

"Good idea," Colin answered. He didn't want to go into those woods alone.

"And take your gun. Just in case."

No kidding.

Colin cradled his father's old single-shot, break-action twelve gauge in his arms as he walked toward the end of the dead-end street. A quick survey of his yard had yielded no clues as to Fang's whereabouts. It was time to bring in some help.

There was only one house between the Hampton's and the end of the road. Tim Forth lived in the old colonial by himself, having lost Sharon, his wife of forty-two years just nine months earlier. They had bought the old fixer-upper a year ago so they'd have a hobby in their retirement. Nearing Tim's residence, Colin could see that all the projects were at a permanent stand-still. He walked up the long driveway, nearly thirty yards, and leaned his gun against the porch railing that spanned the front of the house. A partially used can of stain, its lid ajar, sat to the right of the front door. He let out a sigh before pounding on the half-finished oak door.

The door swung inward to reveal a solid, but somewhat stooped, bald man in his early sixties.

"Hello, Colin," Tim said. "What's up?"

"Fang's off chasing something in the woods. Maybe a bear. Smelled awful. I'm going out to look for him." He knew that Tim liked nothing more than stomping around the woods with his own dog, Zerbert. Tim and his beagle spent countless hours roaming the woods now that Sharon was gone. Colin guessed it gave the man some measure of solace.

Tim's eyebrows creased. "A bear, huh?" He glanced down at his watch, a silver Rolex that Sharon had secretly saved up for, so she could surprise him on their fortieth anniversary. "Gonna get dark soon. I'll get my gun and flashlight."

Colin walked to the backyard where he scanned the trees, looking and listening for any sign of Fang. He was glad to have Tim along on this hunt. It helped him shake off nonsensical worries. The fading sunlight burned the autumn colors and cast deep shadows that reached across the yard like the same skeletal fingers. The leafy wall on the edge of the yard was nearly impenetrable from the outside, but once you breached it, you could see a way through the trees.

"Zerbert!" Tim's voice sang out behind him. "Come on, boy!"

Colin turned to see Tim coming across the yard, his shotgun in hand. Floppy-eared Zerbert came busting out the doggy-door to run circles around his master. Ever the wise and seasoned senior, Tim offered to lead the expedition. Colin was happy to step aside and follow. Though not a fully trained hunting dog, Zerbert charged out front, eagerly seeking game.

After only a few steps, Tim turned with his face contorted in disgust. "What the hell is that smell?"

At the edge of the woods, Zerbert halted, hackles raised, and issued a low growl.

Colin caught the scent a second later, wrinkling his nose. "Yeah. Told you it was bad."

Zerbert worked the air with his nose, following the scent through the thick brush and disappearing from view. Colin heard the dog explode into a barking frenzy before falling into an abrupt and ominous silence.

Tim squinted and brought his shotgun up to his shoulder. He walked closer to the border of leaves and brush and stopped. His body remained still and rigid. Colin felt the blood drain from his face, even as he watched his neighbor's countenance pale. The inexplicable fear returned, quickening his breath and heartbeat. Both men stood motionless for several seconds, eyes combing the edge of the forest, searching. Waiting. Tim turned to face Colin, clearly more than a little anxious.

From the corner of his eye, Colin saw the shape shoot from the barrier of leaves. Blood spiraled away from the stump of the beagle's head as it toppled through the air, hitting Tim square between the shoulder blades. The widower spun around and looked down at Zerbert's bloody face.

When Tim saw the remains of his little friend lying on the grass, his face contorted with rage and despair. The anguished man charged headlong into the trees, shotgun held out like a soldier making a bayonet charge. He'd barely disappeared into the trees when Colin heard him scream out, a shotgun blast, and then nothing.

Colin took a step forward and stopped.

Tim's mangled arm flew out of the leafy wall and landed at his feet. He looked down at the face of the blood-spattered, silver Rolex. Tim had once pointed out to him that a real Rolex had a smooth, continuous-motion second-hand. Not the bouncing, one second lunge of the knock-offs. His eyes locked on that precious time-piece and watched the smooth sweep of the second-hand slide to a stop.

Colin spun and bolted toward the front yard, his shotgun in one hand like a relay baton. Tim was dead. He dared a quick look behind to see if the killer pursued and saw nothing but twitching leaves.

Fear coursed through him, pushing him to run faster.

He reached the little black-topped road and sprinted for his own house, thirty-five-year-old hamstrings tightening with every stride. To his right, he noticed something moving through the trees, paralleling his route. The sinking sun lengthened the darkness that crept toward him from both sides of the road. The thought of the shadows reaching his body filled him with dread. Up the driveway he charged into his garage, mashing the entrance button to send the big bay door on a laborious descent that defied the passage of time. Finally closed, he bolted inside.

He ran to the kitchen, dropped the shotgun on the table, grabbed the telephone, and punched 9-1-1. The line was dead. He swore aloud, slamming the phone back down on the counter-top.

"What's wrong?" Julie asked.

"Phone is out. We gotta call the cops. Something just killed Tim."

Julie gasped and covered her mouth with a hand. "Tim's dead?"

Unaware that Julie had spoken, Colin pulled his cellphone out and ranged through the house, trying in vain to get a decent signal. His road was one of several in the service shadows of the rolling hills in the Saratoga area. "Dammit! Come on," he said to the phone, knowing it was a rare day when he could get the cellphone to work.

"Where's Claire?" he asked, trying to calm his voice.

"Upstairs, playing," Julie answered. Her brows creased as she watched Colin.

"Claire," Colin called. "Come down here, honey. Hurry up." Turning to Julie he said, "We have to get out of here. Whatever killed Tim followed me through the woods. It's out there."

"What happened? What's going on?" Julie asked. When Claire came into the kitchen, Julie wrapped an arm around their daughter and pulled her close, the other arm cradling her abdomen.

Colin threw an exaggerated look at Claire and shook his head. "I'm going to get the car running and open the garage door. I'll come get you when I know it's clear." He didn't want to answer Julie's question. He wasn't sure he could.

With no windows, and little light outside to seep in around the edges of the door, the interior of the garage was near total darkness. He steadied his breath, considering what he might see when the door opened. Knowing they had to get moving, he pressed the glowing button that turned on the overhead light and began raising the double-wide door. He bent to look out through the ever-widening gap. There was nothing there. He reached in to start the car and the putrid stench assailed him, snapping his attention to the driveway. Instantly, he was pounding the garage door button, first stopping, then reversing the door.

"Hurry up, hurry up," he muttered at the slowly descending door, watching and expecting something horrible to skid under it like a player sliding into home plate. Dread saturated his body. When the door finally closed, he darted inside, locking the door behind him.

"Get upstairs and hide," he directed his little family.

"What's out there?" Julie asked.

"Just go," he said through clenched teeth.

With a concerned glare, Julie pushed Claire toward the stairs.

Grabbing the gun off the table, Colin went to the patio door and looked out into the back yard. Still wondering about Fang, he looked at the wood-line, hoping to see the happy mutt come trotting out of the forest, but expecting to see a twisted black monster or alien come striding out with a piece of his dog, or Tim, dangling from bloody jaws.

The long shadows of evening had enveloped the autumn forest, turning the colorful leaves into a threatening storm cloud that clung to the earth's surface. Dapples of yellow, crimson, and fading green highlighted the roiling, tumultuous front. The darkness devoured his backyard like a poisonous fog. And who knew what it concealed?

He tried the telephone again. Still dead. Why wasn't it working?

He turned toward the western horizon, trying to judge through the distant trees how much longer the sun would shine. Nowhere above the surrounding forest could Colin see the sun's golden curve.

The hairs on the back of his neck stood erect. Something watched him. Slowly, he slid the door open a crack so he could listen. He scanned the surrounding area for anything that might be moving. Nothing. Silence had once again smothered the confines of his yard. It seemed that the forest had succumbed to an unnatural, shadowy darkness that oozed slowly across the lawn, making its way determinedly toward Colin.

Just as the tide of shadow reached a small stand of trees and bushes in the yard, the oasis of growth that Claire pretended was her princess castle wherein her daddy had to protect her from imaginary monsters, he saw it. With fluid grace, a dark shape infiltrated the arbor strong-hold, making it an occupied, evil fortress so near his home. He caught only a flashing glimpse. Yet in that glimpse he could tell that whatever it was, walked upright on two legs.

He saw movement within the little patch of foliage, slow, deliberate movement, like a sniper looking for the perfect hide.

A blast of fear crashed into him, forcing him back a step.

The lengthening dark rolled forward more rapidly now. Fighting to control his fear, he watched. Whatever was coming was terrible, but he had to see it himself. He would see what hunted him.

The panic that had nearly taken control of him a moment ago suddenly dissipated. He flipped the switch for the deck light, but the bulb exploded, leaving the backyard a collage of grays and blacks. Confused, Colin flipped the switch several times, trying desperately to shed light on the intruder.

On the heels of the leading edge of blackness came the thing, seeking concealment within the next island of trees. There it waited. The hawk circling the brush pile.

Finally, the darkness took the house.

Without hesitation, the creature raced to the back of the family's home. Whatever it was would only have to climb the four stairs to the deck and he'd be face to face with it. Colin's frantic breathing fogged the glass, and he pulled his head back, wiping the moisture away with his sleeve.

Colin saw a black hand on the stair rail of his deck. The claws extending from each powerful digit looked akin to that of a grizzly bear, but they lacked the worn appearance from grinding through the earth. These were decidedly sharp and wicked. A dark ichor dripped from the pointed tips. What was it? Blood?

He'd seen enough. Courage dissolved like sugar in the rain. He spun around and charged for the staircase. Colin flew up the stairs, taking them two at a time, desperate to get away from the whatever it was that climbed onto his deck. Shotgun still in hand, he ducked into the master bedroom and locked the door. He flew to the master closet and slipped inside, pulling the door tight.

Julie flipped on a flashlight.

Claire was huddled near the back of the big walk-in closet, her mother standing in front of her holding a section of closet rod like a bat. Claire worked her way under the pile of clothes that had fallen to the floor.

Julie lowered the makeshift club. "What is it?"

"I dunno."

Julie bit her lower lip.

A smashing clamor echoed through the house, the sliding glass door shattering. The sound of broken glass being crushed underfoot, followed.

"You have to do something," she said.

The words echoed through his head, banging on the inner surfaces of his skull. He stared at her, seeing all his failures, his lack of doing his very best for her, willing instead to coast through life with little effort or risk. Tears slid down Julie's cheek. The salty droplets caught slivers of the flashlight beam and sparkled like falling stars in the dark closet.

His eyes fell on his daughter, Claire, who, feeding off her parent's fear, had begun to cry quietly, not quite sure what was happening. Though she huddled beneath the pile of clothes, her face radiated trust and hope. Hope that her daddy would make everything alright like he always did because Daddy always killed the monsters.

The horrible intruder thumped its way up the stairs. It did not rush, as though it wanted to prolong the terror. With each step, Colin could hear the clack of claws on the hardwood steps.

Colin and his family were about to die.

Claire let out a shriek when the creature banged on the bedroom door. His daughter's beautiful, big eyes looked up at him, expectant, hopeful. Her right eye twitched, getting ready to spring loose tears. But her eyes were also filled with confidence. Confidence that her daddy would keep them safe.

All three of them jumped when the bulb of the flashlight puffed out.

"I love you," he whispered. Then he opened the closet door and stepped out, pulling it shut behind him.

The dying light outdoors cast the entire room in a muted gray, obscuring the normally vibrant colors of the bed quilt and curtains. The silence and stillness transformed his master bedroom into a crypt. He stopped at the foot of the bed, the shotgun already aimed where he knew the creature's center of mass would appear. The beast's stench crawled under the door and filled the room.

A voice, smooth, deep and foul resonated through the closed door. "Colin, isn't it?" When

Colin failed to respond, the voice continued. "I'll make this easy for you. I just want your wife."

Colin aimed the shotgun at the source of the reprehensible words, bile rising in the back of his throat.

"There isn't need for any of you to die," the creature continued. "Give me your wife or your children will grow up without their daddy."

He could hear the smile form around the end of the threat. He wasn't about to give his wife to that thing. But then he thought of Claire. She'd grow up without a father. And their son would too, assuming he survived whatever wretched act the beast perpetrated on Julie. What kind of sick creature was out there? He tried to swallow, but his mouth had gone dry. The barrel of the gun dropped, suddenly the weight of a canon. If he fought, he would die. That thing had ripped Tim apart. The only other option was to risk his wife and unborn son, and whoever survived would know forever that he had silently condoned whatever befell them now.

"Either way, Colin, I'll have your wife for my pleasure."

The door flew open with a crash, the latch tearing through the frame in a shower of splintered wood. What cover the door had provided, was gone. The thing stepped through the mangled door frame, allowing Colin to get a better look at his doom. Its body was hairless and black. Darker than anything he'd ever seen, like looking at a murderer's soul.

Small horn-like spikes protruded from its spine. For a moment, Colin was a five-year-old boy staring with fascination at the silver-back gorilla at the zoo, blissfully unaware that the creature could smash him on the concrete like a basket of eggs. The monster, alien or demon or whatever the hell it was, stared at him with contempt and loathing. Its judging eyes were over-sized pools of chrome, broken only by a dark crescent that nearly bisected each orb. The small ebony scales that covered its body rippled like wavelets in a pond every time the thing moved. Then it smiled at him with a mouth full of yellow, oozing fangs.

Breathless, Colin raised the barrel and tightened his finger on the trigger.

According to the GPS, Mitch Stackwell was in the right area whether he liked it or not. A small cul-de-sac street, acres of trees all around, and night drowning everything in silent darkness.

He looked at the house to his left, the theoretical epicenter. It looked quiet.

Time to start asking some questions. He approached the house, climbed the front steps and gave the door a solid 'thunking' with his knuckles.

Mitch didn't need his experience to tell him something was wrong. Anyone with a soul could sense the vileness in the environment. He reconsidered knocking again, choosing instead to try and peer inside to assess the situation. Moving toward the window, his foot connected with something and he stumbled. He looked down to see a can of liquid spill onto the porch, its dark contents flowing out to stain the white boards.

The muffled roar of a firearm bit through the still evening. But it came from next door.

The black creature recoiled at the impact of the shotgun blast, buckling slightly. It fixed its mercuric eyes on Colin, allowing him to see the reflection of the closet door in those pocket-mirror-sized orbs. The gun-shot slowed the beast only for a moment. It advanced toward Colin and raised one clawed hand, ready to rip his throat out. Colin quickly changed his grip on the shotgun, wielding it like a club, and swung at the monster, the blow landing solidly on its left shoulder. It shrugged off the attack, increasing Colin's desperation. He felt his fear rising again, threatening to overcome his will to fight. But before he could turn and flee, the creature lashed out with its claws, raking across Colin's chest, spraying blood as the tiny daggers dug deep into flesh. Colin screamed out in agony. The black thing leaped at him, bearing him to the ground, clawed hands digging into his shoulders. Frantic, Colin grabbed the monster's wrists and tried rolling it off him. Twisting to his side, he saw Julie charging out of the closet to hammer its head with the closet rod. The ringing in his ears obscured Julie's scream of fear and rage as she attacked.

"No!" Colin shouted.

At once, the beast let go of Colin and jumped up, throwing Julie backward onto the bed. Weakened, Colin was unable to regain his feet. "Leave her alone," he croaked through pain clenched teeth.

The monster stared at Julie, who lay quivering on the bed. Towering over her, it settled its hands on her swollen abdomen and spoke an obscene sound with a deep, guttural voice. Julie's body fell limp, though her terror-filled eyes remained fixed on the creature. Now the dark horror continued to speak, the words unintelligible.

Though an acid-like fire burned in his chest and shoulders, Colin struggled to his elbows and grabbed one of the thing's black, scaly calves and tried tugging the hellion down. The scales felt paper-thin, but unyielding, with sharp edges that cut into Colin's hands. The monster remained un-phased as it slowly tilted its head back, opening its fang-filled mouth. Colin looked at his wife's limp body and watched in horror as a white spark of light floated reluctantly up from Julie's belly and into the monster's gaping maw.

"No! Stop it," he screamed. He punched a black thigh as hard as he could.

Then it was over. Julie screamed and flailed with her arms and legs when the thing finally stepped away from her. It regarded Colin with those metallic eyes, and he sensed its gratification. With a humorless laugh, it spun and dove through their bedroom window, the shattered pane tinkling shards of broken glass onto the carpet and out onto the lawn.

That's when everything went black.

CHAPTER TWO

A burning pain in his chest penetrated the fog that incapacitated Colin, though it faded as the sounds around him amplified. But what were the sounds? Crying? Julie and Claire. And another voice. A man's voice, one he did not recognize, was saying words that plucked at his memories. He was a sixteen-year-old kid, watching as a priest recited something at the bedside of his foster-mother's dying father. Having been raised Lutheran, he was unfamiliar with the ritual, so he paid close attention to the words the priest spoke. The same words he heard now. The Last Rites.

Panicked and horrified, he opened his eyes to see a middle-aged man with dark hair bending over him, one hand planted on Colin's forehead. He swatted the hand away.

The man's green eyes grew wide and Colin heard a squeal of shock and pleasure from his daughter. Julie and Claire were suddenly hugging him as he laid on the floor, the stranger blocked from view.

"Oh, thank God," Julie said.

"Daddy!"

The man said, "This can't be."

"We thought you were dead," Julie whispered. "There was so much blood."

"Where'd it go?" Colin asked, looking around. "Is it gone?" He struggled to a sitting position, still hugging Claire to his side.

Julie nodded, a worried smile on her face. "We gotta call the cops. Tim..." He trailed off, not wanting to say too much in front of Claire and the stranger.

Julie shook her head. "Phones are still down."

"Dammit!" Colin complained. "We can go down to the police department and —"

"Hold on a second," the stranger said. Then he ejected the spent shell from the shotgun before laying it down empty.

This was the man he'd heard reciting Last Rites? He didn't look like a priest, but rather a survivor in a post-apocalyptic world, wearing a leather jacket with linoleum strips sewn to it like weird, quixotic armor. Colin's brows wrinkled, and he looked at Julie.

"He came running in just after that thing took off," Julie provided.

"Who are you?" Colin demanded.

"Father Mitch Stackwell. Before we go to the police, we have to talk."

"Why?" Colin asked, annoyed.

"After our conversation, we can decide on

the best course of action. I have some questions for you too. I really don't know why you aren't dead. Though I'm glad you're not," he added. With a weak smile, he reached forward toward Colin's shredded shirt. "May I?"

Thoroughly confused, Colin nodded, unsure of what else to say. Mitch pulled the torn fabric away from Colin's chest. Bright pink scars stood out on his skin.

"It's a miracle." Mitch locked eyes with Colin. "A bona-fide miracle." He stood up and held out a hand to help Colin to his feet at which point Colin introduced himself and his family. Mitch looked around the blood-spattered room and then down at Claire, who clung to her daddy's waist.

"Maybe we should go downstairs?"

Julie settled Claire in front of her favorite movie with some mac-and-cheese in the family room and they resumed their conversation in the kitchen, the cool evening air sweeping in through the shattered door.

"What happened, Father?" Colin asked.

"First, please just call me Mitch. As to what happened..." Mitch paused, his eyebrows raised for a moment. "You were attacked by a demon."

"That was a demon? What the hell was it doing in our house?"

"You believe me?"

"Maybe. Frankly, I just saw something that I've never seen before. I thought it was an alien. But your explanation makes as much sense."

"I was trying to find it and exorcise it back to Hell," Mitch said.

"Did you?" Colin asked.

"No. It took off, and I had to get in here. I heard the gun-shot and feared the worst. When I came inside, I witnessed a miracle." He gestured to Colin's chest.

"We thought you were dead," Julie said.

"Usually," Mitch said, "anything more than a superficial scratch from a demon kills the victim after only a few minutes. We call it Demon's Wrath."

Colin rubbed his face with his hands, squeezing his eyes shut. "Wait a minute. A demon from Hell attacked me, and somehow I miraculously survived? I thought demons were spirits, like ghosts."

"Normally, they are. Someone's bringing them into the physical world."

"Why would anyone do that?" Julie asked.

"When I find out, maybe I can stop them."

"Physical world?" Colin scratched his head. "This is too much."

"You had a storm this morning, didn't you?" Mitch asked.

Colin nodded. It had awakened him with its roaring thunder and lightning. Red lightning.

"It wasn't your average storm," Mitch said. "It was a meta-quantum rift, a breaching of the barrier between our world and theirs. Some very smart people have figured out how to detect them."

"You've got to be kidding," Colin said. "Why would someone drop a demon in my backyard?"

"He probably wanted it somewhere else."

Colin's head swam. This was a lot of crazy news. Crazy news with too much potential for truth.

"But something even more unusual happened here," Mitch said. "We've no record of a demon ever attacking a family. They usually don't try to kill humans unless they are attacked themselves. What exactly happened?"

Colin relayed the details of what led to the demon attacking them in their home, finishing with the thing latching onto Julie's baby-belly.

Mitch dropped into a chair, his shoulders drooping, face pale. Julie and Colin exchanged concerned glances.

"What's the matter?" Colin asked.

Mitch shook his head, rubbing his jaw. "I know why he attacked your family."

Colin and Julie watched the priest as he sat silent. "You going to share it with us?"

"I'd really rather not," Mitch said. Then after a moment, "But, I have to." The priest drew in a heavy breath and raised his eyes, face grim. "The demon stole your baby's soul."

Julie covered her mouth with her hands, sobbing and trying to catch her breath.

Colin's head dropped. He reached an arm around Julie and pulled her close. A tear trailing down his cheeks.

"When are you due?"

"In ten days," Julie said, her voice barely a whisper.

"Stole our son's soul?" Colin said. "Why?"

Mitch just shook his head.

"Can we save him?" Julie asked.

"We have to exorcise that demon before you give birth."

"Well, get after it!" Julie demanded.

"We will." Mitch stood up and stared out the surviving patio door into the dark back-yard. For a moment, he stood there, motionless. When he turned to face them again, his countenance was authoritative and determined. "Colin. You need to come with me."

Colin recoiled. "Me? Don't you have a bunch of guys at the Vatican for this?"

"God spared you from the Demon's Wrath. And he let me witness it. I think God has a purpose for you: to help me." After a moment he said, "Or for me to help you."

"I'm not even Catholic. I'm definitely not an exorcist. And what if that thing comes back?"

Julie leaned forward. "You said that you have to exorcise it before I give birth. What happens if I have the baby first?"

Mitch took a deep breath and turned away.

Finally, he turned to face the concerned parents but could only look at their feet. "If we don't exorcise the demon before you give birth, the child will be permanently possessed."

Julie croaked out a groan and slouched against Colin's arm. Without looking up, Colin said, "What does that mean?"

"Short of death, we will not be able to free your child from the demonic soul that possesses him."

"How do you know?" Julie asked, her expression pained.

"Because we have a documented occurrence of this happening once before." He raised his head and looked at the distraught parents. "And it took us fifty-six years to fix it."

Colin didn't like the sound of that. He turned and pulled Julie against his chest, both fighting a new round of tears. "What happened?"

"It's in the past. Right now, we have to find that demon."

"And for some reason you think that I need to go along to help you?"

Mitch yanked up Colin's shirt and pointed to the fresh scars. "God gave you a special gift and brought us together so we could prevent this catastrophe."

Julie looked up at her husband. "Colin, you have to go."

Like many times in the recent past, she tried

to push him to action – an action Colin wasn't quite convinced was the best course. If the demon came back, he'd have to defend them again. He didn't have the slightest idea how to find the damned thing, and he was completely unaware of how to conduct an exorcism if they did find it. What help could he possibly be? He gave Mitch a hard look. "How do we know you're even telling the truth? You could be some nut."

Mitch returned the stern glare. "You fought the beast. Have you ever seen anything like that? Ever?"

"No. But it could be an alien or something." He remembered how the creature drew the glowing spark up into its mouth from Julie's abdomen. Mitch was telling the truth, but he wanted some other explanation.

"Did you see a flying saucer?" Mitch asked, eyebrows raised.

"No."

"And there was a brief, violent storm early this morning, right?"

Colin nodded.

"With red lightning?"

Colin squinted up at the priest. "Yeah," he answered, recalling being awakened by the flash and thunder. He hadn't mentioned the odd color of the lightning to Mitch.

"The meta-quantum rift. And he wasn't the first demon. In fact, he was the third."

Julie's head snapped up. "There are three of those things here?"

"Not any more. He's the only one now. But he's my primary concern. Colin, if you and I don't take that thing out in the next ten days, we won't be able to save your little boy."

Colin looked to his wife, then stared at her baby-belly. He reached out one hand and caressed the bulge, wondering at the miracle that dwelt within. The miracle that could become a nightmare. He sucked in a deep breath and drew himself up to his full height. "How soon do we leave?"

CHAPTER THREE

Apophis had been shocked by the impact that his legs absorbed when he leaped from the window of the house. This was his first time in physical form on Earth. Up until now, his entire existence had been as an ethereal spirit. Gravity had meant nothing to him. But now it showed him that he did have limitations, despite his physical superiority to humans. Standing where he'd landed, he had immediately noticed the human who stood at the yard's edge. At the time, he already knew the man's identity. That was the knowledge that had sent him running. Two of the demon's kind had already been sent reeling back into Hell where the pain of their damned existence reignited like a spark drenched with gasoline. Neither of them had been a soul-thief, like Apophis. Not many other demons were. Which made his mission that much more important. With the precious cargo he carried, Apophis could not become a victim of that miserable exorcist.

Solely concerned with his own survival, Apophis had fled into the confines of the dark forest. He waited and watched, trying to determine if the man was pursuing him. Though it appeared he'd eluded the hunter, he slunk through the shadows quietly, moving ever deeper into the protective darkness.

Strange new scents assailed him. With burning jealousy, he realized that none of them were rancid. The moist, rich smells of earth mixed with the crisp, biting tang of dead leaves were carried to him on clean, refreshing breaths of cool wind. He could smell the trunks of the surrounding trees, the sweet and smoky maples, and the spice of the pines. All these wonderful scents for undeserving men who should smell only the rot of death, and blood, and smoke. Fetid odors that he hoped he could bring to mankind in great quantity.

The one scent he didn't detect was that of the exorcist.

Convinced that there was no immediate threat, Apophis stopped to survey his surroundings and take stock of his situation. A curious feeling permeated his being, one he'd never experienced in the presence of mortal man. Though he'd wanted to kill the exorcist he'd seen, he found that he himself was at risk. He knew the human was capable of ending his physical existence, sending him back into the Abyss, and he did not want that. In fact, with each passing hour he found that he actively *feared* that.

While in his spirit form, Apophis could do as he pleased around mortal men. They could not hurt him. In fact, they never acknowledged his existence, even as he prodded and subtly influenced their actions, causing them to commit all degrees of evil acts.

But now in this physical body, bright light caused him pain, his movements were very limited, and he felt fear – and excitement. He knew these to be human emotions, a sign of weakness. But the excitement he felt now, knowing what it meant to carry this unborn soul, was extremely satisfying. The debt that would be owed to him if he succeeded would be immeasurable. He'd calculated his entrance to this world perfectly. Though he'd had to wait for darkness, it was worth the physical pain he'd endured to resist the draw of the summoner's rite, to steal this little soul. Now he was free to respond to the pull of the ritual that attracted him south.

Apophis frowned. By now he should have felt the death of the man he'd just fought, felt his pathetic soul disconnect from his weak body. But there was nothing. He had severely wounded the worthless waste of a creature. The Demon's Wrath should have taken him by now. And still he felt nothing. Why was the man still alive? It was a question that had no answer, and one that didn't need an answer. Apophis needed to avoid the exorcist before it was too late, and he would earn a significant crown in his world.

Seth Myska's gray eyes scoured the map displayed on his computer screen, searching for the highlighted area the software displayed over the location of interest. He wasn't sure how the hell this software worked, but apparently it did.

"Where'd it go?"

The question was asked with biting, impatient words. Seth bristled. Didn't *he* realize that summoning demons was not something just anyone could do, much less bring them *physically* into existence? How he'd been chosen for this was a mystery, but Seth was willing to take advantage and benefit in any way he could.

"Looks like somewhere up-state, near Saratoga Springs," Seth said aloud, running a weathered hand through his stringy brown hair. In his thirty-two years, Seth had never been to the small, upstate city, but he'd heard it was nice. Probably not so much now, with a demon running around.

Seth had thrown himself into researching the sorcery necessary to manifest a demon in the physical plane. To his delight, he found that he was provided nearly unlimited financial resources, throwing down a credit card that was somehow paid off. He purchased books and talismans and anything else he desired like booze and hookers. The latter being paid for with cash advances on the card.

And as promised, no one bothered him or

interfered.

But that was before he completed the first material summoning. Having been able to summon spirits for several years, Seth hadn't given much thought to the ritualistic nuances necessary to bring a demon into the physical plane. And to make it appear exactly where he wanted it. He remembered seeing something about it in one of the documents he'd read, but certainly hadn't put enough credence into it. Now on his third demon, and with it coming into existence nearly two hundred miles away, his superior was losing his patience and, in Seth's opinion, starting to get growly. This was nerve-wracking enough without the added pressure.

From the shadows behind him the voice said, "What seems to be the problem? I thought you could do this? Maybe you aren't as strong as I thought."

Seth never was one to appreciate authority, no matter what form it came in. But this time... this time he wanted to please, to be successful. Maybe because of the material and carnal rewards that would be involved. And as much as he didn't want to admit it, there was the element of fear if he failed.

Clearing his throat he said, "This one hasn't been exorcised yet. So it should be making its way here."

"When it gets here, you know how to get hold of me," the voice commanded. "And don't give up. I'll make it worth the effort."

Seth thought he heard a door open and close, but couldn't be sure. He suddenly knew he was alone. He could still smell the unique scent drifting through the cool air. Though part of him was glad to be left alone, he didn't relish the thought of being in this dark warehouse by himself when a demon showed up in the flesh.

He looked again at the computer screen, wondering to himself how long it would take the hellion to arrive here in the city, and hoping this one wasn't exorcised before it arrived. Seth had no idea that when he brought one of the fiends into the human plane, he would be bound to it in such a way as to cause him such excruciating pain when it was banished. When the first one had met its end, he thought the creature was ripping his body apart from afar with supernatural powers. He'd never experienced pain like that. But when it was over, he was sure the demon was gone, sent back to the Abyss. Someone had exorcised it. He would like to get his hands on whoever was responsible for the exorcisms and kill him outright because the only thing more painful than that first loss, was the second. Seth was not anxious to find out what the third would feel like.

Of course, the alternative didn't seem much better, to be face-to-face with an actual demon. When he had dealt with the spirit world in the past, every transaction was a barter, or a request, hoping that the spiritual entity would comply and lend its aid. Losing negotiations with a demon in physical form may not end well at all.

But right now, there was nothing to do but review his books and papers, trying again to decipher how he could pinpoint manifesting a devil. He prepared himself for a long night.

CHAPTER FOUR

Colin kissed Claire as he hugged her by the front door, telling her he had to go on a business trip, hoping silently that he would see her again. The few times he'd had to travel for work in the past, she'd not been able to hide her tears. This time was worse, nearly breaking Colin's resolve. Putting on a calm face, he let her go. He gave Julie a light kiss and asked her to wish him luck. She did, though her voice quavered.

Now that the phones were restored, about a half-hour after Colin and Mitch left, Julie would call the police and tell them that her dog was gone and that she hadn't seen her neighbor or his dog all day too. That would set her up to request they conduct a welfare check on him "to make sure he was okay". Obviously, he wasn't, and the cops needed to be involved. Then she would take Claire and stay with her mother who lived on the other side of town. The widow would appreciate the company.

It was well past nine o'clock when Mitch and Colin climbed into Mitch's Jeep to start the three-hour drive to New York, an unexplained destination determined by Mitch. As they pulled out of the small neighborhood, Colin stared out the side window into the darkness.

"I'm glad you decided to come along," Mitch said.

Without turning his head, Colin said, "Julie wouldn't have it any other way."

"What about you? How would you have it?"

Colin shrugged. "I gotta save my family." He shook his head. "But I'm not sure how much help I'll be."

"I can really use your help," Mitch said. His voice was quieter than usual.

Colin scowled. "I was never much of a fighter."

"How so? You took on that demon and survived."

"You said yourself that I should be dead. I fought that thing because there was no other choice."

"That may be," Mitch said. "But this time you won't be fighting it on your own. And we know how to kill it."

Colin fixed Mitch with a hard stare. "Right. I'm a mediocre computer salesman whose wife thinks I've given up on life. I'm the hero you need to help you hunt down a demon."

"Geez, Colin. You're starting to shake my confidence." Mitch laughed. "You don't understand. You're alive for a reason. I found you for a reason.

Julie encouraged you to come with me because she believes in you. God always has a plan and I believe this is how you fit into it."

Colin massaged his forehead. "So how do we go about killing this thing?" Skepticism still bittered his voice.

Mitch's eyes never left the road in front of them. He took his time answering. "It's not so much killing as it is exorcising. We just have to control the demon long enough for me to conduct the exorcism ritual. Luckily, when they are in physical form, the ritual is short and sweet."

Colin took a deep breath. "How do we control them, borrow one of the Ghostbusters' proton guns?"

"Grab that black duffel bag in the back seat and take a look inside."

Colin looked over his shoulder and scanned the floor and seat, trying to locate the bag in the dark. Finally, he reached back on the floor behind Mitch where his fingers closed on a rough, canvas-like sack. He hoisted the bag and set it on his lap. Looking inside, he found several moderately ornate daggers, each ensconced in its own dark velvet bag. He grabbed one and held it up to examine it. This particular knife was completely made of wood, though the blade had been honed down to some semblance of an edge.

"A wooden stake through the heart?" he asked, eyebrows arched.

Mitch laughed. "I wish. You grabbed the Palo Santo dagger. Palo Santo is thought of as holy wood in some parts of South America. At any rate, those are all sanctified weapons. And they are very old. *Very* old. You can carry that one if you'd like, it's just as good as any of the bronze or iron ones."

"So we just stab 'em?"

"No. Those knives can't kill a demon, just help pin 'em down so I can exorcise them. We'll each want..." His voice caught for a moment. "Both of us will have to stab in nice and solid, to weaken it." He exhaled. "But it will still be dangerous."

Colin's head snapped around. "Pin 'em down? Stab in solid?" he asked, his voice rising. "How long do we have to 'pin 'em down'?"

Mitch looked at Colin, his face going hard. "As long as it takes. Usually less than two minutes, if I can get through the Rite without them tearing me open."

Colin closed his eyes and rubbed his face with both hands. "Oh boy. What the hell am I doing here?"

"How did you think we were going to kill them, wave a magic wand?" Mitch's voice took on an edge.

"I guess I didn't really think about it. Don't you have a special gun or something? And why are we the only ones out trying to kill these things? Can't we call in the Army or something?"

Mitch scoffed. "First of all, you'd want to

call the Marines, not the Army," he said with a snarky smile. "But, yeah. I can see it now; 'Mr. President, we need you to deploy the Marines in and around New York city. Why? To battle demons.' As if they'd do any good. Can't kill a demon with mortal weapons. As for your question about the guns... I do have one gun that has been sanctified for battling demons, but it has never been successfully tested, and..."

"And what?"

"It's pretty old too," Mitch said shrugging. "It's actually a flintlock pistol. One shot."

Colin stared at Mitch in the dark interior of the Jeep. "Are you freaking kidding me? You mean to tell me that with all the damned automatics being used to gun down kids, shoppers, co-workers and what not, the best you can come up with is a muzzle-loader?" Colin tipped his head back and stared at the ceiling. "Why not something current, and maybe... useful?"

Mitch shook his head, annoyed. "It takes a very special saint to be able to bless a weapon and the Vatican doesn't believe such a person has actually existed since the late seventeenth century. We just haven't been able to see if this one works yet. My partner used it on the last one but missed. So we don't know if it'll work. Hopefully, we'll get another opportunity. We used knives on the first one, then we got the gun and tried it on the second. Things probably would have..." The priest gave a disgusted grunt.

Colin turned to look at Mitch, respect and a touch of fear in his eyes. It was unbelievable to think that the man sitting next to him had fought and vanquished two demons already. "You and your partner already took two of these things out with just some knives? I guess three against one are better odds. Who's your partner? Are we picking him up somewhere?"

The exorcist stared forward, a blank look on his face. Colin watched him patiently, waiting for an answer. Finally, he said, "No. We're not picking him up."

Colin picked up on the unspoken message but needed to hear it. "Things didn't go well?"

A barely perceptible shake of Mitch's head was followed by, "No. It caught him with its claws along his neck and face. He," he swallowed. "Roy and I had high hopes for the gun. So when he missed, he didn't have his knife ready fast enough."

Colin nodded, a sick feeling developing in his belly.

"Not that he couldn't shoot. But an old muzzle-loader, with a ball, and the adrenaline..." The sad priest shook his head. "Just didn't work out. The 'Demon's Wrath' took him a few minutes after we finished the exorcism."

"'Demon's Wrath'. That's what should have killed me."

Mitch's head bobbed. Then he turned to

Colin. "That's why you are very special."

"And you don't have another partner?"

"I have you. And you have what we call a charismatic gift. A gift from God. It's why you didn't die."

Colin examined the blackness of the roadside. So, someone who was trained for this had already been killed in action. That was not a comforting thought. Now here he was, second string. He looked at the wooden dagger in his hand then slipped it back into the sack, carefully placing the bag in the back-seat. He reached up and rubbed the raised scars across his chest. At least he survived. Apparently because of a God-given gift, the likes of which he'd never heard of.

"You know," he began, "I haven't been trained for any of this. And even if the 'Demon's Wrath' didn't kill me, I really don't want to go through that again. It hurt like hell. No pun intended."

Nodding, Mitch said, "That's what the coat is for. I have three of them. One should fit you."

"Is that the weird leather coat you had on? What was that, linoleum sewn onto it?"

Mitch's eyes sparkled to life. "Yes sir. I learned that from a big game hunter for going after leopards. I made them up after I discharged and went to Africa on a mission trip and got out in the bush once in a while. Was glad I had it when we dealt with those first two demons. I'd probably be dead without that coat."

"Why not just wear chain-mail?"

Mitch glanced quickly at Colin, pursing his lips. "Because I haven't got any chain-mail. This all came about very quickly. It's not really something we were expecting. But chain-mail is something I intend to make a note of in my reports, because yes, that would work pretty darn good." Looking back at the road he continued. "Now, I know how to engage the creatures with a knife, so I think we'll have you carry the pistol. You ever shoot a pistol?"

"Not a flint-lock," Colin answered, an uneasy edge to his voice. "Do we really want to go with the pistol?" He didn't have to add, *because it didn't work out too well for your partner.*

"Yes. I'll be right there with you. And prepared to intercept if you miss." His features wrinkled. "I wasn't thinking straight last time. I was waiting to see a miracle or something. I lost my objectivity." He threw a reassuring look at Colin. "Don't worry about the pistol. It's the same basic thing as the new ones. Just less accurate."

Colin nodded, a small measure of tension dissipating. He still had a lot of reservations about this impromptu mission but having a gun might help, *if* he could hit his target.

Mitch regarded Colin for a moment. "You said that getting cut up by the demon hurt a lot. I've studied demons a long time. Immunity to their soul-rending is unbelievably rare. How did you resist it?"

Colin shrugged. "I don't know. I'm just a plain guy."

Mitch furrowed his brow. "Have you had any extraordinary experiences in your life? Meet anyone who gave you an unusual blessing or had a spiritual experience?"

Colin shook his head. "The only unusual thing I can even think of is that my parents said that I almost died when I was born."

The priest's head snapped around. "Almost died, or did die?"

"They said 'almost'. A nurse gave me mouth-to-mouth and got me going again."

"Do you happen to know the nurse's name?" Mitch asked, eyebrows arched.

Colin gave him an annoyed scowl. "Sorry, I seem to have forgotten because I was zero. Really? If the hospital wasn't the one we use now, I wouldn't even know its name."

Mitch shrugged sheepishly. "I thought maybe your parents would have told you."

Colin nodded in concession. "If they did, I forgot. Do you think her name is important?"

"Who knows? If I'd known her name... well, never mind. Maybe something happened then that resulted in your resilience."

"I don't know what you want me to say," Colin said. "There's nothing special about me. I'm a frigging computer salesman who can't even get promoted. I hardly ever go to church, I never pray, and... ah, screw it."

Mitch fell silent at Colin's negative outburst. Colin stared through the passenger window into the darkness, wondering why he'd survived his battle with the demon. Did God really intervene to save him for some reason? Though he tried to be a good man, he was hardly worth personal attention from the Almighty.

After several moments of awkward silence, Mitch threw up his hand, brushing off the subject. "I dunno. I'll just take it as a needed blessing for now."

Colin sighed. Blessing or a curse?

Sergeant Sean O'Malley was working late tonight, called in because of a welfare check that proved anything but well. Something had gone horribly wrong for a man on the east side of Saratoga Springs. Walking past the 911 operator's area, he overheard something odd.

"A bigfoot? Really? Where did you see it?" Saratoga Springs Sheriff's dispatch asked the caller. "Between Saratoga Lake and the Saratoga Battlefield. Southbound. Yes, I've got it. We'll send a car that direction."

"What the hell was that all about?" O'Malley asked the dispatcher.

"Someone thinks they saw a bigfoot run across Seventy-one. Scared the heck out of 'em."

O'Malley shook his head. "People are nuts.

Drunk probably saw a racoon." A dismembered male. Bigfoot. Sometimes he thought his job couldn't get any weirder.

"I need to ask you some more questions about the demon at your house," Mitch said. "Did you notice anything unusual about it?"

"Other than there was an actual demon, big black and scary looking, stalking me and my family in my house after it killed my neighbor? You mean other than that?"

"All right. Poorly worded. Let me explain. Demons, in physical form have strengths and weaknesses. Think of it like their super-power and their 'kryptonite'. Did you feel any sort of intrusion into your mind? Hear voices? Hallucinate? Feel uncontrollably weak? Anything along those lines?"

"It scared the hell out of me before I even laid eyes on it. And it smelled bad."

"They all smell bad," Mitch said. He wrinkled his nose. "But you hadn't even seen it and it frightened you?"

"When I went into the backyard to see what Fang was barking at, I got this feeling like I was being stalked by a tiger. That's when I smelled it the first time."

In the light of the dashboard, Colin could see Mitch crinkle his eyebrows. "You walked out, presumably right towards it, but it didn't reveal itself?"

"No. I guess it stayed in the woods. Then, when I went over to Tim's, my neighbor, he went in there after it with his shotgun — we didn't know what it was yet —and that's when it killed him." Once again, he relayed how the demon ended up in their house, paying close attention to when he felt the most frightened.

"I saw it when it jumped out your window. It frightened me too." He was silent for a moment. "Maybe it causes fear or panic in people. But not so much that it can't be overcome, if both you and your neighbor were able to attack it. That's good, but something we can't dismiss either. It would be very bad if either of us were to freeze up when we went to kill it."

"That's not entirely encouraging, Father."

"If we hide from the truth, we are more likely to be destroyed ourselves. And please, just call me Mitch."

Colin was thankful that in the dark of the vehicle Mitch couldn't see the worry that sculpted his features.

"What about you? Are you immune to their scratches?"

"No. I'm not. Hence the crazy coats. Superficial scratches will just cause a lot of pain. But if I get a deep wound... Of course, neither one of us could survive if they rip out something important."

Colin's head snapped around to look at Mitch's profile. "What? Seriously? They can rip us apart?" His head tipped back and then rolled to the side as realization set in. "Of course they can. Tim's arm." His chin dropped to his chest.

"I'm sorry. But you need to know the truth. These things are bad to the bone."

"What have I gotten myself into?" A toxic, sick feeling washed over him. He looked at Mitch out of the corner of his eye. What if Mitch was wrong about the soul? He hadn't talked to a real priest before taking off with this guy. Was Mitch wrong about everything? What if he'd just made it up so he'd have another partner, demon-fodder as it were? It felt like the car had grown darker in the last several seconds and his head reeled. Was he doing the right thing?

"You've gotten yourself into God's service," Mitch answered.

Colin stared blankly at the floor, thoughts of never seeing his little family again cluttering his mind. He couldn't let Claire experience anything like what had befallen him when he was fifteen, suddenly left in charge of his brother and sister. Maybe he was better off going back home and taking care of them, while Mitch, who was clearly trained in this kind of thing, took care of business. And what if he just got in the way? Should he risk his life and his family's welfare on the word of this guy he just met? Right now, his pregnant wife, his family, was at home, unprotected.

"What if that thing goes after Julie and Claire? I should be there to protect them."

"He won't. He needs Julie to survive and give birth. Besides, he's being drawn to the sorcerer. He has to complete the ritual."

"Do you really think I'm going to be any help at all?"

"I do," Mitch answered. Mitch glanced over at Colin, contemplative. Finally he said, "Do you want out? This isn't something you 'kinda' do. If you aren't fully dedicated to this effort, I can drop you at the nearest rest stop."

Colin dropped his chin to his chest. "Yeah. Maybe you should."

Mitch tightened his lips but nodded his head. They rode in silence the ten miles to the next rest stop.

Silently, Mitch said a prayer, apologizing to God for screwing up what was possibly the single greatest asset his order had ever found and asking for His help in re-recruiting Colin. Now, with such high stakes, he did not want to go it alone. Not because he feared for his own safety, but because he knew what failure meant. And it terrified him.

CHAPTER FIVE

Mitch swung the Jeep into a parking spot far from the main building despite the availability of spaces. Colin didn't question the choice, he wasn't driving. Mitch climbed out of the vehicle and immediately went to the back and opened it up, grabbing Colin's bag. As Colin came around, Mitch held it out to him with his left hand and extended his right, a grim expression on his face.

"Good luck, Colin. I'm afraid you'll have to find your own way home."

Colin took Mitch's calloused hand and nodded in understanding. "No problem. I'll figure it out." Then he met Mitch's powerful gaze. "Let us know when you get that thing. And be safe, okay?"

"I'm not making any promises." He gestured with his head to the plaza building. "I'm going to grab a quick bite and take a leak before I hit the road." The rugged exorcist strode off with a purpose.

Colin followed him, a step behind. He couldn't help feeling judged by Mitch. The look on the man's face and the tone of his voice radiated disappointment and disapproval. Despite his misgivings, Colin felt he'd made the right choice. What good was he to his family, dead? The cool night air blew gently into his face, filling him with a sense of calm despite the frantic roar of cars and trucks racing along the highway to his left. Looking around at the nearly empty parking lot, Colin felt very alone. He looked at his watch. Nearly ten-thirty. No wonder the plaza was almost empty.

The traffic sounds got louder and changed, taking on the character of raging beasts, dragons. He stopped. The transformation was alarming enough that he looked over at the speeding vehicles to make sure they were still just cars. As soon as his eyes lighted upon the first sedan, the sound slipped back to its normal tone. Realizing that he had stopped, he looked forward again and saw that Mitch was nearly to the doors.

Colin beat a healthy pace toward the service building where he'd find the restaurants and bathrooms. But as he got closer, the acrid stench of burning tires assailed his nostrils. He grimaced and glanced around looking for the source. Around him were a few dark, empty cars, their interiors surprisingly black under the sodium vapor lights. Farther back sat three tractor trailers, dark and idling, like battle tanks waiting for the command to crush everything in their paths. There were no fires anywhere. No vehicles skidding out of control or hot-rods spinning their tires. Just as quickly as it had come, the smell vanished. Colin's face wrinkled as he scanned the area, trying to ascertain the source of the smell, but he saw nothing.

Finally reaching the glass doors, Colin yanked one open and walked into the bluish glow of the fluorescent lights. To his right was a row of four fast-food counters. On his left was a round dining area equipped with solid, plastic table-tops and permanently affixed hard-backed chairs on swivels. His target, the bathroom, was situated on the other side of the building.

Colin looked at the first food counter and was surprised to see a young woman, perhaps a bit younger than he, with a boy of about four, waiting for food at this late hour. Though the woman's shoulders drooped, and her head hung down, she displayed a sad smile for her son as she caressed his hair. As he passed, the boy turned to face Colin and gave him a huge smile and a friendly wave. Colin returned the gesture and his eyes dropped to the boy's army green sweat-shirt with big white lettering announcing, "My Daddy Died a Hero". A small punch of pain and shame struck him in the gut as he turned away. No doubt the boy's father had been in the military and died fighting somewhere over in the middle-east. He was glad to see the boy still had his mother, but silently wished the child had some other fate than what he'd been given. He glanced once more at the shirt which now read "My Daddy is a Hero". The boy's pale blue eyes locked with Colin's, the smile still shining on his countenance. Were his eyes playing tricks on him, or had he misread the shirt the first time? He nodded again at the boy, his own smile dwindling and walked on.

Mitch stood at the counter of the second restaurant, scanning the menu displayed on the wall behind the annoyed-looking young woman waiting to take his order. The exorcist was too engrossed in making his decision to notice Colin walking past.

A television high on the wall played a news story about the owner of Negaré Industries, one of the country's big energy companies. The company had somehow managed to buy a wild-life refuge, so they could build a new power plant. Local residents had protested and in response the owner of the company was quoted as saying "Sometimes the few have to suffer for the good of the many." The story was in regard to the resulting outcry and rage. Colin shook his head in quiet disgust. Rich people.

The bathroom was large, with ten urinals lining the right wall and eight stalls opposite. The room was empty, so Colin had his choice of facilities. Still bewildered by the child's sweatshirt, he stepped up to a urinal and proceeded to drain his bladder. As he finished, his eyes wandered down the wall that was barely a foot from his face and jolted to a halt on the black design marked on the tan tile. A big, foreboding swastika had been scrawled in black marker. He stared at the symbol of hate, subconsciously drawn down into the darkness of its crooked arms. Unblinking and unmoving Colin stood there looking at the vile drawing as if he thought it had an evil life of its own.

"You alright? Or are you gonna stand there playing with it all night?"

Colin blinked, lifting his gaze to the speaker, a large Native American man stood two urinals away with his chin lifted high, his salt- and- pepper hair reaching down to brush his broad shoulder-blades.

"Oh. Kinda falling asleep on my feet, I guess," he said. He promptly zipped up and headed to the sink. He hadn't heard or seen the man come in and felt like an idiot.

"Uh huh. I hope you ain't driving."

"No. No. Good night," he said walking out, embarrassed. He didn't see the little smirk on the man's face or hear him softly chuckle as Colin fled the bathroom.

Stumbling out of the restroom, Colin glanced to his left and noticed another family – mother, father and son, again about four years old – waiting in line at one of the food counters. The boy's father had him by the wrist, and his mother's head bobbed in short, snapping motions as she spoke to her husband. Both had sagging, glassy eyes and Colin could see the man's jaw flexing. The little boy started screaming out something unintelligible and kicked at his father's shin. The father tried to control the child by taking hold of his shoulders and planting him out of kicking range. The kid's tantrum stopped long enough for him to glare at Colin. His little, hate-filled eyes followed Colin until he decided he wanted to return to thumping on his father's leg.

Colin shook his head, hoping that his daughter—no, children—never behaved that badly. Children. One of his children was in peril now, though he hadn't been born.

Colin's mind raced. Images of the holocaust morphed into him bouncing a happy little baby on his knee. Visions of horror and visions of joy were struggling for the limited spotlight of his consciousness. Dizzy, he wobbled over to a table and plunked down into a chair. He anchored his elbows on the table and stabilized his head with both hands. What was going on? The room bounced and spun, now expanding, now contracting. Why did he feel this way? It wasn't something physical, he'd been drunk before, and this was different. No, this was psychological, emotional. He experienced a sort of sensory overload and just wanted to shut down his brain. The two little boys, one smiling, one kicking, the swastika, the bestial sounds of the traffic, and the stench of smoke outside, they all swam in his washing machine mind, churning, screaming, drowning, wanting to be acknowledged. A boy with Colin's face, pleading for help, then being ripped apart by a shadowy, clawed figure.

As much as he wanted to, he could not escape the truth of the matter. He had to—

"Hey man, do you have a light, and maybe some spare cash? I'm starving, man." Colin fought to focus on the person in front of him. The speaker was a disheveled man of about twenty. A baggy, ragged red sweatshirt with the phrase "Fuck the Police" emblazoned in big white letters across the chest, hung limply on his emaciated shoulders. Scraggly stubble marred a pocked face that was covered with about three days' worth of filth, which was presumably the last time he wasn't tripping out on some sort of mind-altering drug. The pupils of his eyes were dilated even now, and his breath smelled like rotting dung. Colin recoiled, scowling.

"I don't smoke," Colin replied. He started to stand up, but the stranger grabbed his wrist, pulling him back down.

"What about some money? I could really use something to eat."

Colin's mind tried to return to what he was thinking about before this interruption, but the man's persistence distracted him.

"How did you even get here if you don't have any money?"

The creepy guy tossed his head from side to side. "Naw, man. I spent my last dime on gas. I'm trying to get to my ma's house. She's sick, probably dying. So I gotta get there. Spent my last dime..."

Annoyed, but trying to extricate himself

from the man's presence without being overly rude, Colin dug into his wallet and dropped a five-dollar bill on the table. "Go get something to eat."

"Nice, man," the guy said. He scooped up the bill as he stood and reached across to grasp Colin's hand in an enthusiastic hand-shake. "Thanks a ton. You rock!" He spun on his heel and headed off toward the bathrooms.

Instantly, the unbidden thoughts came swirling back in. Hitler, swastikas, demons, death, apocalypse, happiness, love, sacrifice... How could he sit here and contemplate abandoning Mitch? His son needed him, more so than Julie and Claire. He needed to reunite his family. So many people had sacrificed their lives for so much less. And right now, his son's soul, his *soul*, lay in the balance.

His mind returned to all those adventure novels he'd read, where seemingly normal, everyday people accomplished amazing acts. The true-life stories of soldiers and cops who succeeded in the face of overwhelming odds humbled him. He'd sat in a Jeep with one of those types of men, who charged headlong into the gun-fire to save the day. Though Colin was afraid, though he may die, though he didn't know what the hell he was doing, he had to rescue his son's soul and repair his fractured family. He could not let Mitch fight this fight alone. Mitch!

He jumped up from his seat and began scanning the food court for the man who would try to save the world on his own. It didn't take long to see that Mitch was nowhere in sight. A growing panic seized him. He ran to the doors and sprinted into the parking lot, hoping to see the priest walking toward his parked Jeep. But after he'd run only a few steps he could see the empty parking space. Mitch was gone.

CHAPTER SIX

Colin whipped out his cellphone and stared at it, silently biting his lip. He didn't have Mitch's number. He hadn't taken the time to get it, thinking he'd be with the priest all night and could get it tomorrow. His eyes closed in regret and frustration as he held the phone against his forehead.

"You were better off sleeping at a urinal than in the middle of a parking lot."

Colin spun around at the sound of the voice. The Native American guy stood there shaking his head, arms folded.

"My ride left me," he said.

"Are you sure you ever had a ride?"

Colin's head dropped. "I may have given him the wrong impression when I told him to drop me off here."

"Looks to me like you gave him exactly the right impression." The trucker walked over to Colin and shook his hand. "Thomas Whitecloud. Why don't you give him a call and tell him to pull over somewhere? I can drop you off with him."

"That'd be great, but..."

"What's the problem?" Thomas asked.

"Uh," Colin shook his head, not sure how to explain. "I have a new phone and haven't programmed in all the numbers yet. His number is, of course, one that isn't in here yet."

"No problem," Thomas said with a smile. "We'll chase him down."

"Really? Okay. I'm Colin Hampton, by the way. I really need to catch up with him. We're..."

"You can explain later," Thomas said, chuckling. "I really don't need the details right now. Come on."

Colin hoisted his duffel bag and scurried after his long-legged rescuer. The darkness of the lot around him tugged and pulled at his arms and shoulders, trying to tangle his feet and bring him down. Unnerved, he looked from side to side, seeking the source of his discomfort. Looking forward, he saw the big Native American moving through the glow of the sodium vapor lights. He tried in vain to read the caption on the big, round patch on the back of Thomas' denim vest. The image was bright orange flames with white lettering both at the top and bottom. On the bottom it looked like it said, "Search and Rescue". But before he could get close enough to clearly see the upper words, Thomas mounted the steps to the driver's side door of an idling, white Kenworth tractor, complete with sleeper. No trailer was attached.

"This is it," he heard Thomas say as he pulled the door open.

Colin trotted over to the passenger side and climbed up into what was the biggest road vehicle he would ever ride in. The interior was cavernous, leaving plenty of room for him to stow his luggage in the sleeper cab behind them. A dreamcatcher hung from the rear-view mirror. Colin buckled himself in.

"No trailer?" he asked.

"On my way to pick it up tonight."

The tractor slipped out of its parking spot under Thomas' expert control. Unladen, the machine jumped forward with peppy acceleration.

"What's your buddy driving and where's he going?" Thomas asked, checking his mirrors as he merged out onto the highway.

"A black Jeep Wrangler. He's going to... uh, New York."

Thomas raised his eyebrows and glanced at Colin. "Can you be more specific? New York is a big place."

Colin thought a moment. He hadn't really known exactly where they were heading, other than the city. Mitch may not have even known. "To be honest, I'm not exactly sure where he's planning on staying."

Thomas smiled at the sparse traffic in front of him. "Then we'd better catch him on the road." With that, Colin felt the truck pick up speed and watched the cars in front of them slide by to either side of the cruising tractor. Colin tried to peek at the speedometer, but it was too far over for him to view it.

"So what has you going to New York?" Whitecloud asked.

"We have a meeting with this guy down there in the morning."

Whitecloud looked at Colin with narrowed eyes. "And for some reason, when you were halfway there, you decided to not go and your buddy just dumped you at a rest stop?"

Colin realized his lie didn't make much sense, but this was unfamiliar ground. Still, he had to try to recover. "We disagreed on how to approach the meeting and kind of got into an argument. I told him to negotiate the deal without me, so he left me there." That seemed reasonable.

"Doesn't sound like this business venture is going to last long with you two fighting and abandoning each other," Whitecloud said. He locked onto Colin out of the corner of his eye. "I've never heard of any successful partnerships where people get into pissing matches over how to run a meeting."

"We're both kind of volatile," Colin replied. He turned to look anywhere but at Whitecloud.

"Yeah. I can see you're a real firecracker."

Colin bit his lip as he stared out the side window.

"Colin, I don't think you're being totally honest with me," Thomas said as he maneuvered through traffic. "I offered to do you a favor. I'd at least like to know why I'm doing it." Colin turned and saw the trucker looking at him. His big kind eyes locked with Colin's for only a moment, but it was enough to make him feel like a lying, despicable, insignificant bug.

"My son's been kidnapped and Mitch, the guy we're chasing, is going to help me get him back." It wasn't exactly a lie.

"Ever hear of the cops?"

"They said no cops."

Thomas squinted at the dark road. "They said that, did they?" He threw a sidelong glance at Colin. "Who is Mitch that he was going on to save your son while you were going to bail? Must be one heck of a guy."

The question hit Colin like a brick to the gut. *Bail? On my unborn son? That's exactly what you were going to do. Loser.* "He's a friend. But I have my wife and daughter to take care of too. And Mitch is definitely more capable of doing this than I am. So I wasn't exactly bailing."

"You know, a shepherd will put himself at risk to rescue one lost sheep and let the whole herd take care of itself until he returns. And this is your kid?" Whitecloud's voice oozed suspicion.

Now Colin felt lousy. He wished that Thomas would just shut up and drive. He didn't need anyone else pointing out the fact that he was not Action-Jackson. But he had taken on a damned *demon* when his family was threatened. Thomas didn't know about that, and that was enough to freak anyone out.

"I already got my ass kicked when he got kidnapped. And Mitch is a specialist at this kind of thing."

"What is he, special forces or something? The 'A-team' or the 'Equalizer'?"

"Something like that."

Whitecloud sneered. "But now you want to hook back up with him, even though you got your ass kicked once already?"

Colin paused. "I guess I just needed more time to think. It's a risk I need to take, to save my son. I can't let them win."

"Let who win?"

"The animals who took him. If we don't get him back..."

In the shadowy confines of the cab, Colin could see Whitecloud's jaw tighten as he slowly nodded his head. "Sounds like you're up against gangsters." Whitecloud's voice had lost its edge.

"The likes of which you've never seen."

"Ah, I dunno," Thomas said. "I've seen shit you wouldn't believe." He fixed Colin with a satisfied grin. "I'm glad you changed your mind. I think things will work out for the best. And even if you're scared, sometimes a father has to take risks for his kids. Sometimes has to die for them."

Colin thought of his battle with the demon.

"When does he have to quit taking risks?"

"When will you quit loving your kids?"

Colin's head snapped up and he looked at Thomas, confused. "Never."

Thomas smiled. "There's your answer."

Colin pondered Thomas' wisdom silently. As he stared out the panoramic windshield he realized that they were cruising along the Garden State Parkway.

"Hey! What are you doing? You can't take this rig on the Parkway. It's too heavy."

"Yeah, it is. But if I were your friend, and I was heading to Lower Manhattan at this hour, this is the way I'd go. Less traffic."

"We're gonna get pulled over," Colin said. He kneaded his hands. "We'll never find Mitch if that happens. Lower Manhattan?" He could hardly sit still.

Thomas scowled at Colin. "Man, you gotta settle down. You're way too tight. Rules are rules and the law is the law. But you have to look at the spirit of the law. Do cops break the law when they go speeding off to a crime scene? Technically they are. But the spirit of the law allows it. We're going after someone who can help you rescue your son from kidnappers, and you're afraid of a traffic violation? How are you going to accomplish anything if you don't take some chances?"

"I just like doing things the right way, according to the rules or, in this case, the law. And I don't want the cops getting involved in this. It'd be way too messy."

"The bad guys don't pay any attention to the law. And if you give them even one inch," he held up his thumb and forefinger, an inch apart for emphasis, "they'll grab a mile." His hand snapped shut into a fist. "Oh, they'll talk a good game, making sense here and there, speaking half-truths and getting you to believe they don't want to hurt you and if you give them what they want, they'll let you walk away. But as soon as you turn your back... wham!" He punched his palm with the meaty fist. "They stick a shank in your neck and laugh as you flop around on the floor, bleeding out. That's the way the bad guys do it."

Colin stared wide-eyed at the lucid and gesticulating Native American. "Hey, why don't you keep both hands on the wheel. You know, ten and two?"

Whitecloud huffed as he took hold of the steering wheel again. The big man talked as though he had infinite experience in dealing with toughs. But he was a truck driver, not a cop. That seemed like it should be a pretty straightforward career. Nonetheless, the trucker was very convincing, if not through logic, then through emotion. There was something in the tone of his voice and the conviction with which the man spoke that seemed to reach deep into Colin's soul and grab hold, demanding to be heard and heeded. The weight of his words plunged Colin into quiet contemplation. He was undoubtedly up against the evilest... what? Men? No. A demon from hell. As impossible as that sounded, he knew it to be true. Only because he'd seen it with his own eyes and felt the pain when it lashed him with its claws. He had no doubt that a creature from the Netherworld would be happy to break every rule on Earth. Anything to throw the world into chaos.

Michael smiled and knelt as the injured animal hopped toward him through the dark cluster of trees, its back-right leg held aloft, never hitting the ground. The roar of traffic behind it was one of the many sounds that were simply part of its life. It regarded Michael with not an ounce of fear. Like a dog seeking solace from its life-long, loving master the coyote approached him, lowering its head in submission when it neared. Michael felt bad for the animal, not intending for it to get injured. Even so, every battle has its casualties. This one was no different. He coaxed the animal to lie on its left side and caressed its damaged hip and leg, asking for the wound to be healed.

The coyote sat up, no longer favoring its right hip, and licked Michael's face, eliciting a chuckle. "Thank you," Michael whispered. Then to the coyote, "All better I see. You wouldn't have gotten hurt if you'd run faster. Are you getting lazy?" The canine tilted its head, ears erect and an insulted look on its furry face. Michael laughed again. "Don't worry. You can go shortly. Not quite done here."

This is crap luck. First, Colin bailing and now this. Mitch raised his face to heaven. "Thanks." He knelt and examined the brush guard on the front of his Jeep. Thankfully, it appeared to have taken the brunt of the damage, which wasn't much. Both headlights were still intact, though the passenger side light appeared to have a small amount of blood splattered on it. *Stupid urban coyotes. That could have really caused a big pile-up.* He gazed into the darkness, lost to the world around him. Who was he fooling? The task in front of him was monumental. Impossible. He'd probably just die in vain. *Everything is possible, with God.* He dropped his head and clung to that hopeful thought.

Taking a deep, cleansing breath, he looked at the trees next to the road, searching for some sign of the animal he'd hit. Not finding it in the ditch, he turned to look back up the road to see if it was lying in the middle of a lane, or on the shoulder. Nothing.

As he walked around to climb back into his vehicle he heard the unmistakable yipping howl of a coyote emanating from the far side of the highway. His brow furrowed, and he stared off in the direction from which he thought the howl originated. The animal he hit would have been coming from that direction. Had he spun it around and sent it back the way it had come? If that was the case, there was nothing he could do about it. He climbed back in behind the wheel.

"You a religious guy?" Thomas asked.

"Uh, not really. No."

"Going up against tough odds... it wouldn't hurt to say a prayer once in a while. You know, to ask for some help." Thomas' dark eyes peered at Colin in the eerie green glow of the dashboard lights. It made Colin feel like he'd just been chastised by his mother for stealing cookies from the pantry, like he'd done something wrong.

"I never found prayer to be helpful."

"I've had some interesting religious experiences in my time," Thomas said, as if Colin hadn't spoken, "and I think it can help. It sure can't hurt. I mean, why not? What better cause than rescuing your stolen child, right? If you want, I can say it for you, here together."

Colin wondered for a minute about the phrase 'stolen child,' but let it go. He wasn't sure what he'd hooked up with on this ride. Maybe Thomas had Attention Deficit Disorder or something. He sure made wild jumps in conversation and he had way too much advice to give. He was like that nosy uncle who would read into one little complaint you made about your life and chart out every move you needed to make over the next year to fix it, and then take the next three hours telling you his plan. That same uncle who thought he knew more about everything than you do. Perhaps it was best to appease him.

"Go ahead," Colin said.

"Dear Lord," Thomas began. "Please help this man— Hold on!" Tires screamed and the cab bucked and jostled as Thomas struggled to keep the tractor in its lane. Colin grabbed hold of the arms on his seat, the seatbelt pressing him into the chair like an invisible hand.

Thomas was off the brakes and back on the accelerator before Colin knew what was happening.

"What was that?" Colin asked, looking in the rear-view mirror outside his window.

"Animal. If I'd had a load, it woulda been road pizza. Don't break like that for animals if I have a trailer." He checked his right-side mirror. "I think he made it."

Colin sucked in a deep breath and glanced at the side of the road, wondering how many animals were running around the New Jersey Turnpike and if his nerves were going to survive this trip.

"See," Michael said. "That's how it's done. Not a scratch on him." He held his hand out to a second coyote that trotted up to him, its tongue lolling out of its mouth. This one got a rough scratch behind the ears and a pat on the head. He could hear the truck engine slow and knew that he'd accomplished what had been asked of him. Smiling down at the two coyotes he said, "Two for two. Nice work." He handed each of them a hunk of meat. "You can run along now." As he watched the two skinny canines bound off through the trees, meat securely in their jaws, he shouted, "And no more fighting with the dogs."

While waiting for traffic to clear enough to pull off the shoulder, Mitch saw a trailer-less tractor swerve over to the shoulder in front of him and turn on its emergency flashers. The passenger side door flew open and Colin jumped out, hollering and running back toward him before gesturing to wait, and then running back to the tractor. The driver of the truck, a big Native American man with long hair and confident smile, came strolling toward the Jeep in a slightly overweight, 'I'm sheriff of this town' stride.

Mitch climbed out of the Jeep and started forward at a friendly pace. When he neared the big truck driver he reached out his hand.

"You must be Mitch," Thomas said. He took Mitch's offered handshake. "Thomas Whitecloud. Found your buddy standing in the middle of the parking lot at the rest-stop up the road. He seemed pretty lost when he saw that you'd left."

Mitch wasn't sure what to say. "I thought he was going to try to get a ride back up to Saratoga."

Thomas turned and looked back at the tractor where Colin had emerged carrying his pack. Returning his eyes to Mitch he continued, "He said he needed to find you. I said I'd help. From what he told me, sounds like you could use his help. Especially since it's his son."

Mitch swallowed and paused a moment. Then he said, "He told you what happened?"

"Not everything," Thomas said through a restrained grin. "But enough to know what you are up against."

Their eyes locked, each man measuring the nature of the other, neither finding the other wanting.

"I told him about my son being kidnapped and your being willing to help me, what with your special skills and all," Colin said.

Thomas continued penetrating Mitch with his deep stare.

"Thank you for giving him a ride. I'm glad to have his help. Can I give you any money for your trouble?"

A big smile broke upon Thomas's lips. "No. I won't take your money. I'm glad I could help. You two go find that little guy and get him back where he belongs." He extended his hand to Colin but pulled the poor computer salesman into a man-hug when Colin took the bait. When he released him, he said, "If you catch up with this kidnapper, don't let him take you out. Give 'im Hell." Then he turned and walked back to his rig.

Mitch watched as the big man walked away. The logo on the back of his vest showed in flashes of the passing headlights. Mitch's breath caught in his chest as he finally saw all the words. It read, "Lake of Fire - Search and Rescue."

Colin spoke up and snapped Mitch out of his trance. "I can't believe we caught you. That guy really knows where he's going." He smiled, then looked at the Jeep and furrowed his brow. "Is everything okay with your car? Why'd you pull over?"

Tearing his attention away from Whitecloud, Mitch said, "I hit a coyote. At least, I thought I did. I was just leaving when you guys pulled up."

"We almost hit something just back there too. Maybe there's a pack of them running around here."

"Maybe," Mitch said. After looking around the area he gave Colin a warm grin. "You changed your mind?"

"Yeah. Sorry I left. I just—I guess I'm scared."

"That's alright," Mitch said. He gripped Colin's shoulder. "You came back. And I don't believe that it was a coincidence that you found me."

Mitch searched the area one more time for a sign of the coyote that he'd hit, but once again found nothing. The only proof he had that he'd hit anything was a couple of red specks on his headlight. Straining his eyes, he scanned the area one more time, looking for anything unusual, but came up empty. "Okay, then," he whispered to himself. Then lifting his eyes, he said, "Thanks."

Colin jumped into the Jeep as Mitch fired up the engine. The tires squawked as Mitch re-entered the sparse traffic and Colin could see the man surveying the road in front of them, no doubt searching out Thomas's rig in the sporadic pockets of light. Did he sense a look of mistrust in those searching eyes, or suspicion?

Mitch asked him what had caused him to change his mind. Colin wasn't quite sure himself, so he described the odd little things he'd seen at the rest stop, the strange sounds, the burning smell, the behavior of the little boys, the swastika, and how they had made him think about what he and Mitch were facing.

"How did you miss me in the parking lot? You must have been right behind me," Mitch said.

Colin thought a minute. Then he remembered the strange man who had bummed money off him for food. He'd talked with him, perhaps just long enough to miss catching Mitch in the parking lot.

"Some guy stopped me. Begging for money for food. Maybe he held me up just long enough for you to leave."

Mitch thought long and hard about that. His lips pursed into a frown.

"What matters now is that you're here. Hopefully, between the two of us, we can kill this bastard."

Colin's head snapped around, shocked at the profanity. "Father! Er... Mitch. What should I call you anyway?"

"Mitch is good. I've never been very good in the 'Father' role. Probably why I ended up doing exorcisms. Possessed people are tough to offend."

"Okay, Mitch. So where are we headed?"

"We'll get checked in to a hotel in lower Manhattan, then get started first thing in the morning."

It was about 1:00 A.M. when they finally checked in to a very nice-looking hotel not far from Battery Park. Mitch was obviously familiar with the clerk working the desk, calling her "Maggie" as though they had coffee on a regular basis. She was a plain looking woman in her early thirties, with mud brown hair and eyes to match. She was pleasant, addressing Mitch as "Mr. Stackwell". Colin thought it odd that she didn't use his religious title.

After receiving two card keys, Mitch turned and handed one to Colin and the men each hoisted his respective baggage and marched off toward the elevator bank.

"We're on the fifteenth floor. Room 1503. I got us one room. Don't know what will be thrown at us and I don't want you out there on your own."

"Sounds good to me."

"I hope you don't mind snoring." Mitch examined Colin's face as the elevator doors opened.

"Do you snore?" Colin stepped into the brass detailed elevator. "So do I. I guess we'll race each other to sleep tonight."

"Want to put money on it?" Mitch chuckled as the doors closed behind him.

When the alarm-clock sounded the next morning, Mitch fixed Colin with a red-eyed death-stare.

"I thought I was going to have to perform the Rite on you last night. That's the only explanation I can figure for the human body making those unholy sounds."

Colin laughed. "Told you, I snore."

Mitch bobbed his head in agreement. "Jump in the shower while I get some coffee going. We can grab a bite to eat when we hit the street."

As Colin showered, he found himself considering the reality of his situation. Yesterday morning he was at home, and more or less happy. Because of his recent disappointment at work, and hence Julie's disappointment in him, perhaps less happy. But he was basically content. Now, here he was in New York City with a man he hardly knew, a priest, who was going to help him hunt down the demon that had stolen the soul of his unborn son right from Julie's womb. A monster that had not been able to kill him, despite putting forth a worthy effort. Why wasn't he dead? Was he some sort of 'chosen one'? Probably not. Mitch had said that a demon could still rip his throat out or—he shook his head, physically throwing the thought from his mind. It would do no good to put too much thought into how dangerous this endeavor was. But the fear of failure didn't stop resonating in his consciousness. If he failed, he would lose his family, let Mitch down and damn the whole world. His past failures sprang to mind, sending a shudder through his already wavering foundation. Hell, he wouldn't even fight for a raise at work. How could he fight evil?

As he dried himself, he considered Mitch and all that the exorcist had told him. He still found this all very hard to comprehend. But he'd seen the physical manifestation of a demon. Fought with it. Felt the rake of its claws, saw the hate in its mercuric eyes, witnessed it suck the unborn soul from his wife's abdomen. Mitch seemed to take this all completely in stride. He didn't seem to fear the demons, or even think failure was possible. The man oozed confidence, knowledge and strength.

Colin could see that if Father Mitch failed in his duties, he would die trying.

Colin wondered about his own role in this. If he died, it would be flailing and trying to escape, trying to avoid any kind of risk and danger. That's why Julie had called him a wimp. That's what he was. He remembered the argument they'd had four weeks ago when he told her he'd been passed up for promotion. It was because he didn't start a big fight at work when that asshole Jim Reuter took credit for developing a big customer. He thought that management saw through Jim's bullshit, but they turned out to be dumber than he thought. And he got screwed out of another nice promotion. Julie was furious that he didn't set the record straight and pitch a fit. That's when she'd disparaged him, saying he wasn't taking care of the family like he could be. But he believed that Karma would come around and he'd get a much better deal. That wasn't really working out. Anger burned within his gut. Not a roaring blaze or even a wavering flame, but a glowing, smoldering ember. She had called him a wimp. But he had fought that demon. Fought a demon from hell! And he did it to protect his family, thinking he would probably die. Why did he do that? Where did that strength come from? Maybe he wasn't such a chicken-shit after all.

"Coffee's hot," Mitch said through the cracked bathroom door.

Colin left the steamy bathroom to Mitch and

sought out the coffee.

By the time he was into clean clothes, Mitch emerged from the bathroom with a towel wrapped around his waist. Colin was impressed by the priest's lean musculature, hoping he would be as fit at that age. As Colin downed his coffee, Mitch threw on some jeans and a long-sleeved T-shirt. Not your typical priestly raiments. In a few short minutes, Mitch hoisted his pack of ancient weapons and they were headed out the door. Where they were going, Colin had no idea.

They opted to leave the Jeep in the valet parking and head out on foot. The sky was filled with a heavy overcast that appeared ready to break loose with a deluge any minute, and a penetrating chill oozed through Colin's jacket as though it were made of cheese-cloth. The grayness of the day did little to boost Colin's spirits.

They grabbed a quick breakfast sandwich and then hailed a taxi. Mitch whispered a destination to the driver. Colin thought that a little strange but chalked it up to Mitch's unorthodox nature. They had hardly settled into the backseat when Mitch reached into his weapon bag and pulled out a pair of extremely dark sunglasses, with side and bottom shields that made them look like some sort of safety or welder's glasses. Handing them to Colin, he said, "Put these on."

Colin laughed out loud before he realized that Mitch was serious.

"Welder's goggles? Why?"

"Because I'm taking you to a secret location."

Colin glanced at the cabbie. "You told him."

"No, I didn't. Please, just trust me."

Colin sighed and put the glasses on. The glasses were completely opaque, preventing Colin from seeing anything at all. "You can't let me walk around like this. I can't see a thing."

"That's the idea. Don't worry, I won't let you bang into anything." To the cabbie he said, "Stop here."

"Are you sure," the dark-skinned driver asked in heavily accented English.

"Yes. Anywhere here is fine."

Colin felt the cab jerk to a halt at the side of the road.

"Keep the change," Mitch said.

"Thank you very much, sir," came the happy reply.

Then Colin was being pulled out the passenger side of the car and guided to his feet. Mitch took him by the right elbow and started to walk.

"We're going to attract a lot of attention, walking around like this," Colin said. He fidgeted with the glasses, trying to get them into a comfortable position.

"It looks like you're a blind guy and I'm helping you get around. No one is going to give us more than a passing thought. Unless they think I'm a classy, selfless guy helping out a fellow citizen with a disability."

Colin scoffed. "If you say so."

"Don't worry. I won't purposely let you walk into anything or trip."

"Purposely?"

Mitch huffed a laugh.

Colin let himself be led down the sidewalk, issuing an "excuse me" whenever he bumped into someone. No one acknowledged his apologies. Occasionally, Mitch would push or yank him this way or that or tell him to watch his step. They turned left, they turned right, they turned right and then left. And so they proceeded to traverse the city streets. Colin lost track of the direction they were walking after the first five minutes, something he was sure was intentional on Mitch's part. They walked for at least thirty minutes and traveled who-knows how far.

"Step up twice," Mitch said. He guided Colin up some concrete stairs.

Colin heard the groan and squeak of what must be a heavy door. Then Mitch guided him into what felt like a small room that smelled of wood and candles. Their footsteps thudded dully as they walked forward about eight feet. A click followed by the sound of wood rolling on wood. Then an electronic jumble and four distinct beeps. Kachunk! Like someone hitting the side of a car with a sledge-hammer. The sound of a doorknob being turned in another heavy, probably steel, door. Mitch pushed him through another doorway before he heard the door slam to behind him, along with a cacophony of other sounds that made Colin think of some mysterious vault from "Indiana Jones" sealing itself up.

"Where are you taking me? Sounds like Fort Knox."

"You'll see in a minute."

He felt walls close in on him from both sides and Mitch guided him down broad, stone steps that arced right in a lazy spiral. The air was cool, still, and smelled musty and damp. Down and down they went, at least four floors. When they reached the bottom, or perhaps a landing, Mitch turned them to the right and knocked on a solid wooden door. Without delay, the door opened, and Mitch pushed Colin through the portal ahead of himself.

Two pairs of hands locked onto each of Colin's arms and flung him to one side and forced his back against an extremely hard wall.

"He's okay. He's with me." Mitch's voice.

"We'll be the judge of that," growled a male voice on Colin's left.

One of the two hands securing his right arm let go and another fixed itself firmly around his throat. Whoever held his left arm, released it and started violently probing Colin's legs, waist, chest and armpits.

"One wrong move and I'll end you. Got it," the searching voice threatened as he groped Colin's pockets.

"You're being a bit dramatic," said an English accented male voice belonging to whoever held him by the throat. "Mitch said he's clean. I think he knows what he's talking about."

The English man's hands released him and pulled the blackened glasses off. It didn't take long for Colin's eyes to adjust to the dimly lit chamber in which he stood. It seemed that most of the light emanated from the plethora of various sized computer monitors arrayed around the roughly forty-by-forty-foot room. The walls were made of rough-hewn stone block that looked like it had been quarried in the middle ages and the high ceiling that appeared to have been carved out of the Earth itself was solid stone, reinforced by one-foot diameter wooden beams.

Colin checked out the men who'd just threatened and searched him. He was astonished to find that both looked like they had just landed here off the cover of Men's Health or Wired magazine. Despite being straight as an arrow, Colin immediately classified both guys as the most handsome he'd ever seen. He could imagine women swooning as they walked past. The wisdom swirling in the eyes of both young men seemed well beyond their years.

"Colin, meet the Cecidit Angelus Vigilum.

'Cavemen' for short."

"Cavemen?"

"Roughly translated: fallen angel watchmen. They've made a study of identifying, locating, and classifying demonic activity. They research scientific, and paranormal ways to help me do my work. These are the guys who wrote the program to detect the meta-quantum rifts that led me to your street." Quietly Mitch whispered, "They are... very unique."

Colin looked at the two men in awe, forgetting about how roughly he'd just been handled.

The English guy held out a hand, "Reginald." Reginald looked more Persian than English, with black hair, brown eyes, bronze skin, five o'clock shadow accenting a triangular jaw and a warm disarming smile.

Colin shook his hand, too dumbfounded to speak, then turned to the guy who'd searched him and was still scrutinizing him, but offered his hand none-the-less.

"Benjamin. Ben is fine. Sorry 'bout before. Gotta be careful."

Colin nodded as he shook Ben's strong hand. With pale, blue eyes, golden-blond hair, strong jaw, straight nose, broad shoulders, flat stomach, the young man conjured images of the mythological Norwegian god, Thor.

"And this is Colin Hampton. The only

person I've ever seen to survive the rake of a demon's claw," Mitch said.

It was Ben's and Reginald's turn to stare in awe. Their stares were amplified by the abrupt halt of conversation, leaving Colin feeling like a microbe under the scope. Neither of the handsome men were able to hide the gleam of fascination that overtook their features. Colin detected something else there too. Hope? For the first time since leaving Saratoga Springs, Colin felt like maybe he had *not* made a huge mistake.

"How do you know this to be true?" Benjamin asked.

"I saw it with my own eyes." Mitch recounted the events that had occurred at the Hampton residence.

"Let me see," Benjamin said. He yanked Colin's shirt up high enough to reveal four horizontal pink scars. Colin slapped Ben's hands away and pulled his shirt back down into place, clearly annoyed.

"That's why you brought him. To help you hunt the demons," Reginald stated.

"That, and because the demon he fought stole the soul of his unborn son."

"Oh shit!" Benjamin spun a circle, his hands entangled in his perfect blond hair. "How long do we have?"

"She's due in about ten days," Mitch said.

"Double shit," Reginald said. His cool

English demeanor wavering. "We can't risk another holocaust. "

"Wait. What?" Colin asked, snapping his attention to Reginald.

"The last time this happened, we learned far too late. You've heard of Adolph Hitler?" Reginald said.

Colin's jaw fell open and he looked over at Mitch who massaged his temple, clearly not happy. "Adolph Hitler?"

Mitch nodded.

"You said it took fifty-six years to fix that mistake," Colin accused. "How did you fix that?"

"Do you really think a guy like Hitler would commit suicide?" Reginald supplied. "Bonhoeffer almost had him with Valkyrie, but we finally caught him at the Eagle's Nest. If we'd known about him earlier, we could have—"

"Enough about Hitler," Mitch said.

"How old are you guys?" Colin asked.

"Not us personally," Ben responded, glancing at Reginald. "He just meant, us, the good guys."

"Let's focus on finding this demon," Mitch commanded, his voice growing in volume.

"Or whoever summoned it," Benjamin amended as Reginald nodded in agreement.

Colin sat down in a chair near one of the computers, overwhelmed by what he'd just learned. If he hadn't grasped the gravity of the situation before, he did now. He tuned into Mitch who'd resumed speaking.

"How do we find this sorcerer? First, would you agree that it appears that he's here in New York City, based on what we learned from the previous manifestations?"

Reginald plunked himself down in front of a computer and started banging away at the keyboard. He pulled up a map of the eastern United States. Pinpoints showed on the map at Durham, North Carolina, Pittsburgh, Pennsylvania, and Saratoga Springs, New York. Reginald punched in a command and numbers sprang up on the bottom of the screen.

"The first one appeared in Durham and you killed it after it had moved northward. The second one was in Pittsburgh and it had been headed east. Plotting the vectors of both of those do vaguely point here so it would make sense. Especially if he is getting progressively better at bringing them into our realm nearer to his location. But we don't know if he is getting better or getting worse. I hate to say it, but we may not know for sure until he summons another. And if we don't exorcise this one, he may not."

Colin hung his head. This was not good news. How the hell were they going to find a demon that didn't want to be found? The damn thing could hide in the woods until it was too late.

"How can we even hope to find it?" Colin

asked. "Why would it bother doing anything other than hiding and waiting for my wife to give birth?"

Mitch stepped forward, crossing his arms in a defiant gesture. "Because one of those weird, unwritten laws that we don't quite understand, compels the demons to seek out whoever summoned it. They have very little leeway to do otherwise until they meet their summoner and make physical contact. Your demon was, unfortunately, very lucky to have stumbled across your wife before the 'draw' became too painful. I have no doubt that as soon as he left, he headed toward the sorcerer."

"So, he's under control of whoever brought him here?"

"No. That's why the whole 'draw' phenomenon is so weird. Once they make physical contact with the summoner they can pretty much do as they please."

"Why the hell would anyone bring one here? That's insane."

Reginald took a breath and interjected. "People are always overestimating their self-worth and their power. Someone gets it in their head that they know just how to control a demon in physical form when really, all they can master is the summoning. Their arrogance ultimately leads to their demise."

"You say that like it happens a lot," Colin said.

"Hardly," Ben answered, his voice that of a

man about to start a bar-room brawl. "This is the first instance of it in your lifetime. But we do have very good institutional knowledge and history books that taught us how to fight one. We also learned of the unique weather that accompanies their coming across; the red lightning, small diameter vortex winds, and barometric pressure drop. That's how we made our app."

"So now we need to find the sorcerer as soon as possible, before the demon finds him. Because we want to be there waiting when it gets there," Mitch said with a smile. "If the demon makes contact before we get there, our job becomes a lot tougher."

"Then we are looking for a person? Exactly how does looking for one person, whose name we don't even know, in New York City make our jobs easier?" Colin asked.

"Because someone who is trying to learn how to conjure up a demon in physical form will have asked questions. And we know the people who will have heard about someone asking those questions," Mitch said.

"And you have us and our technology," Reginald added. "We're working on identifying the presence signature of a demon in physical form and are very close to being able to track one."

Colin looked at Reginald, dumbfounded. "How could you possibly track one?"

Benjamin sneered a satisfied grin. "Because

demons significantly affect various forms of energy around them. Electro-magnetic fields, spiritual fields, visible and invisible light radiation, radio signals. When they're in our dimension, they operate under the same laws of physics as you and I, but their bodies are variably more capable of challenging those physics. If we can put it all together, we should be able to tell you the exact GPS coordinates of one. As it is, with the data we've gathered from the three conjurings so far, by this time tomorrow, we hope to have an algorithm together that will be able to put you to within a two-block radius of the thing."

Mitch clapped Ben on the back. "That's outstanding! The sooner the better. What have you got for me now? Anything new?"

"Not really. We think we've tightened up the radius on detecting the vortexes, though," Reginald said. "And we have a little more predictability. Maybe five minutes heads-up."

"That could help. Hopefully we'll find him before he tries bringing any more across."

"Don't count on it," Ben said. "If you exorcise this one, I'm sure he'll conjure up another, until he gets what he's looking for."

Mitch shrugged. "True. But first things first. Colin and I have to go find this demon and kill it. Then we can worry about any others."

Reginald walked over and whispered something to Ben who nodded and grabbed something from one of the five desks in their strange office space. He approached Colin. "Hold your hand out," he said.

Colin held his hand out and Ben flipped it palm up and then snapped something against the tip of Colin's finger, drawing a spot of blood. "Ow. What are you doing?"

Instead of answering, Ben drew the small drop of blood up into a glass capillary tube. "We gotta do some testing. Figure out why you're immune."

"You ever think of asking first?" Colin complained.

Ben gave him a blank stare. "No."

He looked over at Mitch who watched the exchange with a dire expression. "You good to go?" Mitch asked.

Colin felt himself nod but couldn't help thinking they were already too late. They had to find one person, in New York City. That, by itself, seemed a monumental task. As far as finding the actual demon, he didn't believe he brought anything to the table. All he'd done was live through an attack – live, when everyone else here thought he should have died. That certainly wasn't going to help them find the thing. And the next time, the demon would not be satisfied to just scratch at him. It would tear his heart out, or his throat out, or some vital organ out. His mind went back to the little boy at the rest-stop, holding his mother's hand, wearing that t-shirt declaring that his father was a hero. He hoped one day his son could wear something like that. But he hoped he would be there to see it.

CHAPTER SEVEN

Myska moved around the warehouse with a purpose, stepping carefully around the big pentagram painted on the concrete floor. Looking at the three diagrams he held in his hand, the sorcerer tried to discern which diagram went with which point of the star. The first two he was fairly confident about, but these last three were still a mystery. He laid the pictures down in the pentagram, each in its own elongated, triangular, point. His attention danced around the new design, looking for the flows and counter-flows created by the new layout.

Nodding to himself, he used a wet rag to erase some of the existing glyphs on the floor and then dried the spot with a towel. After he'd created three blank spaces, he grabbed the plastic bucket and the artist's paintbrush. He frowned when he looked into the pail and saw that the blood was almost gone, and what was left was congealed almost to the point of being useless. Before it could get any worse, he went to work, carefully painting the new drawings in the blank spaces, referring to the diagrams he'd laid out next to each one. He put the finishing touches on the final design with the last dollop of blood. Stepping back, he looked from one arm of the pentagram to the next, observing the bloody diagrams and running their individual meanings through his mind, imagining the flow of energy as it hooked and weaved through the complex arrangement of symbols.

It seemed right. But the first three times he did this, it seemed right then too.

He stepped to the desk and scanned through one of the fragile old books that laid open. Then he compared the artifacts at the points of the pentagram with the ones in the book. If the book was right, and his interpretation of the artifacts was right, everything should work fine. Should. He just needed one more talisman to place in the center of the whole diagram. Unfortunately, this was the one position of the pentagram that all the documentation seemed to ignore. He knew something had to go there but wasn't sure what or why. It was as if whoever had written these books thought it so elementary, or so dangerous, that they didn't mention it.

Before experiencing the pain of having one of his demons exorcised, Myska wasn't concerned about a little trial and error. So what, if the demon appeared half-way across the country? It would find its way to him eventually. The books were very clear on that point. But after two separations — a term he came up with for being ripped apart from one of his summoned beings — he wanted nothing more than to drop the next demon right here in this warehouse. He wanted to be done with this business and start reaping rewards.

Now he carefully considered the artifact that he would place at the center of the pentagram. Unfortunately, he had little to no feedback on the first three creatures he'd brought forth, so he couldn't even guess as to its purpose. He perused the various items he had laid out on his table. One in particular caught his eye; an iron Triskele. It resembled a three-leafed clover, but each of the leaves was a spiral design terminating at the center of the leaf. He wasn't sure what it was about the Triskele that intrigued him. Perhaps it just looked the least ominous. He placed it at the center of the pentagram.

"Are you ready?"

The voice made Myska jump. He hadn't heard his benefactor enter the warehouse. He never did. He gave himself a minute to recover his wits.

"Just now, yes," Myska answered. Then he moved away from the diagram on the floor, knelt and started to recite the ritualistic words. There was no telling how many times he'd have to repeat them, but it would be brutally obvious when he was finished.

As some unfortunate New Yorkers would discover.

As soon as the subterranean door slammed shut behind them, Mitch fumbled through his pack and pulled out the wooden Palo Santo dagger. He handed it to Colin.

"Here. Keep it hidden and only use it on demons. I don't want you stabbing some innocent weirdo because you think he's possessed. Demons only. Got it?"

Colin tucked the dagger into his inside jacket pocket. As soon as he'd done that, Mitch put the dark glasses on him. Walking up the stairs was a bit easier than the descent, only because he had some idea of what to expect. He hoped that as soon as they were outside he'd be allowed to see again, but he was disappointed. They walked several zig-zagging blocks before Mitch finally stopped and removed the glasses. He squinted his light-dazzled eyes as he looked around at a typical New York city block.

"Why all the secrecy with the Cavemen?" he asked.

"Because Satan would love to dismantle our capabilities. If no one knows about it, they can't compromise it."

"You and Reggie and Ben know about it."

"I didn't say it was fool-proof. We just mitigate the risk as well as we can. Plus, some of our tech capabilities are... maybe a little beyond legal."

Colin wasn't quite sure how to respond to that. He looked around at the bustling city. "Where to now?" he asked Mitch.

"Now we go talk to some people who may be able to help us figure out who is summoning these damned demons. This first guy we're going to talk to is... unique. I simply refer to him as 'Rat Man'."

"Rat Man?"

"You'll figure it out when you meet him."

Mitch turned and led Colin to the nearest subway station, about one block away. He purchased a fare-card for Colin and the two walked through the turn-style to the platform.

Colin studied the wide variety of bystanders. He saw people of all shapes and sizes, races, ages, sexes, and economic statures. About fifteen feet away, a woman, with exquisite attire, stared intently at him. She was slightly older than he and had impeccably done black hair that framed a regal face highlighted by dark brown eyes. He quickly became uncomfortable under her gaze and looked away. When he looked back, she gave him a cold smile. Colin turned his back to her.

"That woman about fifteen feet behind me is staring at me," he whispered to Mitch.

Mitch glanced over Colin's shoulder and then returned to watching up the tracks.

"Yeah, I got her. Don't sweat her yet. Just keep an eye out for her. If she turns up again, it could mean she's being used by the other side."

Colin turned his full attention on Mitch, ignoring those around him. "Used by the other side?"

"If she's full-on possessed, they could use her to try and follow us, or kill us."

"They'd do that?"

Mitch looked him in the eye. "To protect the hostage they have? You bet they would. Luckily, it isn't that easy for them to make someone commit murder. But they'd try."

"Why don't they just follow us in spirit form or something?"

Colin felt a rush of air as the train approached the station. Mitch didn't answer as he waited for the cars to come to a halt and open the doors. When it did, he nonchalantly stepped on and ushered Colin to a seat next to him. The train jolted forward and began accelerating, mechanical noises providing a semblance of privacy.

"Their powers aren't unlimited. They can't be more than one place at a time. They can communicate pretty much instantaneously, it seems. But one of them is going to have to be able to 'see' you, much like we see one another, before they can say where you are."

"But aren't there hundreds of thousands of them? They could be anywhere," Colin stated.

"We don't know how many there really are, but we believe there are a lot less than you think.

These aren't deceased evil souls we're talking about. These are fallen angels. We don't know how many angels there are either. Could be a hundred million, or less, putting the demon count at about a third of that. At any rate, there are plenty of things going on all over the world that require their attention."

Colin wanted to feel better knowing they faced only a small army of demons, but it was still an army and he felt naked and exposed. He glanced down the center isle of the subway car, trying to locate the mysterious woman, but didn't see her, though he was pretty sure she'd gotten on this car.

He watched for the woman as the subway made two stops, letting people off and on, but never saw her. As the train approached the third stop, Mitch indicated they would be getting off.

When Colin stood up to exit, he finally located her sitting at the other end of the car. Through the bustle of moving bodies, he could see her looking in his direction. Their eyes met momentarily, and she flashed him a somewhat warmer grin. As the train pulled away, he watched through the windows and saw her give him a small wave. Then the train was gone.

Mitch slapped him on the arm, smiling.

"She was probably just looking for love, and you meet her criteria."

Colin let out a sigh of relief. Despite the false alarm, the tension bloomed in his body and mind. How was he going to make it through this ordeal if he was seeing demons in lonely women? He consciously forced himself to focus on what they were doing now.

He expected Mitch to lead him up to street level again, but instead he stood stationary near a door marked 'no entry'. Mitch watched as most of their fellow passengers headed up to the street. At this time of the morning, most of the commuters were already at work so it didn't take long for the crowd to thin. Mitch reached in his pocket and pulled out a key, fitting it into the door's lock. He slipped through the door, pulling Colin with him.

They were now standing in a well-lit hallway that extended in both directions, the walls the same cheap polished tile that were in the rest of the station. They turned left and walked down the corridor like they belonged there. On their right, they passed a large glass window that looked out on a room divided into two small cubicles. One was occupied by a heavy-set man with salt-and-pepper hair, and glasses that rested half-way down his nose. He glanced up as they passed and gave Mitch a cursory nod. They continued, the hallway curving slowly to their right, passing several gray, steel doors and two more empty offices. Then they were at a door that stood in their path. Without hesitation, Mitch opened it and they went through.

Stairs descended into a shadowy depth, a faint glow evident below. Upon reaching the bottom of the staircase, Colin peered down an old brick lined tunnel, lit sporadically by small, overhead light bulbs that dangled like mummified insects at the ends of spider webs. Near the end of his vision, Colin glimpsed a rat scurrying across the floor, only to disappear through a hole in the wall.

"Where are we going?"

"I told you. We're going to see the Rat Man," Mitch answered.

"What the hell is he doing down here?"

Mitch looked at Colin as if he were simple. "He lives down here."

Colin raised his eyebrows. "How could he possibly know about anything that is going on, if he lives down here?"

"He's not like you and me. He has insights and knowledge that we don't really understand. It's as though he sees and hears by a different spectrum. He picks up on energies that we don't even know exist. At least that's what we think."

"Sounds like some sort of oracle."

"Kind of. But not quite. He's an interesting guy, no doubt."

As they walked down the tunnel, their shuffling foot-falls echoed lightly off the decrepit, brick walls. Colin heard water dripping here and there, and he dodged puddles where they accumulated on the wildly uneven concrete floor. He and Mitch found themselves side-stepping and skipping over some of the larger ones. The cool, damp air smelled slightly of decay and mold.

Though the stench wasn't overpowering, Colin was anxious to abandon the fetid shaft nonetheless.

"Do you call him the Rat Man because he lives here with all the rats? Are they his pets or something?"

Mitch shook his head. "They are quite definitely *not* his pets. You'll see when we get there."

As they walked down the tunnel, Mitch kicked at a rat that sat eyeballing the two men and sent it running for its hole. "Huh," he said.

"What?" Colin asked.

"Bold rat," Mitch answered, shrugging.

They approached a ragged breach in the right-side wall, the bricks fallen in haphazard fashion to form a makeshift portal. Colin wasn't sure if this section of the wall had collapsed or been torn away. Behind the hole was only pure black darkness. Mitch stopped in front of the dark void.

"Take my hand. The terrain is a little tricky in here."

Colin's body clenched. "We're going in there? Don't you have a light?"

In the shadowy light from a distant bulb, Colin could see Mitch's face grow grave.

"We can't use a light here. There are very strict protocols for dealing with the Rat Man. He's an ally, but that doesn't mean he isn't dangerous. We approach in the dark."

Colin didn't like this situation at all. After

seeing a demon in the flesh, the dark now held new terrors for him. They wouldn't know if one lurked until it tore both of their hearts out. But, Mitch seemed to know what he was doing. Reluctantly, Colin grasped the exorcist's hand firmly. Before stepping into the unknown, Mitch said, "And one more thing. Don't speak."

With that, the unorthodox priest pulled his apprehensive young ward into the pitch black. Colin stubbed his toes repeatedly, the floor rising and falling and strewn with rubble. He quickly learned that Mitch would tug upward or downward on his hand to signal having to step up or down, respectively. But there was not much warning he could provide about the debris. Slowly they went, Colin careful to establish his footing so as not to roll an ankle. He wondered how Mitch knew where he was going. He reached out his left hand into the darkness, expecting to feel a jagged wall close to him. But he felt only emptiness. He stuck his right elbow out, sure they must be near a wall on the right. But again, there was nothing there. Quietly, he wondered how big this tunnel was through which they clambered. Could it even be a cavern? He listened intently and noticed a slight echo when he or Mitch kicked a stone and sent it bouncing along the stony floor. It must be big, he thought. He desperately wanted to ask Mitch how he knew where he was going but remembered the man's dire warning.

He wasn't sure how long they'd walked when he heard something, much larger than a rat, move, off to his left. Mitch stopped cold at the sound and Colin's heart leapt like a thorough-bred leaving the gate. Colin strained to hear anything more, but try as he might, all he could hear was his own pulse pounding in his ears. Finally, he heard Mitch take a deep breath and they continued.

Finally, after what must have been an hour, Colin could see a ray of light up ahead. Dim and fluid, the light danced and shook, sending the darkness reeling in random vectors. A fire? Then he could smell the smoke, sweet and clean, like a campfire in the woods. As they neared, he could see that it was a fire, set in a small alcove. The rear wall of the little niche had another hole in it, like the one they'd passed through to start this blind journey. An empty spit was suspended above the fire, and of its creator, he saw no sign. A makeshift cot near the right-hand wall was also empty. Mitch stopped abruptly and pulled Colin close.

"This isn't right," he whispered. "He's always here, because he always knows I'm coming."

Not what Colin wanted to hear. But before he could ask anything, Mitch released his hand and said, "Wait here."

Colin stood in the darkness, well out of the ring of light, and watched Mitch make his way closer to the fire. He turned and looked back, trying to hear anything that might be approaching unseen from the rear. Frustrated at his blindness he turned back to watch Mitch only to see him disappear through the hole in the far wall. Uneasiness gave way to a gripping snake of fear that constricted his body, seeking to swallow him whole. Fighting to take calm, steady breaths, he watched the breach, waiting to see his friend emerge. When after five minutes, Mitch still hadn't returned, Colin considered moving into the light to wait.

Ignoring the priest's warning, he called out in a normal voice, "Mitch."

He caught a whiff of burned flesh and he sensed a subtle warmth in the air around him. He paused and listened. A hand clamped over his mouth and a wiry arm wrapped around his chest, pinning his arms with incredible strength. The hand stank of death and Colin was sure he'd found his, here, alone, in the dark underbelly of the city.

And then a voice, like bark being peeled from a birch tree, whispered quietly in his ear, "Don't... move..."

Colin could feel his attacker's grip loosen, testing the wary prey's ability to follow a command. Knowing he was at a complete disadvantage, Colin remained still. After all, if this stranger had wanted him dead, he already would be. He didn't hear the stranger move and couldn't be sure the man wasn't standing right behind him. His knees weakened, and his limbs trembled.

WHACK! About ten feet to his right the

sound came at him like a thunder-clap. Colin's resolve gave out and he dropped to his knees, raising his arms to ward off the blows that were surely coming. As he tried to see around him, movement near the fire caught his eye. Mitch emerged from the dark fissure, walking calmly and confidently.

"You can come in now, Colin," Mitch said.

Then a tall, gangling man of about twenty-five years walked into the light, a huge dead rat dangling by its tail in his right hand, a wooden club in his left. His tightly trimmed hair might have been blond, but it was darkened with filth. His clothes hung loosely from his skeletal frame, mismatched and grimy. Colin walked to the fire, making sure he kept his distance from the "Rat Man". He watched in revulsion as the Rat Man placed the dead rat, its head a pulpy mess, on a large flat brick. Grabbing a cleaver that hung from a spike driven into a crack in the wall, the grungy man loped off its head and then in one quick motion yanked the skin from the dead animal's body, revealing the sinewy, red, muscle fibers that lay beneath. Rat Man held the corpse aloft, perhaps for Colin's approval.

"They watch. They cannot see," Rat Man said.

Colin looked to Mitch, unsure what he should do.

"Thanks to you, there are less of them," Mitch said.

Rat Man turned to Mitch, nodded and then slit open his prey to pull out its entrails. The handful of guts went into the fire, followed quickly by the head. Then he stabbed the spit through the creature and placed it over the flames. The scene of the cooking rat and the stench of burning entrails spun Colin's stomach like a blender. He looked away to keep from spewing his own half-digested meal out on the floor.

"Rat Man kills the rats that are possessed. They can take control of a rat and use them as spies." Mitch said.

"Demons possess rats? I don't understand the point of that, or the harm. Better rats than humans, right?"

"Drive them from every hole! They cannot see," Rat Man muttered.

"Yes, better rats than humans. But better they be confined to spirit form. In physical form, demons can get a thorough experience and understanding of what is going on here on Earth. What I mean by that is this; imagine that you could see people eating hamburgers and drinking beer, but you yourself could not take a bite or a drink. You would not have a full understanding of the meal, thus you would not be able to communicate it to anyone. Similarly, while in spirit form, they can see us and know we are communicating, but they don't really understand or hear the words or see us as we truly are. In physical form, they hear and understand all that we say and how we say it. So though they are powerful in spirit form, they are not omniscient."

Colin stared at Mitch, pursing his lips.

"It sounds pretty confusing, I guess," Mitch continued. "Think of it this way; a demon in physical form, even a rat, makes a better spy than one in spiritual form."

"Okay. Fair enough," Colin said. Then he pointed at Rat Man. "So how does he know which ones are possessed? I'm guessing this one was."

"Honestly, I don't know," Mitch answered. "But he does. And this one was setting himself up to spy on us. And no way Rat Man will put up with that." He clapped Rat Man on the back, eliciting a nod of agreement.

Without provocation, Rat Man's head snapped up, his pale eyes locking on Colin's face. Several seconds the bedraggled man stared at the computer salesman, beads of sweat forming on his high forehead. Squinting, Rat Man stood up, extending one hand toward Colin's chest until three fingers made contact. Mitch watched in silence. Colin remained still, unsure of what to do about the strange behavior. For a sliver of time, Colin thought he saw a small smile form on Rat Man's lips, but if there had been one, it fizzled away with a blink.

"Always trouble with demons," Rat Man said. Like a wary eel in a reef, he withdrew back to his seat.

Mitch regarded Colin for a moment, his face betraying suspicion. Returning his attention to Rat Man he said, "Which brings us to why we are here. Someone has been summoning demons in physical form. Do you know why?"

"My lips are sealed."

Colin looked at Mitch, scowling. "Not the answer we were hoping for," he said before being shushed by Mitch.

"Are you afraid? Has someone threatened you?"

"Starry, starry, night," answered Rat Man.

Colin shrugged and Mitch walked over and whispered to him. "No one's threatened him."

"Really?" Colin frowned in confusion. "I hope you know what he means. Sounds like nonsense to me."

"The painting? By Vincent Van Gogh?" Mitch asked, turning back to the filthy man.

Rat Man raised cold eyes to Mitch. "Dead ringer."

Colin watched as Mitch's face faded to white. He placed his hand on Mitch's shoulder, hoping the exorcist wasn't going to fall over. Finally, Mitch licked his lips and spoke in a dry, hoarse voice.

"Was it lost?"

"Is it found? The score is three points to three points."

"It can't be," Mitch muttered to himself.

"Who?" he demanded.

"It's never enough, never enough."

"Who!"

Rat Man stood, his face contorted with anger. "How the hell should I know? Think!" Then he sat down, took the meat from over the fire and sank his teeth into the flesh, ripping a piece free as hot dark blood ran down his chin.

"We're done here," Mitch announced.

"Good," Colin replied, just before he threw up.

They stopped when they reached the lit, bricked, subterranean passage, just after stumbling out of the dark caverns. Again, they had been silent during the return trip through the darkness. Colin felt markedly better, having left the aroma of burning rat meat behind. Now he stood looking at Mitch, confused as ever. Mitch took off walking and Colin jumped to keep up.

"What was all that nonsense?"

"That's the way he speaks," Mitch said.

"How did you find this guy, anyway?"

"I got him from his previous handler. He's been reporting to us for over twenty years."

"Holy cow! How old was he when he started reporting? Ten?"

"We don't know. He really hasn't changed much in all those years."

"Did he tell us anything that is going to be helpful?"

They reached the platform of the subway station and Mitch lead Colin to the stairs up to the street level where they continued down the sidewalk. A light rain had begun to mist down through the smothered, gray daylight.

Mitch took a deep breath. "Unfortunately, yes."

"Unfortunately? How can things get any worse?"

"According to Rat Man, someone thinks they have found Solomon's Seal." He fixed deeply troubled eyes on Colin.

Colin squinted and shook his head. "I don't know what that means."

"Rat Man was talking about stars. You've heard of King Solomon, right?" Colin nodded. "He's long dead, but one of the legends of King Solomon was that he had a ring, the Seal of Solomon. It has an engraving of a six-pointed star, or you can think of it as two three-pointed triangles laid atop one another. One right side up, the other upside down. Three points to three points, is how Ratman put it. Legend has it the ring gave Solomon the ability to control demons."

"Oh, that would be helpful," Colin interjected.

"If it existed, and it worked, and you knew how to use it. But even according to legend, the ring was lost long before the birth of Christ. And there is no mention of it in the Bible. Chances are, it doesn't exist."

"So whoever is summoning these demons thinks he can control them?"

"Yep. And he will be in for a rude awakening when he meets one face to face."

"You said that the demons would be drawn to whoever summoned them. Could that be because of the ring?"

Mitch thought about that for a minute. "Our research shows that demons will be inexorably drawn to whoever called it. But if the ring is real, I imagine it could enhance that pull. But the question still comes down to this: who is doing this? Finding them will help us find the demon we are hunting."

"What was all that about never enough? What'd that mean?"

Mitch shrugged. "I'm not sure if he was talking about us, about people in general, or whoever might have the ring."

"What if it has been found? Why would someone want to control demons? To what end?"

Mitch shook his head. "If we can figure that out, it might help us find whoever thinks they have the ring. Can't say I can think of any philanthropic uses for demons."

Colin agreed. But the concept of a ring being able to help someone control demons was extremely far-fetched. He was still conflicted with this whole situation, and throwing one more piece of biblical, or non-biblical, legend into the mix didn't help. However, this time yesterday he never would have believed someone who told him that demons were roaming around the earth, tearing people apart and stealing the souls of the unborn. Subconsciously, he rubbed his chest where the devil's claws had raked him. If he hadn't seen one, and fought one himself, he wouldn't believe any of it. He quietly hoped that Mitch was right about the ring, because it could help them find the sorcerer.

Colin felt a slight tickle in his back pocket, followed by a muffled tinkling sound. He pulled out his cellphone, saw his wife's number on the display, and took the call.

"Hey, Julie. What's up?"

"Something's wrong with the baby," she cried. "It feels like contractions, but not. It hurts."

"What? Are you okay?"

"No. It feels like I'm having contractions or something. But they're different. What if I'm miscarrying because of what the demon did?"

This is not what he needed. What the hell was happening? "Settle down. Is it still hurting?"

"No. It's gone now."

"It's gone now? Good. Any bleeding or anything like that? Did your water break?"

"No. Just the weird pain. It's really better now."

"Good. Probably just Bronson Flix—"

"Braxton Hicks."

"Yeah, whatever those things are called. Probably just that. Keep track of the timing and if you have any question, get to the hospital. Okay?"

"Okay. But I don't think it was Braxton Hicks contractions. I'm scared."

"Don't worry. It's going to be all right. Just make sure you get to the hospital if you think you're in labor or the weird pain comes again. Right?"

"Yes. I will. Colin, this is awful. We can't lose the baby."

"We won't," he said with more confidence than he felt.

Silence hung on the line for an uncomfortable moment, Colin waiting for her to say something more. "The police found Tim. They said it was pretty bad. They questioned me for an hour and a half. They wanted to know where you were."

Colin rubbed his forehead. "Oh, crap. What'd you tell them?"

"I told them you were in New York on a business trip. That you left yesterday. They thought that was convenient. I told them you were with me until you left, but they still want to talk to you. They told me to tell you to come home right away."

"Perfect. Understandable, I guess. Tell them I'll be back in a couple of days."

"The detective still wants you to call him right away. He gave me his number."

Colin exhaled a toxic breath. "Text me his

number, I'll have to figure out what to say to him."

Mitch was shaking his head.

"When are you going to be home? I'm scared that we're going to lose the baby." Julie's voice sounded lost again.

"I don't know. I'll be home as soon as I can."

"Hurry up, okay? I don't want the baby to..."

He could hear her sniffling on the other end of the line and it tore at his insides. "I know. We'll get this done. Just do your best to relax and I'll call you when I get a chance or have any news."

"Okay. Bye."

He shook his head at Mitch and swiped his brow.

Mitch raised his eyebrows. "Everything alright?"

"Not exactly. She had some weird contractions or cramps or something. She's worried that she's going into labor or miscarrying. I think they were those Braxon Chicks contractions."

"Braxton Hicks," Mitch corrected.

Colin explained the gist of the conversation, finishing with the detective's request for a call.

"Complications. Ignore him for now. We have more important things to do."

"I should call the detective," Colin said. "I mean, he is the police."

"No. Don't do that. He *thinks* he has a job to do, a killer to catch. But we know the truth of the matter. A demon killed Tim and we are down here hunting it. Do you think he's going to believe that?"

Colin thought. "Well..."

"Nothing you tell him is going to be anything other than a lie. And cops don't like being lied to, and they know when they are being lied to. You'll just make yourself look more like a suspect. Leave it be, and let's focus on getting this monster."

Reluctantly, Colin slid his phone back into his pocket. "So what now?" he asked, defeated.

"Now we have one more lead," Mitch said. "We have someone who's probably been asking around about the Seal of Solomon or trying to validate its authenticity. And they're going to have to learn how to summon demons in physical form. Fortunately, in my line of work, I know a gal who may have the inside track on both of those questions."

"She doesn't eat rats, does she?"

Mitch laughed aloud. "No. She is much more normal. Of course, that depends on your definition of normal."

CHAPTER EIGHT

Mitch told Colin they had to make a detour before they talked to their next source. They made their way to an affluent part of the city, each man captive to his own thoughts. The priest stopped, grabbing Colin by the arm and staring ahead. Colin followed Mitch's focus and saw a well-dressed, gray-haired man duck into an expensive looking, copper colored sedan that was idling in front of an elegant, three story residence. They waited as the car sped away from the curb.

Mitch started forward.

"What was that about?"

"Dunno. But I don't want to draw too much attention here," Mitch said as he mounted the wide staircase that lead up to the big, oak doors of the residence. The door opened nearly as soon as Mitch knocked, and they were invited in by a man wearing a black cassock. He told the men to take a seat, the Bishop would be there in a moment.

"Bishop?" Colin asked.

"This is bigger than we originally thought."

The Bishop emerged from a closed room, his raiment robes of purple. The image of grace and confidence, the elder man glided across the room and extended his hand to Mitch who grasped it and touched it to his forehead as he momentarily dropped to one knee.

"How are you doing, Mitch?"

"Hanging in there, your Excellency," Mitch said, standing. He introduced Colin and the Bishop took Colin's hand in a traditional handshake, caution and curiosity plain in his expression.

The three all settled down in Victorian-styled chairs. The man who'd opened the door once again appeared, bringing them a small pot of tea that emanated the faint smell of oranges. With a level of formality that Colin hadn't seen before, Mitch relayed their visit with the Rat Man and the nature of what they'd been told. The balding, gray-haired Bishop nodded in agreement with Mitch's assessment of its meaning, complimenting him on his efforts and insight.

"If you find this ring, you must bring it to me," the Bishop commanded. "If it is genuine, we must watch over it."

"Certainly, your Excellency." Then Mitch looked at Colin and took a deep breath. "Thank you for trusting in my judgment. Now let me explain why Colin is here." He went on to tell the story of the attack on the Hamptons and Colin's miraculous survival.

"Praise to the Lord God," the Bishop said. His eyes were wide as he made the sign of the cross.

"May I see the wounds?"

Colin felt his face warm as he opened his shirt to reveal the four raised scars. Like a little boy reaching out to pet the first dog he'd ever laid eyes on, the Holy man reached out and touched where Colin had been scored by the demon's claws.

"You have been set upon by the demon but held fast by God. He will not abandon you, Colin." Then he leaned over and whispered something to Mitch, who swallowed hard. Out loud, he said, "I will inform the rest of the Order." With that, he stood up and hustled from the room.

Mitch motioned toward the door and they left without another word. Once outside Colin asked, "The rest of the Order?"

"The Order of Saint Anthony," Mitch replied in a whisper. "The cavemen and I belong to it. We fight demonic influence in the world."

"So he has to tell them about my son's soul?"

"He will. But he has something even more important to discuss with them."

"What's more important than getting my son's soul back?"

Mitch stopped walking and scrutinized the computer salesman before answering. "You."

The thought caught him completely off guard. It took a second for him to realize that Mitch had started walking again, so he had to trot to catch up. Finally next to the priest, he said, "Me? How am

I so important?"

"It's the Order of Saint Anthony."

Colin waited for Mitch to elaborate. When it was clear no explanation was forthcoming, Colin pressed. "That means nothing to me. Who the hell is Saint Anthony?" he said.

"He survived an attack by demons, too. Had his body all gouged up, into stripes, and lived."

Colin considered that for a moment, his mind overloaded. He could only offer Mitch a confused stare.

"Do you still wonder if you are meant to be here?"

Colin shrugged. "I don't know what to think." He thought what he'd heard before, about demons coming into the physical plane, was nuts. But there was too much evidence to the contrary, scars included. This latest revelation raised a whole new series of questions. Had he been spared just to fight demons? Was he some special hero who was supposed to fight for good? And what about what he'd learned about the possibility of his son becoming...what? The next Hitler? The next anti-Christ? The questions drew his mind into sharp focus on the immediate goal: they had to get his son's soul back. He hoped that if he focused on that, maybe he wouldn't go crazy.

They were on their way to lunch when

Mitch's phone rang.

Mitch answered and listened for a second. Then he said, "Hold on. Let me put you on speaker."

He pressed a button on the screen of his phone and said, "Go ahead, Reginald."

"We have another manifestation being indicated in the Brownsville area of the city. Ben and I are watching it occur on the monitor right now."

"In the middle of the afternoon? That's new. Do you have an address or anything?" Mitch asked.

"Come on, man. We haven't gotten the software tuned in that tight yet. Be glad we can tell you it's Brownsville. I'd head there and follow the screams. Ben has the police scanner on so if we get anything that can help you zero in on it, we'll let you know."

"Thanks." Mitch disconnected the call and stuck the phone back in his pocket. Leaning close to Colin he said, "We have to catch a cab to Brownsville. We gotta find this new demon and take it out."

Colin's limbs went numb and cold. Another demon meant that they would have to go and try to exorcise it. Another fight with a creature born of evil and on parole from Hell. A chance for him to die prematurely, leaving his daughter fatherless and his wife a pregnant widow. And this one was not the one who'd stolen his unborn son's soul. What if he did die, without killing his actual target? Mitch would move on, he knew. But if Colin fell, would Mitch still be alive?

"I didn't sign up to go demon hunting. I'm just after the demon that took my son's soul."

Mitch stared at Colin as though he'd just dropped the f-bomb in church. "There is no half-way on this, Colin. You're either in or you're out, and you chose to be in."

"Yeah. In to hunt down this one demon. Not to hunt down every demon from now until the end of time."

"Haven't you heard anything I've said?" Mitch said. He raised a hand to hail a cab. "We can't pick and choose which demons to fight. We have to take them as they come until we can stop the sorcerer. Besides, maybe this one will lead us to him."

Colin's brow creased. "But what if we die trying to exorcise this one? Then what? Julie gives birth to the next anti-Christ?"

Mitch squared up with Colin and returned the man's frown. "Between the two of us, which one has some sort of weird immunity, a charismatic gift? Not me. So which one of us should be acting chicken-shit?" Colin recoiled as Mitch continued unabated. "I've already done two of these."

"Then do this one," Colin said.

Mitch's face reddened. "I had help. What if I die? How the hell are you going to even *begin* to exorcise your demon? You need to come and get some experience, with me, while you have the chance. You aren't going to want to have a big learning curve when it really matters."

Colin scowled at the exorcist, but he could hear the logic in Mitch's words. His eyes dropped momentarily and Mitch seized the moment to press the attack.

"God brought us together for a reason. You're an important part of the team, otherwise you wouldn't have survived. This is the right thing to do. It's the only thing to do." He placed his hand on Colin's shoulder in a friendly gesture, his anger diffusing.

Mitch made valid points. But he was already putting himself at risk, something that could be devastating to his little family if things went wrong. But this demon did offer a good chance at finding the idiot who summoned it. As much as he didn't want to, he had to admit that Mitch was right. Colin raised his eyes to the exorcist and without saying a word, nodded.

Nephalen's dwarfish, vaguely humanoid form appeared to have been scarred by burns, though one would have to look him directly in the face or at his exposed hands to be able to see the shriveled, dark-red skin. His clothes were not outdated but evidenced a poor, homeless person, a persona magnified by the way he slowly shuffled down the sidewalk of the crime plagued neighborhood. No one would pay much attention to him, and if they did, they would feel pity. They couldn't help it. It was this power that allowed him to move unnoticed amongst human kind. While they were busy feeling their weak empathy, he was free to cause pain, angst and anger. All with the goal of giving the wretched beings a reason to do harm to one another. He most liked it when that harm came in the form of violence.

As he approached the corner, he noticed the group of young men, their head dresses all the same color, if not the same style, and jeans hanging limply from their hips, proudly displaying the boxers beneath. Loathing seeped from the bloodshot eyes of the gang member who saw Nephalen approaching. But these humans were not his targets. They were too easy to affect while in spirit form. In physical form, as he was now, Nephalen would seek bigger, more important prey. When he got close enough, his empathetic sway would allow him to pass, both on the street and from their memories.

"Lookit the little freak," the red-eyed thug said. The other three gang-bangers turned to jeer at the shriveled demon. The hostile display surprised Nephalen. Usually, at this distance, people would avert their eyes or give him a wan smile out of pity. These men, no, *boys*, seemed unaffected by his power thus far. But then, it had been several hundred years since he'd had the opportunity to walk the face of the earth. He continued on his route, undeterred, until one of the young men stepped into his path and shoved him backwards.

"Where you going, you little prick? This is *our* street." His comrades surrounded the diminutive monster. As unusual as the verbal attack was, Nephalen was anything but afraid.

"Hey, motherfucker. He asked you a question." This comment came from behind him, followed up with a slap to the imp's head and group laughter.

Nephalen turned to look at his assailant, a mischievous smile on his cracked lips. Like a striking viper, his hand shot out and latched onto the young man's testicles, his clawed fingertips piercing denim and digging deep into flesh. With a quick yank, the demon tore out the reproductive organs, sending a splash of urine and blood and innards onto the concrete. Three guns materialized from the waistbands of the remaining three men. But not nearly fast enough. Before the first two could even raise their weapons, one had his throat ripped completely out and the other had been disemboweled, both men left thrashing and twitching on the ground. The final thug managed to raise his pistol and fire one shot into Nephalen's torso before the demon jumped and drove his long, black thumbnails into the boy's eyes, ramming them deep into his skull.

Nephalen licked the blood and fluids from his dripping hands before plodding on down the cracked sidewalk. He smiled meekly at the next person he encountered, but they were too distracted by the grisly carnage on the street in front of them to pay a pathetic, disfigured midget any notice.

Mitch yanked open the door of the cab that squealed over to the curb and yelled at Colin to get in. As soon as the car pulled into traffic, Mitch issued an order to the cabbie to drop them at a main intersection in the middle of Brownsville.

"What de hell, man," the dark-skinned driver asked. "You doin' some sorta survival program in de hood? You boys got better places to go than that."

"Just drop us where I asked."

"You're the boss."

The cab veered in and out of traffic, twice nearly running over the feet of pedestrians too anxious to cross the street. The driver never missed an opportunity to shout obscenities at the curb encroaching folk he'd nearly hit. Colin looked frantically for a seat belt, found one end, but not the other. An egg without its carton. He looked at the crack between the seat back and the seat and quickly decided against an expedition into that netherworld. He would put his faith in propping his knees against the seat in front of him. Mitch seemed unfazed. Finally, the cab took a quick right at a busy intersection and bounced off the curb as it jerked to a stop on the side street.

"Forty-five dollars," the cab driver said. Mitch handed over a fifty and told the man to keep the change. "Don' stay here past dark," he added before zooming away.

Somewhere behind the clouds, the sun slid on its way to a rendezvous with the horizon, though after checking his watch Colin figured there were still about three hours of light left. He wondered if the demon they hunted was holed up somewhere in a dark pit, waiting for sunset to fall.

Colin looked around at the neighborhood, suddenly worried that the demon might be the least of his problems. He checked to make sure that the Palo Santo dagger was still in his inside coat pocket, taking a small measure of security when he felt its wooden form. Then he looked to make sure Mitch still had the pack of knives on his back and hoped the flint-lock pistol was in there as well. He could feel the pull of his own backpack containing the two linoleum fortified leather jackets.

Mitch had just started walking briskly down the street when a police car went racing by in the opposite direction with lights flashing and siren screaming. Mitch spun around and grabbed Colin's arm, giving it a tug.

"Let's go," he said. He broke into a jog as he followed the squad car. "And keep your eyes open."

Reluctantly, Colin matched his pace, his head on a swivel. What was the cop car responding to? In this neighborhood, it could be any number of bad things. But in the deepest fibers of his being, Colin knew whatever it was, was related to the demon that now roamed the streets. Mitch seemed to know it too. And, like the police, instead of running away like any sane person would, they were heading into the jaws of the fight.

As the dark gray sidewalk slid underfoot, his eyes scanned alleys and both sides of the street. The tires of passing cars made a swooshing sound as they kicked up the light moisture from the misty rain that had settled over the city. In his mind, it was the sound of Hell's creatures zipping around him, working to surround him before they dug into him with their claws and dripping teeth. Despite the dank weather, Colin's tongue stuck to the roof of his mouth, pasty and dry. The overcast prevented shadows and rendered the world in shades of gray and black. Only the occasional traffic light cut through the dreary, colorless images, like the sole objects that have been artificially colorized in the old black and white movies. He was too jacked up to even realize that he was jogging, his body easily adjusting his breathing to accommodate.

One step in front of him, Mitch looked like a soldier double-timing it through a war-torn hell-hole of a city, his ruck sack in place on his back. All that he lacked was a rifle and uniform.

"Hey," Colin called. "Maybe we should put these jackets on."

Mitch stopped immediately, turned around nodding, and spun Colin around to help him get the pack off his back. Not wasting any time, he pulled out the two jackets that had been unceremoniously crammed into the big back pack and tossed one to Colin as he slipped into one himself and hoisted his own bag back in place.

"Grab the pistol. You still have the Palo Santo dagger, right?" He turned around so Colin could dig through Mitch's pack for the flint-lock pistol.

"Yep," Colin said as he withdrew the antique firearm and slid it into the custom tailored inside pocket of his leather jacket. The two fit together amazingly well.

"This reminds me of gearing up in Iraq."

That caught Colin's attention. "Iraq? Were you in the Army?"

"Oh, hell no. I was a Navy chaplain assigned to the Marine Corps, but I was in the middle of some serious fire-fights. So, despite the fact that I wasn't assigned to carry a rifle, I know how to use one. Rifleman first, everything else comes after that. You ain't much good if you're dead."

"No wonder you're not afraid of these demons."

Mitch patted him on the shoulder. "Make no mistake, I'm scared shitless of these demons. Let's get moving." He turned and started trotting off again.

Surprised at the foul bluntness of Mitch's statement, Colin wasn't sure if he should feel good or bad about the fact that the priest was scared too. He decided that he would have preferred it if Mitch weren't frightened. He carried enough fear for the both of them.

They jogged up to a corner where they'd seen the squad car turn right and followed in that direction. As soon as they made the turn themselves, they could see the bursts of red and blue lights of the police vehicle illuminating the clouds and foggy air. It was pulled over at a haphazard angle at the next block, the driver apparently expecting action when he stopped. Upon nearing the scene, they could see about eight people milling around, and the two police officers from the parked unit trying to get them all to back up, away from the four destroyed bodies that lay crumpled in the street. One officer talked into his radio calling in support and the coroner. Colin saw another police car closing on their location from far down the street, and heard another approaching from behind them, its siren muted by the light rain.

As Colin got close enough to see the bodies, it was plain to see how they'd died. His arms tingled and he struggled to breathe normally, the air coming in weak gasps. He remembered his neighbor, Tim. Just when he thought his knees would give out,

Mitch grabbed him by the shoulders and wrenched his face around until they were looking each other square in the eye.

"Hey! I need you here, with me, right now." Mitch's eyes were intense and had a grip of their own, not letting go of Colin's attention. "We're leaving here ASAP because somewhere out there is a very pissed off demon. This changes the plan. Can't follow it if it's a killer. We have to kill it, first chance we get. Sit over here and wait a minute while I try to figure out what it looks like and where it went." He ushered Colin over to sit on a concrete step in front of a two-story brick building that probably held no more than eight apartments. Then he went over and started talking to some of the bystanders.

Colin let his head drop down toward his knees as he wrung his hands together. He tried to concentrate on breathing normally, in fact, to focus on his breathing so he could banish the images of the broken bodies. How did he think he could help Mitch fight something that could accomplish that? It just mutilated four guys on a street corner who were, judging from the surroundings, probably not unaccustomed to perpetrating violence themselves. He reached up and felt the reassuring bulk of the antique pistol in his jacket.

"Damn. That little guy had one hell of a gleam in his eye. I could see it from way over here. Mean little fucker."

Not sure if he was being spoken to or overhearing a conversation, Colin turned and looked up over his left shoulder to see a man in his sixties, wearing a white tee-shirt, leaning out the second-floor window just above. The white at his temples was fluorescent compared to his dark skin.

"You saw who did this?" Colin asked.

"Sure did. When I hear all this hollerin' and screamin', I figured I'd better take a peek. Didn't expect to see that," he said. The man shook his head. "Looked like a midget. Barely come up to them boys' belly buttons. But fast! Hmm, hmm, hmm." The man closed his eyes as his head continued to sway. "Wish I hadn't seen it."

"What'd he look like," Colin said. He stood to face the man.

"Short little fella. Wearing a hoody, like everybody else 'round here. And dark trousers. Kinda felt bad for him as he walked away. Them boys are nothing but trouble anyhow. I imagine they had it comin'. Still, coulda gone my whole life without seein' a guy get his junk ripped off."

Colin cringed. "Where'd he go?"

The man crinkled his brow and thought, his eyes darting side to side. He scratched his chin as he looked up and down the dark, rainy, street.

"You know, I can't really recall. I think he headed that way." The man pointed down the street in the direction opposite from which Colin and Mitch had come. He smiled down at Colin. "And I gotta say, that is one weird-ass coat you're wearing there."

"New fashion thing," Colin said. Embarrassed, he looked down at his linoleum adorned jacket. "Thanks for the info," he said. He gave the witness a parting wave and turned to see Mitch striding toward him, his visage grim.

"Crap," Mitch spat. "I overheard the cops talking to the only two witnesses who saw anything and they both say it was a little guy, maybe a kid or a little person. But neither one can remember which way he went."

"A guy over here saw it too and thinks he went that way." Colin pointed down the street.

"Good enough." Mitch took off at a fast jog in that direction. Making sure his gun was firmly in place, Colin set off on his heels.

As they ran, they scanned every alley way or vacant lot, hoping to catch a glimpse of the diminutive but deadly demon. When they were about one hundred yards from the next intersection, Mitch abruptly shifted into a walk and grabbed Colin's arm as he slowed next to him. He pointed directly ahead. Through the gloomy mist and spray, Colin could make out the black shape of a small but sturdy figure walking away from them with an unusual gait. When it reached the corner, it turned right and disappeared behind a brick building.

"Fast now. This way," Mitch ordered, leading them at a near sprint on a parallel course through an alley.

Colin's legs protested the speed. He jogged regularly, but this pace had his hamstrings going taught and feeling like dry, frayed ropes. Somehow, he managed to keep up with Mitch who made running look as fluid and comfortable as a hawk gliding on a soft breeze, waiting to swoop down on unsuspecting prey. Mitch dashed left into another alley that would intersect with the street where the demon strode, Colin close behind. When they were about thirty feet from the sidewalk where they hoped to see the imp, Mitch stopped.

"Get the gun," he whispered to Colin as he drew a tarnished, bronze dagger. "Take off that safety. You ever shoot a pistol before?"

"Yes, of course," Colin snapped, trying to mask his rising fear with annoyance. He looked at the featureless pistol barrel and winced. "Though without sights on it, I'm not making promises." The scars on his chest itched and burned slightly. He scrubbed at them as he stepped behind a dumpster and raised the flintlock pistol, using the top of the smelly garbage bin as a prop to steady his arms. In the desolate silence of the alley, the 'clack' the hammer made as Colin cocked the weapon sounded like someone breaking a pine two-by-four. Both men winced, hoping the noise of the rain and the limited traffic provided some auditory cover.

Colin imagined himself on a duck-blind, waiting for a mallard to land near his decoys. The moisture of the day, having accumulated in his hair, ran down his forehead to cling to his eyebrows and lashes until he blinked the droplets away. He heard soft shuffling foot-falls approaching the end of the alley beyond his gun barrel. Though he had once mastered his ability to manage his pulse when prey approached, he found any hope of that vaporized as he thought about the demon he now hunted. The burning of his scars intensified, becoming painful. He tried unsuccessfully not to squirm as he watched for the demon. His heart raced and as the moment of opportunity drew closer, he felt like a murderer, lying in wait for a hapless victim. But this was a creature of hell he sought to destroy. Surely, he was no murderer. Still, how could he ambush this poor little dwarf without it having a fighting chance?

The huddled figure stepped into the left side of Colin's field of fire, the brick apartment building effectively belching the devil from cover. Colin didn't have long before the demon would disappear behind the building on the right side of the one lane alley. His finger tightened against the trigger, finding no slack in its movement. He forced himself to quit breathing and did his best to line up the top of the smooth gun barrel with his target. But he hesitated, wondering as to the fate of the poor creature, sympathizing with it in its ignorance.

"Shoot it," Mitch huffed.

The pint-sized hellion stopped and turned toward them. Colin saw venomous fangs and flashing claws. Then everything exploded in a fury.

The muzzle flash of the flint-lock pistol blinded both Colin and Mitch, and the thunder of the explosion rang in their ears. Colin tried to clear his vision and see through the huge white cloud of smoke that hung in the damp air. From the corner of his eye he saw Mitch lunge forward.

"You missed!"

"Dammit!" Colin dropped the gun and pulled out his Palo Santo dagger only in time to see the demon fling itself onto Mitch. A hideous wail tried to echo down the rain and mist deadened alley. Colin shrugged his shoulders upward, trying to muffle his ears as he stared at Mitch and the demon, not sure of what to do. The dwarfish monster was on its back, flailing feebly at Mitch who clung to the grip of a sanctified dagger that was hilt deep in the demon's right shoulder.

"Stab it," Mitch commanded.

Colin dove forward and sunk the wooden knife into the creature's left shoulder. He was met by a crushing feeling of sorrow and pity. Incredible pain wracked him as his scars felt torn asunder once more. Still, he held the dagger fast. The tortured soul turned its eyes on him, its plea for mercy highlighted within. The revulsion at his own actions was so strong that Colin nearly retched in its face. He closed his eyes and turned away.

Mitch began a rapid recitation of Latin phrases, drawing forth more anguished cries from the writhing demon. Colin tried to listen to the words but was instantly lost. From nowhere, overwhelming feelings of guilt and pity squeezed him in an ever-tightening knot. What were they doing? This little guy never did anything to them. They must be monsters, the two big thugs stabbing into a diminutive, defenseless creature. Why not go club some puppies too? The increasing emotional pain grew so strong that Colin could feel his eyes water and he started to snivel. He glanced at Mitch and watched the trace of a salty tear cut its way through the rainy sheen on the exorcist's cheek. He couldn't bear it any longer. Slowly, he began to withdraw his dagger and his agony lessened.

Like a striking rattle-snake the small demon's arm shot forth, the curved claws seeking Colin's throat. He snapped to the side and the poisonous razors cleaved through the flesh of Colin's cheek, sending scalding pain through his head. He turned and looked at Mitch who looked to be fighting his own losing battle, his words uttering slowly through racking sobs. The demon was unable to reach the priest with his left hand, as if an invisible barrier prevented it. But Colin could see the fingers of its right hand starting to flex as Mitch reluctantly started to draw back his own dagger.

Colin's face screwed up in confusion as the pumping beat of AC/DC's "Highway to Hell" resonated louder and louder in the alley. As the volume increased, he could feel the shroud of pity fall away to be washed down the sewer. The impish demon writhed and wailed anew. Colin touched his cheek and glanced at the dark red blood he took away. Feeling no pity now, he eyed the supine devil and lunged forward, sinking the Palo Santo dagger into where the heart should be, driving it home with all his weight. Simultaneously, Mitch pinned the creature's right shoulder down again and continued his recitation.

The passing car, whose radio blasted out the music through lowered windows, receded and the demon, now unable to fight with the holy knives piercing it and Mitch's words hammering it, began to buck and thrash violently. Random twitches sent raking claws across the protective coats of both men. Colin struggled to hold his knife in place as Mitch spoke his words. On a particularly wild convulsion, Colin accidentally pulled his dagger out of the demon's body. He frantically tried to push the sanctified wooden blade back into its demonic sheath, but a bone-jarring blast of thunder racked his entire body, knocking him forward onto the cold pavement where the demon had been just a split second before.

He spun around on his back, holding the dagger upward in imitation of a fighting cat. But nothing was there to attack him. He looked around the alley, trying to find the evil being. Mitch rolled over onto his back, laid his bronze knife on his chest and let his arms flop out to his sides.

"It's done," Mitch said, trying to catch his breath. "We sent it back to Hell. That wasn't so hard was it? Ow," he said. He reached up to touch his neck.

Colin turned to the exorcist, concerned. He watched as Mitch rubbed his neck and pull his hand away, gloved in blood.

CHAPTER NINE

"Oh shit. You're cut," Colin said. Frantic, he sat up and scrambled to Mitch's side. "Let me see it." He pushed the priest's head to the side and examined the wound. Two deep scratches marred the underside of Mitch's chin, each of them oozing blood. "Crap, crap, crap." He sought out the man's eyes. "Are you going to die? From the, the curse, the scratch?"

Mitch looked again at his hand and grimaced. "I don't think so. I've had at least this bad before, maybe worse. Sure hurts a ton, though." His mouth tightened, accentuating the lines that flared out from the corners.

"How many times have you been scratched? I thought you said you only killed the two?"

Mitch nodded gently. "Yeah. And each one of them got me a little bit."

"Are you crazy? You've been scratched twice before? I thought you said their scratch was lethal, some sort of demonic poison?" Colin sat back on his butt, arms going limp at his sides. He couldn't lose Mitch, the only guy who could do the exorcisms. This is exactly the type of disaster that he'd feared.

"True. But not a superficial scratch. This is just really bloody, it's not too deep." He looked again at his hand. "I'm not *sure* I'm not going to die. I just don't think it's my time." He produced a weak smile. "We'll know in a couple of minutes." He reached into the inside pocket of his leather coat, his hand pausing. "If I do go... I'll need you to deliver something."

Colin's heart thundered in his chest. He couldn't believe what he was hearing. If Mitch died, he was thoroughly screwed. He didn't know how to exorcise anything and didn't know how to find the sorcerer. More than that, he liked Mitch. He stared at Mitch's stationary hand, stuffed inside his jacket and waited impatiently.

Mitch withdrew his hand from his coat, empty. "Never mind. I'm good. The pain is starting to subside. I don't think it'd feel better if it was going to do me in." He smiled at Colin.

"Jesus."

The priest scowled at Colin. "I hope that's the beginning of a prayer of thanks."

Colin caressed his closed eyelids. "Sorry. I just really need your help."

Mitch chuckled. "And I need yours. Maybe you really should say a prayer."

Like an obedient five-year-old, the computer salesman clasped his hands, closed his eyes, and said a silent prayer of thanks. He didn't see Father

Mitch's pained look of relief or hear his prayer of elation and gratitude. But when he opened his eyes, he saw a man who knew he'd just narrowly escaped death and was deeply shaken by it. Mitch's face was pale, and he stared blankly at the ground, his hand stuck back inside his coat.

"Done." Colin announced as he climbed to his feet, pretending not to notice Mitch's demeanor. He looked around the dark alley, making sure the demon wasn't just hiding, waiting for an opportunity to rip his throat out. "That was awful," Colin said. "You're sure you're going to be okay?"

Mitch huffed out an exhausted laugh. "That was definitely the toughest one yet. I don't know if I could have done it without you here. I wanted to stop. I felt pity for it." Mitch stood up, sheathed his dagger in a pocket and dug into his pack, pulling out a small tube of antibiotic. He squeezed some ointment onto a finger and applied it to his neck.

Colin watched, one eyebrow raised in confusion. "Antibiotic?"

"He ripped those four gang-bangers apart. Who knows what was on those claws?"

Colin groaned in disgust.

"How's your face?" Mitch asked leaning in with ointment to touch the area where rendered flesh was fusing back into place. "That's incredible. I've never seen anything like that. Of course, this last couple of days has been a series of firsts. But I've never even *heard* of something like that."

"I've never heard of *any* of this craziness." Colin felt his cheek. In his concern for Mitch, he'd totally forgotten he'd been injured himself. Three tender scars ran across it from his ear to near his bottom lip. He wondered what it would look like. Julie might see it as another indicator of his abject failure. *How could you let a demon from hell damage the one thing you had going for you?* But he thought it might look a bit bad-ass. He sighed and looked at the priest.

"Face feels okay. Hurt like hell again but seems pretty good now." He shrugged, happy to be alive. "He was a tough little guy."

Mitch's mouth was screwed up in a knot, his brow creased.

"Something wrong?" Colin asked.

"Up until now, the demons have looked like the monsters they are. This one had enough power to pass as a human, albeit a unique one. Our sorcerer is bringing more powerful demons into our world. The lesser demons can't modify their appearance much, if at all." He looked up at Colin, his eyes serious. "Believe me, that little guy doesn't look like that on his home turf."

"Great. At least the one we are after should be easier than this, right?"

"Theoretically."

Now it was Colin's turn to look thoughtful. "What were you saying during the fight?"

"The Rite. It's an exorcism, after all. I'll have

to bring you up to speed on it." He paused and turned to Colin. "I can't believe you missed it. I thought you said you'd fired pistols before?"

Colin scoffed. He looked around and found the old weapon lying where he'd dropped it. He hoisted it up in front of his face. "How could anyone hit anything with this friggin' antique? Maybe if I could have put the barrel in the thing's mouth it'd have worked."

A sly smile slowly spread on the priest's face.

"What?" Colin asked.

"Antique. That's what it is, isn't it? You know what else is an antique? Solomon's Seal."

"And?"

"You've given us an even better lead. I know a guy who deals in antiques who is so well versed in historical items that he'll know if someone had claimed to find it or were asking around about it. We need to talk to him."

"As long as he doesn't eat rats."

"Speaking of eating rats, are you hungry?"

The cab ride to the restaurant Mitch picked out was quiet, both men lost in their own thoughts. Colin stared out the window at the lights that created star-bursts in the droplets clinging to the glass. Around them, the city churned on, no one having the slightest idea what had transpired within the last hour. He tried to wrap his head around it himself. He and Mitch just sent a demon from hell, back to hell. Or somewhere like that. Somewhere it didn't want to go anyway. And that was what? The third or fourth demon Mitch had banished? Colin was so far out of his league. This was not something a computer salesman was cut out for. He wondered again why he was dumb enough to be here.

Then an unbidden image materialized in his mind; a smiling, cooing, little baby boy. *God, how did I end up in this nightmare?*

Colin thought about his family, wondering if Claire was going to be okay. She was used to Daddy having to go off for a couple of days on sales trips, but she was aware, if not wholly, that something horrible had happened at their house. The broken sliding-glass door and bedroom window by themselves could scare kids her age who had such a limited grasp of their real world. He wanted to see her and Julie again.

The thought reminded him of the detective back home who wanted to speak with him. Here he was torn. Mitch made some good points, but how could he just ignore the police? Maybe he could buy some time if he just gave the guy a quick call and let him know he'd be right in to talk as soon as he got home. Whenever that was. After all, the police had a job to do protecting people. And if he could somehow allay their fears, maybe they could work on some other more pressing cases?

He felt the bulk of the backpack on the floor, smashed between his legs and the front seat. Now it contained his coat, the gun and the wooden dagger. They had decided it would be best if they each carried their own complete set of gear in case they got separated. Though if that happened, Colin was doomed. He couldn't banish a demon by himself. He had no idea what to say or how to say it. It was tough enough fighting that pint-sized hellion without having to try to exorcise it. If he'd had to fight the one he encountered at his house alone, he would have failed. There was no way he'd get lucky enough to escape being ripped apart the next time.

He let his head thump against the side window as despair and doubt permeated his spirit. The shapes of bodies walking by on the sidewalk went unnoticed. Every one of them a black, faceless figure who didn't care a whit about the computer salesman riding past them in the cab. He felt the car swerve sharply to the curb and jerk to a halt.

Mindlessly, he gathered up his things and climbed out to stand on the sidewalk in the cold rain, waiting for Mitch to settle up with the driver. Mitch slid out of the passenger door, a big smile on his face, and slapped Colin on the back.

"One more down. One to go. You getting the hang of it?" He pulled Colin down the sidewalk with him.

"Hardly," Colin answered. "I couldn't hit the damn thing with the pistol, and then I almost gave up because I felt bad. And I did nothing to exorcise it. That was all you."

"Hey, don't worry. You did fine," Mitch said. "You haven't been trained to do any of this, and let's face it; it's scary as hell. Besides, I really don't think I could have done that one without you. He was tough. I never thought I'd have to worry about feeling bad for taking one of these things out."

Colin pursed his lips, unconvinced.

Mitch turned and pulled open a solid wooden door, holding it so Colin could enter. "Here we are. Best Irish pub in town."

Colin looked through the doorway and gave Mitch a doubtful headshake before proceeding inside. Irish pub it was. Darkly lit, with wooden booths against the wall opposite an ebony bar that stretched the length of the front room, and a couple of regulars that glared at them when they came in. Mitch stepped past him and walked to the far end of the bar where an open doorway led into another room filled with tables. He picked a booth in the corner and ushered Colin to have a seat.

"Order me a Guinness and whatever you want for yourself. I gotta hit the bathroom, clean up and what not." Mitch looked at the dried blood on his hand. "It may take a little while, so don't be afraid to order a second round." He spun and strode to a fragile-looking door labeled "Real Men" and disappeared inside.

The waitress, a disinterested-looking young woman wearing a tight black t-shirt that matched her pony-tailed hair came over and took Colin's drink order. She tossed two laminated menus down on the table, displaying a tired smile as she left.

Colin pulled his cellphone from his pocket and quickly dialed. It was answered before the second ring.

"Detective Keller."

"Hi, Detective. This is Colin Hampton. I heard about Tim, my neighbor. Julie asked that I give you a call. What happened?"

"I was hoping you could tell me. When was the last time you saw Tim?"

"It was the morning the day I left. He's really dead?" Colin felt his mouth dehydrate.

"I'm afraid so. What time did you see him and why?"

"Our dog went missing and I went over to see if he'd wandered over to Tim's place. Tim said his dog was gone too and that he thought he'd seen a bear the day before."

"A bear?"

"That's what he said. Come to think of it, I saw something back in the woods too. I thought it was, maybe, just a really dark deer or something. But now I'm not so sure. Maybe it got our dogs." This wasn't going as well as he'd hoped it would. But he couldn't turn back now.

"Uh huh. Look, I need you to come in for a

full interview. How soon can you be back here?"

"Oh. I uh… I'm on an important business trip and it might be a few days. I'll come right in when I get back."

"I'm conducting a murder investigation, Mr. Hampton. And frankly, you are my biggest lead, and I find it a bit disconcerting that you left town right around the time your neighbor was killed, and you were the last to see him alive. Are you now telling me that you aren't willing to come back, even after hearing what's happened?"

"Murder investigation? Whoa. You're telling me that Tim was murdered?"

"I'm investigating it as a homicide. Yes."

Keller didn't say another word. The silence that spilled from the telephone was nerve-racking. Colin wasn't sure how to respond, but he knew he had to. "I understand," Colin said. The door to the men's room opened and Mitch came out shaking water from his hands. "But I'm about to start a sales meeting so I have to go now. I promise I'll come and see you just as soon as I'm back in town." He pressed the 'end' button on his phone and pocketed it.

Detective Keller immediately placed a call to his office. "Keller here. I spoke with Hampton and he won't come in. When I spoke to his boss earlier today, he said Hampton had no plans to go to

New York for business. Go ahead and send his information to NYPD and have them pick him up as a person of interest in this murder. Have them notify me on my cellphone when they do so I can get right down there and talk to him. Thanks." The old detective shook his head, the greasy salt and pepper hair motionless. "Why do they always have to do things the hard way?"

"Who was that?" Mitch asked as he slid into the booth.

"Oh, I was just leaving a message for my boss that I would be out a couple of days. Didn't want to raise any flags there."

Mitch examined Colin's face. "Sure. Good idea." He picked up one of the menus and perused it quickly with his eyes before snapping it shut. "I highly recommend the bar-b-que burger."

"Doesn't sound very Irish."

"It's not. That's why I recommend it."

Both men laughed lightly, the stress of the day squirting out in small doses. The dark-haired waitress arrived carrying two creamy-headed, Guinness beers, a small beige trickle of the tiny bubbles sliding down the side of each clear glass. She saw Mitch and her face transformed into a radiant countenance of pleasure.

"Father Mitch. How are you?" she asked. After she set the tray of beer down she slid into

Mitch's lap and wrapped her arms around his neck and gave him a sweet kiss on the cheek.

"I'm good, Lily. Thank you," Mitch answered.

Colin couldn't help but notice the relaxed demeanor with which Mitch dealt with the young lady.

She squeezed his shoulders. "You seem tense. You know I got my massage therapy degree, right? You should make an appointment and let me work those knots out." She threw Colin a devious smile.

"Maybe some other time," Mitch said. He squirmed in his seat, lips pursed. "And be careful who you take as clients. Wouldn't want anything happening to my favorite waitress." He obviously felt uncomfortable with the young woman's subtle sensuality. He gestured to Colin. "Lily, this is my friend, Colin. Colin, Lily."

With that, the young waitress bounced out of Mitch's lap, a sad smile playing across her lips. She inclined her head politely at Colin, long lashes batting over green eyes. "Nice to meet you." She pulled her order pad out of the back pocket of her tight jeans. "Well then, what can I get you?"

The men placed their orders and the waitress headed for the kitchen, a noticeable bounce in her step. Colin raised his eyebrows and stared at Mitch.

"My, my. You have a fan."

Mitch's face soured. "She's a sweet young

lady. Though I wish she wouldn't be quite so forward with me. She does it just to make me uncomfortable, out of fun. I'm a priest who can take a joke. I come in here a lot so I've gotten to know her." Mitch's eyes followed her until she disappeared behind the swinging metal door to the kitchen. Colin thought he caught a sense of longing in the priest's eyes.

"The vow of celibacy must be really challenging."

Mitch's eyebrows drew down. Then he looked back to where the young woman had disappeared, and his face lightened with an amused, but sad smile. "Get your mind out of the gutter."

"You're a priest. But you're a man too. Of course, if you don't know what you're missing..."

"I do," Mitch said.

"So, you've had a relationship with a woman?"

Mitch clenched his lips and nodded, his eyes descending. "Yes. Before I took my vows, I was ready to marry her but it didn't work out. It wasn't long after that I got the calling."

"Sorry," Colin said. He didn't know what to say to a man who had lost his love. He tried to find something, anything less awkward to stare at. Mitch said no more on the subject, and Colin was more than willing to let it drop. He didn't like prying into people's private affairs.

Visually changing gear, Mitch took a big

swig of beer and wiped the creamy foam residue off his upper lip. "Hopefully, we can get some information from my antique dealer tomorrow," Mitch said.

"What if we can't?"

"We still have my other lead to follow up on. We won't be wasting any time."

Colin was glad for that. Whenever he thought of his unborn son's hostage soul, he felt a nauseating grip wrap itself around his insides. They had to find that chrome-eyed devil and send it back to hell, without his son. And he felt they weren't any closer to doing that than they had been. Now, here they sat, drinking beer and waiting for a stupid burger. He knew that Mitch was optimistic, but what did he have to lose? A family? No, he didn't even have a girlfriend. That was always one of his problems with priests; they wanted to counsel you on relationships and none of them ever had a family. What the hell did they know? He was doing the best he could for his wife and daughter, but it was becoming more and more clear that for Julie, it wasn't enough. When he got screwed out of that last promotion, Julie leaped on top of the "pile on Colin" heap, adding her disapproval to his bosses, something she hadn't done before. She chastised him for not being more assertive and speaking up for himself, knowing that the other guy had claimed credit for something Colin had done. She belabored him for not taking the extended assignments out of town that would show how valuable and dedicated he was. At first she had understood, knowing how he'd lost his parents. But Colin had used up her supply of emotional support and encouragement and was now left with disappointment and frustration. Saving their unborn son was his last chance to redeem himself and put his marriage back on track. If he wasn't too late. And if he didn't die doing it.

"I'm sorry," Colin said. He hadn't realized that Mitch had been speaking.

"Kind of distracted, huh?"

"Yeah."

Mitch reached across the table and seized Colin's wrists with his vices, giving a little tug to doubly gain Colin's attention. "We're going to find that son-of-a-bitch. And we're going to send him back to hell. I can feel it in my bones."

"I hope you're right."

"I'm three for four so far, with number four pending. Plus, I have you to help me."

Colin examined Mitch's determined features. "Speaking of that, what happens if you can't say your rite?"

Mitch's face darkened. "That wouldn't be good. At all. I should teach you the verses so that you can recite along with me. I guess we can't discount the prospect that you may have to do it alone sometime, if we get separated."

Or if you get killed. The thought made Colin cringe. He couldn't imagine facing a creature from hell alone. He got lucky the first time because the damned thing wanted something else more than he wanted to kill Colin and his family. He reached up and ran his fingers delicately along the length of the scar on his face. Like the ones on his chest, this one was starting to lose its sensitivity already. Healing from a scratch was one thing, being able to fend off a wild, animal-like being that was determined to pull your spine out through your belly-button was quite another.

"Why am I not affected by their scratches? This thing on my face is already healed."

Mitch smiled. "You have a charismatic gift. Some lay people have received special blessings. We will sometimes have one of these folks along for particularly tough exorcisms. But I wouldn't have thought of bringing one of them along on this nightmare. The gifts I've seen demonstrated before wouldn't help a bit dealing with material demons. But you– you're exactly what I need right now. I think God must have brought us together to fight this evil."

"The scars on my chest started to itch and burn when we were waiting in the alley. Then, when we were fighting that demon, they really hurt. A lot."

Mitch considered Colin's words. "How are they now?"

"They're fine," Colin said. He ran his fingers over his chest. "Don't even know I've been wounded."

The priest rubbed his chin as he eyed Colin. "You may be more gifted than I thought. Let me know if your scars start to hurt again. And if they do, get ready for action."

"You think they react when I'm near a demon?" Colin asked, flabbergasted.

"Maybe. At any rate, we should pay attention if they start acting up."

Colin took a swig of his beer. "But why do you even need me? You banished or exorcised the first two demons without me."

"I had a partner. And when I'm faced with my biggest challenge, one I would have failed with on my own, I had you here and together we got it done. Isn't that just a little too convenient?"

Colin had to admit that the timing was fortunate, terrifying though it was. "How did I get this gift? I haven't done anything great. I hardly even go to church."

Mitch shrugged his shoulders. "Like I said, maybe you received a special blessing as a child. Maybe God gave it to you when you made the decision to attack that demon in your house. I don't know. I just know that you have the gift and I'm not going to second guess His reason for giving it to you."

Colin tried to wrap his head around the idea of God reaching down and stamping him with a 'charismatic gift', some sort of magical power. Of all the people on Earth, he couldn't believe he was on the list of deserving of any special attention from God. Then again, was it a gift or a curse?

"Do you really think I can do it? An exorcism? I thought you had to go through a mess of training?"

"The education and background is certainly helpful in dealing with the variety of demons that you may run up against. However, Jesus himself directed his disciples to go out and exorcise demons, among other things. I don't recall seeing any mention in the Bible of him putting on a class to teach them how. But those were men of faith. Are you a man of faith?"

Mitch's intense green eyes bore into Colin's. "I don't know. I guess I'd say I am more a man of faith after seeing those demons and seeing you exorcise one."

"It's gonna take more than that, Colin," Mitch said. He leaned back on his bench and contemplated the computer salesman. "Believing what you've seen is not the same as believing in what you can't see, that God has absolute power and that He may allow you to exorcise a demon in His name. You aren't going to do anything on your own. If you don't put complete faith in God, you'll fail."

The words hit Colin hard, shallowing his breath. He had never been a very religious guy, his scientific mind coming into conflict with biblical teachings. And his co-workers treated religion as passé' and trite. He did believe in God, he thought. But he had never achieved the level of belief of which Mitch spoke. Had it become stronger over the last two days? Yes. Undoubtedly. But could he give himself over to God like a child trusting his or her father to catch them if they jumped from the window of a burning building? He didn't know. But he was going to try. He had to, because he was standing in a burning building.

Lily brought their sandwiches over, smiling sweetly at Mitch the entire time, her breasts straining against the black tee-shirt. Colin hoped he wouldn't get caught staring. Mitch, in his best priestly way, averted his eyes, choosing to take in her pleasant face. As she walked away, a moment of sadness clouded the exorcist's eyes, replaced by burning determination as he chomped into his burger.

"I'm definitely going to work on building my faith. But at the same time, I think you should teach me the Rite, like you said."

Mitch eyed Colin and caressed his upper lip with the fingers of one hand, a father judging the veracity of a disobedient child's repentance. "Yes, I'll teach you. But I will also minister to your soul as well. It does no good to give you bullets if you haven't got a gun."

Colin smiled a weak smile. "So I'm going to have to learn a little Latin, huh?"

Mitch grinned. "Actually, no. I'm going to

teach you the Rite in English. I'm just used to using Latin because I use it for spiritual exorcisms. It helps to root out people who are faking their possession. If I said 'your boots are dirty' in Latin, and they thrash around acting crazy, they're probably faking it."

"People do that? That's weird. But how do you know it'll work if I say it in English?"

"Demons speak all languages my friend. They aren't as dumb as you and I," Mitch said. His eyes gripped Colin's over the rim of his beer mug as he took another sip. "It's important for you to know the meaning as well as the words. It'll make it easier for you to remember and the exact wording isn't as important as the message. But recitation helps you to focus on the words and message and not worry so much about what the demon is saying or doing. Though it's pretty tough to ignore a crazed beast trying to kill you. I'd go back to regular exorcisms any day."

"Amen," Colin said as the two men clanked their mugs together.

As they finished eating their meals Mitch began teaching Colin the prayers of the Rite as well as their meaning and biblical basis. Colin proved to be a quick study, picking up several of the prayers very quickly. He felt some comfort in his progress, but Mitch didn't heap praise upon him, knowing there was too much left to learn. After a while, Mitch went to work on Colin's faith, trying to elicit a level of spiritual realization that took most adults a lifetime to achieve – if they ever did. Colin would never know the intense prayer that Mitch would conduct on his behalf in the quiet hours of the night.

Mitch took a sip of his beer and turned toward the bar. Lily seemed to have disappeared into the kitchen or somewhere. Colin noticed Mitch squint as he took in the only two men who sat at the bar. The younger, thin guy was engaged in a conversation with the bartender, but the thick, gray-haired man sat alone and seemed a little tapped. He wasn't sure who Mitch was watching, but he could feel the intensity in the priest's stare. Colin's pulse quickened. It wasn't another demon, was it?

Ralph Means sat alone at the bar, working on his sixth beer and feeling ornery. His gray-haired head hung between hunched shoulders, swimming in the effects of the alcohol. He didn't know why, but he was in a very black mood, hating everything and everyone. Maybe it was because of the alimony check he had to deliver just after getting off work. Bitch.

Normally, he was a live-and-let-live kind of guy. Not tonight.

His eyes swayed around the tavern, looking for that hot little waitress. Damn. Why wasn't she the bartender instead of the fat old Mick that leaned against the back of the bar as he chattered away at another customer. That waitress was delightful. The tight jeans and tight black tee-shirt really showed off her dynamite body. If he had a chance to charm her... After all, he was in good shape for fifty-one. Some aches and pains maybe, but that was because he tried to stay active. He could still take care of business in the sack and was sure she'd learn some things from him.

A couple entered the bar and sat down in a booth near the front door. Means glanced in their direction and sneered. Stupid couples.

Out of the kitchen came his vision, carrying two menus, silverware and her notepad. He flashed a charming smile at her as she passed. "Hey there." She gave a curt smile and strode over to the table of newcomers. Means watched her over his shoulder. At least he watched her butt.

When she turned to return to the kitchen, he saw his chance. Spinning his stool around he waved his hand. "Excuse me."

She stopped in front of him and raised her eyebrows. "Yes?"

"You should sit down and let me buy you a drink. You race around here so fast, you must be thirsty."

She smiled a patronizing smile and said, "I get water in the kitchen. Thanks anyway."

As she made to walk away, Means grabbed her arm. "When do you get off work? I could buy you a drink then. I think you'd find me to be great company."

"I'm sorry. I don't date customers." She started to pull away but Means tightened his grip. "Hey! Let go of me."

"Let go of her," a voice boomed like it rained down from Heaven above. Means released the waitress and glared at the two men closing in on him.

"Why don't you mind your own business, dickhead?" Means said. He drew himself up to his full six-foot-three. He noticed the second man was looking on wide-eyed, fearful. Means started to ball his hands into fists. Then he looked into the green eyes of the man who'd yelled at him and was now nearly chest to chest with him.

"Keep your hands off of her and get the hell out of here." The words were spoken with subdued rage, breathy and low.

The confidence and power that radiated out of those eyes convinced Means that maybe it was time to head home for the night. He relaxed his hands and dropped a bill on the bar, only then catching a glimpse of the bat wielding bartender. With a grunt he spun around and stalked out onto the street, letting the heavy door slam behind him.

Colin had watched Mitch confront the drunk in stunned silence, desperately hoping to avoid a fight. He had been very impressed at how Mitch engaged the demon, seemingly without fear, and exorcised it. In hindsight Mitch's actions seemed dutiful, professional, like an exterminator doing his job. What he'd just witnessed was different. It was personal, with an element of rage Colin hadn't believed Mitch was capable of.

"Father, you didn't need to jump in there," the bartender said. "I'd have handled it."

"I know," Mitch said. "But we were on our way out and I didn't want anyone messing with my favorite waitress. And for crying out loud, call me Mitch."

The bartender chuckled. "Very good, Mitch. Drinks are on me next time you come in." With that he gave a friendly wave and went back to serving up drinks to the few other bar patrons.

"Thank you so much, Father," Lily said. "I hate creeps like that."

"Glad to help," Mitch said. "Don't let idiots like that know you're a massage therapist or you'll have to hire a body-guard."

As they left the tavern, Mitch gave Lily a tender, yet awkward hug. Colin opted for shaking her hand and wishing her well. He noticed again the look of longing in Mitch's eyes and was struck by how lonely the priest's life seemed. He wondered how many true friends Mitch had.

He was ashamed, feeling that he did not offer Mitch much in the way of friendship. He truly liked the man, but their relationship was too akin to teacher/student. Perhaps even father/son, though Mitch was probably only ten to fifteen years older than he was. But the priest managed to evoke memories of the father he'd lost so many years ago, filling a place in Colin's world that had been vacated too early. Colin watched Mitch in silent awe as they left the bar.

They jumped a cab back to their hotel, both men winding down quickly in the darkness of the backseat. Colin replayed the exorcism of the little demon over in his head, the whole event seeming like a bad dream or a movie. He wondered about the pain he felt in his scars, about relenting and pulling back with his knife, about the music that suddenly roared from a passing car.

"Did you hear that music, in the alley, when we both had started to back off?" he asked.

Mitch squinted his eyes in thought. "Yeah. What was it? Highway to Hell?"

"Do you think that had anything to do with our being able to finish the job?" Colin watched his words, glancing at the cab driver.

"Most likely," Mitch said. "Things sure went our way when that started playing. Maybe that was his weakness."

"Never thought I'd be glad to hear that song blasting from a car."

"Thank God it did."

The taxi lurched to a halt in front of their hotel. Mitch paid the driver and they proceeded to their room in silence where they both crashed into their beds, beyond tired. Mitch spent several minutes in silent prayer that only God could possibly have heard over Colin's snoring.

Mitch's phone playing Battle Hymn of the Republic the next morning awakened both men. Trying to get his tongue working again, Mitch answered.

"Hello. No, we haven't even got out of bed yet. Kind of a rough day yesterday." He rolled his legs over the side of the bed rubbing his eyes. "Crap." The sudden exclamation roused Colin completely from the groggy state he'd been in since the phone rang. Mitch turned and looked at him, his face sour. "Hmm. Before you go, how is that tracking algorithm coming along?" Mitch caressed his forehead as he listened. "The sooner you get it done, the better. We gotta find that black demon and do it quick. I don't want to risk Julie going into labor." With that he hung up the phone and turned to Colin who was propped up on one elbow, watching him with concern.

Mitch sucked in a big breath, let it out and asked, "Did you happen to call that detective from Saratoga?"

Colin was caught off guard. He felt bad that he had lied earlier and knew he had to come clean.

"Yeah. I know you told me not to, but

they're the cops. I didn't kill Tim, so I have nothing to hide."

"You do have something to hide: the truth. Because the police aren't going to believe it. And they apparently didn't buy whatever you told them because your face was all over the early news as being sought by the police in a heinous murder upstate."

"Oh shit," Colin said dropping his face into the pillow.

"You can say that again. What's the guy's name?"

Colin looked up. "The detective? Uh, Keller."

"Seems Detective Keller is determined to talk to you. Has he tried calling you back?"

"No. I blocked the number when I called, and Julie won't give him my number."

"If he's real determined, he'll get your number and then track it. We should assume we only have a couple days at best before that happens."

Colin stared at the ground. *Dammit.* He wondered at his own stupidity and blind adherence to the rules. Swinging his feet to the floor he climbed out of bed, disgusted with himself and his inability to get outside the box. He sneaked a peek at Mitch but couldn't get a good look at his face, though he could imagine what he was thinking. He was going to have to start putting more credence into what Mitch told him.

Climbing into the hot shower Colin felt awful, knowing that he'd possibly made an already daunting task even harder. But it was possible that the police would have issued that alert regardless of whether or not he'd called. The fact remained that if he got picked up, he'd lose a couple of days at best. At worst he'd be held until long after Julie gave birth. He could not get picked up. He was going to have to maintain a very low profile and wondered if it was wise to go out.

"Not possible," Mitch said when Colin asked him about skipping the meeting with the next contact. "You have to be with me. What if we get a break and find the demon that has your son? I can't be trying to coordinate getting you on target. We need to stick together. Just try to keep your face down. We'll get you a hat too."

Colin rubbed his eyes with the heels of both hands. He'd really screwed up. One thing New York seemed to have a ton of was cops. And they'd all be on the lookout for him.

Mitch picked up on his distress. "Don't worry about the cops. There are a lot of people in this town, and they do a great job of keeping the police occupied. As long as you don't bump into one face-to-face, and then stare at him like a deer in the headlights, we should be fine."

That thought gave Colin some hope, something he was profoundly short of at the moment.

They finished getting dressed and jumped in the elevator down to the lobby. Colin stood sipping complimentary coffee from a small Styrofoam cup while Mitch ducked into the hotel's gift shop. When he emerged, he snapped an NYPD baseball cap on Colin's head.

"Really?" Colin said as he arced the bill and then pulled it low on his forehead. "This is subtle."

"Would you be looking for a guy wearing that hat?"

Colin shrugged. They stepped through the doors into the bright morning light to seek out a knowledgeable antique collector.

The cab ride was uneventful, even if Colin thought the driver was stealing glances at him in the mirror. He made sure to stare out the side window as much as possible. Then it seemed as though everyone on the sidewalk was transfixed and locked onto his portrait as they drove by. It wasn't long before sweat beaded on his brow, then broke and dripped onto his cheek. On one occasion, as they passed a pair of police officers walking their beat, Colin almost folded himself into the size of a suitcase onto the floor before Mitch backhanded him and asked him if he'd dropped something before whispering for him to settle down.

Eventually Colin could only focus on the

soul of his unborn son, being carried around by a black-scaled demon. Maybe somewhere in this very city. He wondered what he would do if they failed to exorcise the fiend. What if his son was born permanently possessed? How do you raise a child with the knowledge that he will dedicate his life to destroying as much of mankind as possible? Did Adolph Hitler's parents know? It made him sick to think that the only fix would be to kill him, your own child. Colin's stomach clenched and he became restless, shifting this way and that in the back of the cab. His eyes burned and tears gathered at the corners, one squirting down his cheek. Moisture condensed on the insides of his nostrils, threatening to drip onto his upper lip. There was no way he would allow his son to die. He and Mitch would find this demon. They had to.

Mitch's firm grip on his wrist stopped his squirming. Colin looked at the older man, whom he was beginning to think of as a friend, and saw the cold, hard, courage that emanated from his being. And the concern, and the empathy, and the warmth. The rugged exorcist didn't say anything, he didn't need to. His bearing and presence said it all. Mitch had no intention of failing, and he would not let Colin entertain the thought either. Even if it was to just save one soul. And they were trying to save all of mankind.

The taxi jerked to a halt near the curb. Colin and Mitch exited after Mitch dropped some bills in the driver's hand telling him no change was necessary. The cab shot back into the flow of traffic like a leaf being pulled away from shore by a raging current.

Mitch tugged on Colin's arm and led him down the sidewalk a short distance before he turned over to the worn, wood and glass door of a small shop. Through the display window Colin saw an old spinning wheel and a rustic trunk made of black wood. To him, it looked like any other antique store. That impression wouldn't last long.

Jingle-bells tinkled as they thrust open the door and walked in, a primitive anti-intruder alarm. Colin followed Mitch to the back end of the store where an elderly man, probably in his seventies, was behind a counter, elbows resting on its surface, examining some small item with a monocular magnifier strapped to his head. The man had a regal air about him, his white hair combed with precision, a neat and perfectly straight cardigan sweater hugging his lean but robust frame. He handled the item of his intrigue with agile fingers, turning it this way and that, checking it from all sides and angles. He hadn't even noticed their entrance, despite the clanking bells that were affixed to the handle of the door.

"Good morning, Horace," Mitch said.

The white-haired man merely raised one finger to signify that he'd heard, but it was clear he was not going to interrupt his work just yet. Mitch crossed his hands politely and gave Colin a patient grin.

Colin decided he'd look around the shop while the old man doddered. Almost at once his eyes fell onto an item displayed within a locked, glass cabinet. It was a dagger. Hieroglyphic etchings were black on its surprisingly white blade. The handle appeared to be some sort of bone, yellowed and carved to easily accommodate the wielder's grip. The knife reminded Colin of the various blades that Mitch carried, one of which was in Colin's own pack. Atop the display case was a tented, little sign that read "Not for Sale".

"Don't touch the case," the old man's voice commanded, brooking no argument.

Colin looked back to see both Mitch and the old man watching him intently. Feeling awkward, he re-joined Mitch while the old man, Horace, followed his every move.

When he was finally standing at attention at Mitch's side, Horace smiled and extended a bony hand to the exorcist.

"Father Mitch. How delightful to see you again. And you've brought someone with you?"

"Please, just Mitch," Mitch said. He took the elder's hand. "Horace, this is Colin Hampton, an apprentice of sorts," Mitch said.

Colin's heart skipped a beat when Mitch used his real name. He envisioned the old man making a quick call to the police.

"Yes. The young man who was on the news this morning?" Colin almost swallowed his tongue. "Sounds like you've got yourself into a bit of trouble."

Mitch shook his head. "Colin is innocent. I can attest to that. But we don't have time to go to the police just now."

Horace tented his fingers in front of his mouth and said through them, "That doesn't bode well, Father. Something must really be amiss if you are avoiding the police where a gruesome murder is involved. It doesn't bode well at all."

Mitch planted his hands on top of the counter. "We were hoping you might be able to help us out. We're looking for someone and we need to find him quickly. He may have come in here."

"I'm always happy to help, Father. Whether or not I can, is another matter. What does he look like?"

"I don't know. But he may have been asking about the Seal of Solomon."

Horace's face turned grave. "The mythological ring. It's said to give the bearer the ability to control demons." He rubbed his chin and squinted his eyes. "There was a man a couple of weeks back, maybe a month or two actually, who was asking about it."

Colin perked up and Mitch straightened, both instantly alert.

"What did he want? Did he say he had the

ring or anything like that?"

Horace chuckled. "No. No. He wanted to know about its history, just general knowledge. I told him that if it ever really existed, it was said to have been lost, perhaps swallowed by a fish over in the Mediterranean. Unfortunately, I don't know who the man is and haven't seen him since."

The air came out of Mitch's sails. "What did he look like?"

Horace's eyebrows jumped. "He isn't what I typically see in here. Young, maybe a bit younger than your apprentice here. White man with black, longish hair that was just awful. I swear the man didn't know what a comb is. And he had a silver... knob, or earring, or whatever in the side of his nose." Horace steepled his fingers again, bouncing them together. "A violent murder, the Seal of Solomon... has someone found the ring? Are they killing to facilitate conjurings?"

Mitch stared hard at Horace as the question hung on the air. "I don't think that's quite it. But this guy may *think* he found the ring. And whatever the case, someone is summoning demons into the material world."

The color left Horace's cheeks and he grasped the counter with both bony hands, steadying himself.

"Do you remember how this guy was dressed?"

Horace shrugged. "Not too unusual. Jeans, I

think. And a dark shirt. No coat, so it must have still been warm outside."

"Did you ever install security cameras?"

The old man cast a grim smile. "No. You know that anyone who breaks in here or tries to rob me isn't getting out."

Mitch sighed. Colin gave him an inquisitive stare. "The building locks itself down until Horace enters a code. Barred windows and doors. The whole deal."

"Did he buy anything?" Colin asked.

Horace regarded him and then silently shook his head. Colin could see the mistrust in the old man's face. Did he believe that Colin had something to do with Tim's death? Horace turned to Mitch.

"You know," Horace began, "if someone is conjuring demons to the material world, they would have to do some research. And that kind of thing isn't on the Internet. It's in books. Very old, very rare, books." He looked at Mitch, his eyes communicating silently.

"Yeah," Mitch agreed. The old man smiled, loving the intrigue and mystery. "And there aren't that many places one can find rare books, are there?"

"That's where I'd go," Horace said. He nodded like a teacher approving of a learned student.

"Libraries won't help," Mitch said to Colin, his eyes asking if he had any more questions.

Colin glanced at the dagger in the display case. "What's with that knife? Looks pretty dang old."

Horace came out from behind his counter and led them over to the object.

"Don't touch the case," he said. "This is an ancient Egyptian sacrificial dagger. We think."

That caught Colin by surprise. His brow furrowed as he threw a questioning glance at Mitch who simply shrugged his shoulders.

"The wording on it translates to 'Destroy or Set Free'," Horace explained. "But we can find no context or any other occurrences of that phrase. It is made in a fashion similar to other sacrificial daggers, but none have this type of blade."

"What is the blade made of? It looks like some sort of metal but it's so white," Colin said.

"We don't know," Mitch interjected. "It doesn't seem to be any alloy they would have had available to them at the time. We're going to have it fully evaluated to determine its nature, but it may require doing irreparable damage to the blade. We're hoping to be able to do something spectroscopically. But we don't have a profile that is even close yet."

Colin stared at the pale weapon, his focus narrowing so that it filled his vision. He was intrigued by its incredible age. Something about it made him want to wrap his hand around its grip, to hold it up to his face for closer scrutiny. The handle would feel comfortable, familiar as it molded to his palm and fingers. In his imagination he could see himself wielding it against their foe, driving it deep into the demon's chest, forcing light into the monster's body until it exploded with a flash, like an overfilled balloon. He reached forward to touch it.

Someone yelled the word 'no', and then everything went black.

When he opened his eyes, his arm and leg throbbed, as did the back of his head. He was looking up at Mitch and Horace who knelt over him.

"Do you not understand the words 'Don't touch the case'?" the old man asked.

"Sorry. What the hell happened?" he asked sitting up, flexing his sore arm.

"It's electrified. Anti-theft," Mitch said. "You okay?"

"My arm hurts like hell, and my leg. And did I hit my head?"

"It bounced a little on the floor," Horace said. "Of course, I've always held that stupidity should hurt."

Colin grunted. "Lose many customers this way?"

Horace suddenly looked like he'd heard a door-bell that was only audible to him. He began to smile.

"'Stupidity should hurt.' Do you know where I learned that expression? Adon Negaré. He is one of my regular customers and he is very well versed in religious artifacts. As a matter of fact, he and I once discussed the Seal of Solomon, several years ago."

"Adon Negaré? Really? I didn't realize he was a collector," Mitch said.

"Oh yes. He has more connections in the world of antiquities than I do and he's quite versed in the lore."

The old man and the exorcist stared at each other a moment, each showing the barest hint of a smile.

"Thank you," Mitch said. He shook Horace's hand. "I'm glad you're a good guy."

"I like to think I'm a good man," Horace said. "The only thing necessary for the triumph of evil, is for good men to do nothing."

Colin felt the old man's eyes on his back as they walked out the door.

CHAPTER TEN

"Adon Negaré? The guy who owns Negaré Power?" Colin said as the two men strode down the sidewalk.

"Yep. Apparently, he's a collector. The funny thing is, the guy is very philanthropic when it comes to helping us out."

"Us who? The church?"

Mitch shot a quick look around. "Specifically, our order."

"I never pegged him as a church going guy. More of an 'eat the poor' type."

"He's a bit narcissistic, but he has contributed significantly to my little branch of the church for quite a while. Our expense account is basically limitless, thanks to him."

"Weird. Maybe he's trying to figure out how to buy off the devil."

Mitch chuckled. "At any rate, if someone has been looking for the ring, he may know about it." He opened the door to a diner and waved Colin inside. "Let's get some brunch. After we eat, we'll head over to Negaré Tower and see if we can get a meeting."

Over their late breakfast, Mitch schooled Colin in the exorcism rite once again. He had Colin recite back the different stages as well as the phrases he'd most likely use during the ritual. Colin knew the stages well enough but was still stumbling on the lines Mitch wanted him to memorize. Colin put a lot of effort into getting the phrases down, not unlike a college student cramming for the big final. But deep inside, he sincerely hoped he would never have to take that exam. Because to fail in this, meant death.

Having finished their meal, they stepped outside where Mitch hailed a cab. After a forty-five-minute ride of stops and starts, they were standing on the sidewalk looking up at the artistically sculpted sky-scraper that rose like a stone god at the end of a concrete courtyard. Trees spaced around the approach provided an aesthetic appeal in the man-made surroundings, especially with the leaves burning with the reds and oranges of autumn. Colin fell in behind Mitch, trying to make sure not to look up at any of the people leaving the building. For the most part, everyone completely ignored them. Colin did not doubt that their casual attire put them far below the radar of the power-brokers they passed.

Inside the towering building, their shoes

squeaked on the black marble floor as they approached a long, curving reception desk stationed to the right of the hall that lead to the elevators. Mitch marched directly to the stern looking man who sat watching them. He was somewhere in his early thirties and, even sitting down, looked to be very fit.

"Can I help you?" the man asked. Colin turned to look at the doors when the man's eyes lingered a fraction too long.

"We're here to see Mr. Negaré," Mitch said. He rested both arms on the high counter between him and the receptionist.

"Is he expecting you?" the man asked.

"Yes. He should be. I'm Mitch Stackwell."

A look of mild amusement fixed on the young man's face. "And what time is your appointment?"

Mitch looked at his watch. "It was actually at eleven-thirty. We're a little late. Traffic was worse than we expected."

The man eyed Mitch with a skeptical scowl. "Just a minute." He picked up a phone with no buttons or dials on its surface and held it to his ear. "I have a Mitch Stackwell here for Mr. Negaré. He says he and his friend have an eleven-thirty." He raised his penetrating gaze to Mitch. "Yes, I'll wait."

The receptionist glanced to his right and slightly raised his chin. Two extremely tough looking security guards materialized out of a door

Colin hadn't noticed and took up positions between the elevators and the reception desk. Colin turned his back to them, leaning his left arm on the reception counter.

Still on the phone, the unfriendly receptionist's brow crinkled. "Yes. I see. Okay, I'll send them up." He replaced the phone on the receiver and looked up at Mitch assuming a very apologetic demeanor. "Mr. Negaré will see you presently. Just to your left, Carmine will get you on the elevator." He signaled to one of the guards. "Mr. Negaré's suite."

Mitch and Colin walked to the elevator bank where one of the rough-looking guards, presumably Carmine, stuck a key into the call button for an elevator that stood apart from the rest. In a moment the door opened, and the guard escorted them into the interior, placed the key into the control panel, gave it a twist and then stepped back out, wishing them both a fine day. The interior of the elevator car was luxurious, with two leather chairs and a flat screen television displaying one of the financial network programs. They eschewed the chairs, curious as to their necessity.

Like any other elevator, the ride lasted just over a minute. Apparently Mr. Negaré was used to comfort. The ostentatious display disgusted Colin. Rich people were so into their own little worlds. It brought back the bitter taste left in his mouth by his foster parents, who to their credit, did care for him for two years. But their disdain for the families who cared for his brother and sister never sat well with him.

The elevator doors opened onto a lavish office with a bank of windows on the opposite side of the room, through which only sky and a few other towering buildings could be seen. Directly centered in the room and facing the elevator was a huge mahogany desk with a middle aged, attractive blond woman sitting behind it. Her blue eyes smiled in concert with her full lips as she rose behind the desk. Mitch walked forward, Colin a step behind.

"Mr. Stackwell?"

"Yes," Mitch said.

"And?" Her eyes drifted to Colin who was milling around behind Mitch, trying to obscure his face with little effect.

Mitch threw a quick glance over his shoulder. "My apprentice."

The answer seemed to satisfy her curiosity and she picked up the phone on her desk. "Mr. Stackwell and his apprentice have arrived. Yes, I'll send them in."

She walked from behind her desk revealing a proper, yet strangely seductive short skirt that hugged firm but narrow hips leading the eye down to shapely legs. Colin couldn't help but notice that she was very well proportioned and not afraid to show it off, but in a professional manner as opposed to tawdry. His eyes involuntarily fell to her tight posterior as they followed her to the twin oaken doors that were on the left side of the room. He pried them loose when she turned and opened one of the doors and held it wide.

"Right in here, gentlemen," she said. They walked through the doorway and Colin heard the subdued click of the latch as she closed it behind them.

They entered from the left corner of Negaré's office. Colin had never seen such a decadent room. He'd seen some amazing things on TV shows about the shamelessly wealthy, but even those didn't compare with where he now stood. The opposite wall and the wall to their far right made up the corner of the building and were all windows, stretching at least twenty feet high. There was a fountain, a damn *fountain,* on the far side of the room. It was three tiers high, concentric circles decreasing in size as they went up. It reminded Colin of pictures of the public fountains he'd seen pictured in Italy. An alcove off the fountain looked like it was set up for having drinks, with four high-backed leather chairs and cherry side tables next to each. The floor was a highly glossed white marble with gray and black streaks spiraling around with the natural randomness of foreboding storm clouds. Two massive pillars, each centered at opposite ends of the room, led the eye up to a ceiling painted with an angelic fresco that would make Michelangelo smile.

Colin recognized the man who stood up behind a massive cherry desk. He'd seen Adon Negaré's thinning gray hair, wire rimmed glasses, and tall, lean frame many times on news stories. He never thought he'd ever have cause, or the misfortune, to meet such a wealthy, powerful, and despicable man. Negaré smiled and came out from behind his desk, hand extended toward Mitch. Colin had the feeling that Negaré didn't often venture out from behind his desk to greet guests.

"Father Mitch Stackwell. What a pleasure to finally meet you." He grasped Mitch's hand firmly.

"Please. Just call me Mitch," Mitch corrected. "The pleasure's mine."

Negaré then turned a curious eye on Colin as he redirected his outstretched palm.

"Colin Hampton." Colin said. Despite his disdain for the man, he reached out politely all the same.

Negaré's eyebrows lifted briefly. His blue-gray eyes shifted their fire from Colin to Mitch. "I'll admit that I was excited to meet the acclaimed exorcist in person, but I'm at a loss as to why you are traveling with a suspected murderer."

Right to the point.

Mitch shifted uneasily. "I can vouch that he hasn't killed anyone. But the story behind what brings us here may be a little," he paused, "hard to swallow."

"Falling oil and gas prices are what I find

hard to swallow. I've been funding a lot of the research those — what do you call them, Cavemen — have been doing. So I am a lot more open minded than you might think."

At Colin's confused look, out of the side of his mouth Mitch said, "Cavemen, Ben and Reginald."

Colin sucked in a breath of recollection and nodded as though he was intimately familiar with their research.

"Why don't we have a seat over here and you can tell me what's going on."

Negaré led them over to the alcove, sat down and then gestured for the men to sit. Mitch sat forward on the edge of his seat, elbows on his knees while Colin grasped both arm rests like an uncomfortable airline passenger. The elder man leaned back, crossed his legs and folded his hands in his lap, radiating confidence as he waited for Mitch to begin.

"There's no beating around the bush on this," Mitch said. "Someone has discovered how to conjure demons into the physical world and it looks like they are doing it from somewhere here in New York. Colin and I are hunting them down."

Surprised flashed across Negaré's face and was gone like the darkening after a lightning flash. If Colin hadn't been looking right at him, he'd have thought that Negaré had heard this type of thing a hundred times. He could see why the man was such a successful negotiator.

"Why, in the name of all that is Holy, would someone be doing that?" Negaré asked.

Mitch glanced uncomfortably at Colin. "Why? Ultimately, we don't know. But we think whoever is doing it may believe they've found the Seal of Solomon."

Negaré's eyebrows raised and a smile tugged at the corners of his mouth. "Ahh. The famous ring that allows the bearer to control demons." His brows furrowed. "I believe that ring has been forever lost or destroyed. Most likely, it was a myth. But if someone thinks they've found it, and they successfully summon a demon, they are going to be in for a rude awakening."

"That's pretty much what we figured. But that may be the least of our problems."

Colin's breath caught in his throat as Mitch looked over at him.

"One of the demons stole the soul of an unborn child."

Negaré's eyes squinted. "That," he said, "is definitely an unfortunate side effect. I assume it was the soul of some urchin the sorcerer is familiar with? Kid is probably better off being born soulless."

Mitch looked as though he swallowed his tongue as he snapped his head around to look at Colin.

Colin felt the nearly uncontrollable desire to

punch Negaré right in the mouth. That pompous son-of-a-bitch. It was exactly the kind of selfish, misinformed bullshit attitude he expected from the rich prick.

"It was the soul of my son," Colin said. He bit off the last word, knuckles turning white as his grip tightened on the chair's arms.

"I apologize," Negaré said. "I misspoke." He regarded Colin cautiously, obviously seeing his demeanor edging toward violence.

Mitch went on to explain the implications of the stolen soul and what would happen if the child was born permanently possessed.

Now the color drained from Negaré's face, making him look like he was on Death's doorstep. He fixed Colin with a serious countenance.

"I am very sorry about my insensitive comment. Please, pardon me." Folding his hands, he asked, "When is your wife due?"

"About nine days."

Negaré shook his head slowly. "I hadn't even thought of that possibility. What are the odds?"

"I hadn't thought about it either until I ran into Colin and his wife after the attack," Mitch said.

"What happened upstate that the police want to talk to you? Is your wife okay?"

"Yeah, for the most part," Colin answered. "My neighbor didn't come out so well though. The thing ripped him apart before it came after me and my family. Since Mitch and I had to leave right after it happened, the cops think I had something to do with it."

Negaré set both feet on the ground and leaned forward, gripping the arm rests with his elbows raised as though about to lift himself like a gymnast on the parallel bars. "Where do we stand?"

"The Cavemen are working on some software that can help us locate the demons when they are summoned. So far, four have been summoned and we've sent three back to hell where they belong. We haven't had any luck with Colin's demon. But according to the archives, an evil spirit conjured in physical form has no choice but to seek out its summoner to complete the ritual." Negaré nodded as Mitch spoke. "So it should be coming to New York, if it isn't already here. We're trying to find whoever is conjuring the damned things before the demon does."

"And you can really exorcise these demons in physical form?"

"Yes. It isn't easy, but I've been able to do two with my partner, Roy, and one with Colin's help." He gave Colin a respectful glance. "Roy was killed when we encountered the second demon."

Negaré ran his hands together as his eyes danced around. "Your partner's been killed. This sounds worse every minute." His head bobbed in a barely perceptible nod. "I can see why you came to me. I have several contacts in the antiquities world.

I will make some calls and see if anyone has been asking around about the Seal of Solomon. As soon as I hear something useful, I'll give you a call. You just make sure you find that fourth demon and take him out before Colin's wife gives birth. Is there anything else I can do?"

Mitch shrugged. "Do you have any pull with the police department?"

Negaré pursed his lips and drew the corners of his mouth back tightly. "I'm afraid I don't think I'll be of much service to you there. I'll make a call but assume that Colin is going to be picked up if he's caught. If it were something less than murder, I might be able to buy you some time. But they won't want to hear it in a case like this. I'm sorry."

Colin had momentarily gotten his hopes up but realized that because of the heinous nature of the crime, there was going to be no quarter given. He really wished he hadn't made that call to the detective. He followed Mitch's lead and got to his feet, feeling somewhat better knowing that Adon Negaré was going to see what he could find out. That didn't make him like Negaré though. They shook hands with the executive who headed back behind his desk and gestured toward the door, trusting them to find their own way out. As they left the office, Colin glanced back and was satisfied to see Negaré with the phone to his ear and a smile on his face, already jumping into action.

As they walked through the courtyard Colin felt his phone buzzing in his pocket. He looked at the display. Julie. He bit his lip as he touched the "take the call" button.

"Hey," he said. "Everything okay?"

"Colin, something's not right. I think I'm having contractions again and they aren't going away! Did you kill that thing yet?"

He could hear her crying through the phone. "No. Not yet. How long has it been happening?" He looked over at Mitch who watched him, concern evident.

"Couple of hours. Mom is going to watch the kids and I'm going to the hospital. Come home. I'm scared."

"Julie, I can't. Not until we get this taken care of." Colin looked around at the people passing by, intentionally being vague.

"Dammit, Colin! I don't know what's wrong. It's awful. Do I have to put up with this myself?"

She groaned in pain then. Colin put his hand to his forehead, caressing it with his thumb and forefinger. "You *know* what will happen if I give up on this. How the hell is that taking care of our child, our family?" He'd made up his mind on this, tough as it was. "Get to the hospital and call me when they tell you what is going on. But I can't come back until I get this done. We're making progress, but I have to go. I love you." He disconnected the call and it nearly killed him. That was the first time he'd been so unsympathetic, and it was when she most needed him.

Mitch stared at him and reached out to place both hands on Colin's shoulders. "How's she doing? Didn't sound good."

"No. She's still having pain, like contractions again. But she says it's different this time. She's heading to the hospital. Do you think we're too late?" His eyes started to glass over.

Father Mitch took a deep breath and looked skyward for a moment. When he looked back into Colin's eyes, he looked like a fatherly, old, priest, not a demon-hunter. "I don't know what is going on. It could be complications brought about by the... well, you know. But I believe that we have a divine purpose. And you and I are going to do our utmost to carry it out." Mitch pulled back one hand and got Colin walking again with the other. "Let's get this thing done so you can get back home."

Mitch felt sick to his stomach. The underworld would do anything to usher in one of their own. And now it sounded like they'd sped up the clock. He and Colin were running out of time and they were no closer to killing their target.

CHAPTER ELEVEN

Kylova.

The word echoed in Seth Myska's head as he hunkered alone in the dark warehouse, recovering. With effort, he blinked his eyes as his world came back to him. The bright light of the morning sun made no appearance in the windowless building. A few dim lights hung from strands of wire, metallic shades reflecting the faint light downward as they rested on the fragile bulbs. But that feeble light was enough to make him squint and cringe. He shivered and wiped the sweat from his body as well as he could with trembling hands. All night it had been like this. Hot. Cold. Hot. Cold. When he did sleep, in a ball on the floor where he'd collapsed, he'd wake up drenched in sweat and shaking, covered in goose-pimples. And wracked with pain. Now, at least the pain had subsided. When his imp had been exorcised the night before, he thought he was going to die of agony. Each time the son-of-a-bitch who was out there banishing his demons was successful, it caused Seth to reel in pain. And it was getting progressively worse. This was the third time and it had caused him to black out from the anguish.

When he'd regained consciousness, it felt as though someone had wrapped a white-hot metal strand around his spine and made him swallow a cactus. He whimpered and cried through most of the night, trying to sleep with little success. If he kept summoning demons that appeared anywhere but right here, he would just be giving the exorcist fodder and he could very well die when the next one got exorcised.

Kylova.

Like the stubborn fog that recedes away from shore with the rising sun, his mind was clearing. Who the hell had said "Kylova"?

He rotated his head from side to side, eyes searching and finding no one. The farthest reaches of the huge warehouse were lost to his weakened sight. Slowly he raised himself from the cold concrete floor, finally having the strength. He got to his hands and knees so he could crawl over to his desk chair and pull himself up into it. He flopped onto the utilitarian folding chair and slumped there, listless. His head pounded as he tried to figure out what had happened last night and what had gone wrong.

He remembered doing the conjuring ritual, pretty sure he'd included the new parts that should have brought the demon into existence right here in the warehouse. He had felt the shroud between the physical world and the spiritual world rip as the evil being came through. But then... nothing. No demon.

He remembered someone yelling at him, rage, disappointment...

Seth looked around. There was no sign of anyone else in the warehouse. If there were, he'd easily be able to see them as the rectangular building was basically empty except for where he'd set up his desk, cot, and research equipment. The solitude suited him fine. He didn't want to talk to anyone just now.

He remembered going back over his research, trying to figure out what had gone wrong. But he'd known, no *felt,* that his demon was brought through much closer to the warehouse this time. As a matter of fact, he had been sure that while he was going over the ritual again, the damned thing would come strolling in through one of the doors, looking for him. But before that could happen, the exorcist had struck. Somehow the bastard had found the creature, with alarming efficiency, and exorcised it, sending Seth into fits of misery, writhing on the floor.

Details floated like dispersing rain clouds in his mind, but not before he had the gist of what had happened. At least he thought he did.

His mind leapt to the demon that was still out there, the one that had so far eluded whatever fricking priest or paranormal investigating dickhead was sending them all back to hell. The thought of that one getting sent back to the abyss terrified him now. How far away could that last one be? It had to be getting close. It would be a bad day if the demonic creature found him in this weakened state. He didn't think the thing would kill him since he'd been the one to bring it into this plane. But it wouldn't obey him. Not without the ring. Seth was starting to wonder if he'd gotten in over his head. After all, he was bringing real, physical demons into the world. All because of the discovery of a ring. A ring that he was told could somehow control them. If this worked, he'd be a rich, well pleasured man.

A wave of dizziness overcame him, and Seth clumsily dropped his head down on the desk, thoughts of carnal payoffs flitting into the dark recesses of the warehouse. His head spun and his breath grew choppy and erratic. Here came the swell of heat, followed closely by his pores bursting with sweat that stank of garlic and sulfur. He gripped the sides of the desk and waited for the feeling to pass.

When it subsided, he looked at the duffel bag laying next to his cot, trying to remember if there was another shirt he could don in place of the smelly, perspiration drenched one he now wore. Shivering, he decided it was worth the effort to look. He got up and wobbled over and dropped onto the cot, grabbing the bag and rummaging through it until he found a sweatshirt. He pulled off the soaked tee-shirt and slid into the clean, dry garment, reveling in its warmth.

"Man, I need to get some fluids in me," Seth

said aloud.

He looked at the far corner where an old refrigerator rested, shrouded in shadows near the maintenance closet. It looked like a long walk. Somewhat reluctantly, Seth started across the floor on his forty-mile (fifty-foot) trek to get re-hydrated. The far side of the warehouse was much darker than where he'd set up shop under the best lighting. On the far side, no daylight stole in through faulty ceiling joints or cracks in the brick wall and light sockets were empty or neglected. As he walked a sudden chill took him, reminding him that it was autumn and probably cool outside this morning. Where the frigid draft had come from, he couldn't surmise, though he looked suspiciously at the aged roof. His mood soured the closer he got to the refrigerator, the aches in his body driving his mind to dark thoughts.

Kylova.

It whispered in his head again. Was it something from a song? Had he heard it somewhere recently? No. This wasn't his imagination, it was a *voice* inside his head, speaking directly and only to him. But how? He was afraid he knew the answer and it was more than a little unnerving. This whole damned operation was more than a little unnerving. He re-focused his mind on the task at hand. It was the only defense he had.

When he finally put his hands on the door to the fridge, he didn't open it. He steadied himself there for a moment, suddenly feeling both pissy and sorry for himself. Why the hell was he putting himself through this? Was he fooling himself about how much control he had, or would have? He shook his head, clearing his mind and pulled open the door of the refrigerator, energizing the magic light that dwelt inside. The light was extraordinarily bright, piercing the depths of the unusual darkness that swirled around him. He bent and saw his prize, a can of Coke. His hand wrapped around the cylindrical body, the coolness of the aluminum sucking the warmth from Seth's fingers. It took no more than thirty seconds for him to pop the can open and down its syrupy-sweet contents. He crumpled the empty can and tossed it into the blackest corner of the building. Then he reached in and seized another can to carry back to his desk, slamming the door closed and extinguishing the light.

As he walked back toward his desk, something hard struck him between the shoulder-blades. Still aching from the previous night's ordeal, he turned slowly and looked down to see the crumpled Coke can lying on the floor. His eyes snapped to the corner where he'd thrown it.

"What the hell?"

And then a voice, maybe no longer just in his head: *Kylova.*

Confused, he tried in vain to pierce the impenetrable dark with his eyes. His dismay morphed into unease. Seth picked up the can and threw it gently back into the corner where he heard it land on the concrete floor. He waited. Nothing happened. Tentatively, he turned around and resumed his march to the desk.

He had just walked below one of the hanging light fixtures when the bulb exploded with a loud 'pop', making him flinch involuntarily, his head ducking down between his shoulders. Once again he was bathed in a black veil.

"Fuck!"

Seth was no stranger to demonic powers and the shit they liked to pull. But he had never been the one on the receiving end of the contemptuous threats and violence. He'd seen things fly across rooms, people slam against the ceiling like spiders, even heard unholy, inhuman voices. But he was always a spectator, the emcee of the events. Now, it seemed, he was the target of the evil spirit's aggression.

"Just leave me be, okay," he said to the swirling shadows. "I'm doing something that you'd be very happy about, so don't mess with me because I'm not done yet. I just gotta figure some shit out. How do you not know this?" His eyes scanned the emptiness that surrounded him, looking for anything that might indicate compliance or understanding. He saw nothing.

Cautiously optimistic, he continued over to the desk and sank into his chair. It was so damned uncomfortable... he should have gotten himself a nice high-backed leather chair that swiveled and was on wheels, like the fat-cats had in their offices.

He perused the piles of documents scattered haphazardly across the desk in front of him. He had been close this time, very close. And still the demon didn't make it to him before being cast back into hell. Was the exorcist so close? He must be, unless something else very unusual happened.

His fingers settled onto a small sheet of paper and he held it up to read. A name appeared on the note; Belphegor. He sighed.

KYLOVA! It was damn near a shout.

"Stop it," Seth shouted back, refusing to be intimidated.

The note he'd found was a reminder that not only did he need to perfect bringing the demons into existence right in this warehouse, but his real goal was to bring this one in particular. He hoped that his experience in contacting specific spirits would prove beneficial in this task. Several times during seances he'd been able to establish communications with a specific entity. At least he believed he had. There was the possibility that the spirits were just claiming to be the one he sought. Liars.

The papers on his desk exploded up into the air like someone flipping a deck of cards skyward in a game of fifty-two pick-up. Instinctively his hand shot out and caught hold of one of the fluttering sheets. As quickly as it had begun, the papers drifted slowly back down, free from the power that had propelled them. Seth looked at the page he'd latched onto and was suddenly filled with enlightenment. A wicked smile grew upon his lips. How had he missed it? Looking at the information contained on the document made him realize where he'd gone wrong. Now he knew, he *knew*, that he could bring a creature from the netherworld into our world and do it right here in this warehouse. And somehow, he knew the name of the spirit that he'd try it on first, and it wasn't the name on the note. He chuckled to himself as he realized how stupid he'd been. *Kylova* had shown him the way, and *Kylova* would be here soon.

CHAPTER TWELVE

Ralph Means wasn't in a particularly jovial mood. As a matter of fact, he felt downright foul. His embarrassment from the tavern last night and the gray, gloomy, weather combined to sour his attitude. What was worse was the fact that he didn't usually act so forward with women. He was proud of his normally subtle charms. Something was eating him and he didn't know what.

His joints ached, though at fifty-one that wasn't unusual. Especially given all the rough sports he'd played up through high-school. And his ex-wife insisting her alimony check be delivered yesterday was irking him more than it usually did.

His gripes didn't stop there.

Ralph's new boss at the shop was a snot-nosed prick who felt he had to constantly put down the workers to show how smart he was. Not being fortunate enough to be able to go to college didn't mean that Ralph was stupid, though that was definitely the message his boss liked to send. So now here he was, the unlucky chosen one who got to walk a couple of blocks to pick up the shit-head's new business cards, like he's some kind of personal assistant, not a qualified machinist. What kind of lily-livered, weak piece, arrogant, son-of-a-bitch can't even go pick up his own business cards?

He shook his head, trying to scatter the dismal thoughts to the autumn wind. The weather wasn't half bad. Maybe he could enjoy the fresh air. Maybe he could stop for a cup of joe on the way back and people watch. There was a great coffee shop with tight-bodied little baristas just up the street. If shit-for-brains asked what took him so long, he'd just tell him he had to wait for them to find the order.

That was the plan.

But after picking up the small, brown, paper-wrapped package and settling down with a hot cup of coffee, his mood devolved further. The whooshing sound of the espresso maker pierced his head with painful barbs. He couldn't see past the counter to enjoy the curve of the barista's ass. And the women walking by outside the picture window were all clad in utilitarian fall fashions that rarely showed off their forms. Most who walked by were rich, pompous-looking men with their fancy suits and impeccable hair – businessmen coming and going from the snobby Negaré Tower. Pricks, no doubt, all of 'em. None of them knew what an actual day of *hard* work was, sitting in their comfortable leather chairs behind their mahogany desks with their big-breasted secretaries. He was better than any of these guys. Only difference was he didn't make as much money.

Ralph didn't feel himself let go. Didn't feel the slow intrusion as a dark presence oozed into his being. He didn't realize he was leaving the coffee shop and moving toward the grand courtyard in front of the decadent office building, didn't feel the evil wrap itself around his conscious like a python, squeezing away any resistance, transforming him into a living puppet. All he felt was anger. Anger that could only be relieved through violence. And his perfect opportunity was walking right at him.

Colin realized that Mitch was right. The best way for him to help Julie now was to finish what they'd come here to do. But he was still torn. He was so used to dropping everything to take care of his family. They were, without doubt, his number-one priority, though he and his wife disagreed on how he could best take care of them. He didn't want to be an absentee dad and cut-throat salesman who stomped on anyone who showed signs of weakness. One more reason why his career had stagnated. His conscience told him he should be holding Julie's hand right now, as she went through this scary time. But for the first time in his married life, he knew that the best thing for his family was for him to not be with them.

He was too distracted by his thoughts to pay attention to where he was going. When Ralph

Means' shoulder slammed into him, it spun him around and sent him stumbling.

"Hey! Dumbass! You got some sort of problem?" Means shouted as he shoved Colin with both hands.

"Oh. I'm sorry..."

"Sorry my ass. You think you're better 'n me? Coming out of the high and mighty Negaré Plaza. You some rich, arrogant, prick who thinks everyone should just get out of your way?"

Colin was shocked. The man was obviously overreacting and wasn't going to calm down on his own. "No. I'm sorry. I just wasn't watching where I was going."

Means' voice rose, his irritation growing to critical mass. Mitch's eyes darted around as the scene developed. Bystanders all around the plaza and on the sidewalk were taking more than a passing interest, concerned faces watching on.

"Bullshit," Means said. He shoved Colin again. Harder.

Colin tried to walk away, hoping to escape this irrational mad-man. Far too many scrutinizing eyes were turned his way. But before he got two steps, Means grabbed his arm and spun him around, throwing a wild, roundhouse punch aimed at Colin's head. Colin ducked the punch but couldn't escape Means' reaching arms. Arms and legs flailing, they tumbled to the ground.

"Shit," Mitch muttered. "Break it up. Break

it up fellas," he said, rushing to pry the men apart.

Colin thrashed at the man, trying to escape, but Means held him fast with one arm as he pounded away with the other.

"Motherfucker wants to fight," Means screamed. "I got some fight for you. Teach you to pick on a working man."

Now people were starting to gather around, hesitant to intercede. Some pulled their phones out to video-record the fray. Others put their phones to their ears and started relating the events to the 9-1-1 operator.

Mitch was able to get Colin out from under the man, but they remained side by side on the ground the assailant clinging to Colin like a tick, his free hand swinging wildly. Then the man made a peculiar change in strategy. He began hitting himself in the face and banging the back of his own head on the concrete. As Colin stared in amazement he realized that this was the guy who'd been hitting on Lily in the Irish tavern. What the hell? He'd just about extricated himself from the maniac's grasp when—

"Police! Knock it off." The booming voice pounded into Mitch making him cringe. Discretely, he stepped back to allow the police access to the men. As soon as he did so, Means released Colin and pushed him away.

"Look at this," Means said. He climbed to his knees and pointed at his self-inflicted injuries,

"This son-of-a-bitch attacked me for no reason."

"What?" Colin's voice squeaked with dismay. "Are you crazy? You attacked *me.*"

Mitch faded into the crowd, taking up a position of obscurity. Thankfully, Colin avoided looking in his direction.

Mitch stepped back as two police officers quickly made space between Colin and Means, one cop addressing each of the men. Seeing that the police had things under control, the crowd quickly dispersed and Mitch headed over to the edge of the courtyard where he watched, unnoticed.

After handcuffing both men, one officer spoke in Colin's ear as he stood behind him and reached into his back pocket, retrieving his wallet. It was then that Mitch realized that Colin's backpack was lying there at the officer's feet. When the officer looked at Colin's identification, his eyes narrowed, deep in thought. Then he raised his hand to key the microphone secured to his right shoulder and turned his head to speak into it. Colin glanced around, surreptitiously trying to locate Mitch. When his eyes finally found him, Mitch made a calming gesture with his hands and nodded, mouthing the words "It's okay". But Colin did not look okay. He looked desperate, as if he were a rabbit in a snare.

Mitch heard the officer shout to his partner but couldn't make out what he was saying. But he didn't have to, he knew what was going on. They knew who Colin was, that he was wanted for questioning. Now his partner, who'd handcuffed Colin's attacker, walked Means over and sat him down a short distance from Colin. Then he grabbed the backpack at Colin's feet and unzipped it. Mitch could see Colin's eyes close and his shoulders slump as the officer's eyebrows jumped to his forehead. Slowly the officer pulled the flintlock pistol out of the bag. Luckily, Mitch hadn't reloaded the weapon yet, for what that was worth. Then the Palo Santo dagger was drawn forth from Colin's pack and held aloft for the other officer to see. After returning both items to the backpack, the officers marched both men to the squad car and put Colin in the back seat, keeping Means standing on the curb. Shortly thereafter, another squad car arrived into which Means was stuffed. Mitch stole forward and got a look at the squad cars. He looked at the rear quarter-panel of one and saw what he needed to see: "17 Pct". Looked like Colin was a guest of the 17th Precinct of New York's Finest.

Seth Myska dropped the crust of his fourth piece of pizza into the open box and took a swig of beer from the bottle sitting on his cluttered desk. Having a full belly on top of his recent revelation in bringing forth a demon with pinpoint accuracy put him in a positively superior mood. He wasn't sure he had recovered completely from the exorcism of the last demon he'd brought into this world, but his excitement drove him forward without fear of the physical and psychological taxes demanded by the summoning ritual. Especially when he considered the payoff.

Myska got up from his desk and went to what he had come to call the 'summoning portal', the inverted pentagram painted on the floor in animal blood, with elaborate script in each of the five points and the center of the star. He scanned the points of the design, making a mental note of the items that needed to be placed precisely on each tip. Of the talismans currently occupying those points, only two of the items were even needed and those were in the wrong positions. Annoyed at his own ignorance, Myska kicked the other three antique objects, sending them skittering across the concrete. Then he carefully placed the remaining two in their correct positions. He strode over to his stash of artifacts and surveyed the collection. Patiently he pulled first one, then two, and finally three of the items from the group, placing each on its appropriate point.

He stared at the section at the very center of the diagram and laughed quietly to himself. How could he have been so stupid? So blind? There, in the center, he would have to change the seal drawn into the space and then place a very specific item. One that was uniquely associated with the desired being. Though in this case, he was not summoning a simple imp. He would bring forth a full-fledged devil. One of Satan's captains.

Myska returned to his desk and shuffled through his printouts and books, looking for one specific seal. He knew it was here, somewhere. His jaw tightened as he perused the photos and titles in vain. It *had* to be here. He remembered seeing it, making a mental note of it. Then a breeze, originating from out of the still shadows, wafted across the desk, scattering the papers onto the floor but leaving one still anchored to the desktop. Myska smiled as his eyes beheld the diagram he sought. Snatching up the paper, he quickly stuffed it into the pocket of his torn jeans.

He went to the maintenance closet and pulled out a bucket and rag. After splashing some cleanser into the pail and filling it with warm water from the utility sink he carried it over and got to work scrubbing clean the nonsense he'd scrawled into the center section of the pentagram. The dried blood symbols came off easily. He stepped back and admired the work he'd done. The new portal was well on its way to being complete. Five talismans rested at the proper points of the star and the script from the center had been erased. He'd at least gotten the scripts right in each of the arms of the pentagram, but this time everything would be perfect. Now all he needed was fresh blood for the central diagram and the precise talisman, also to be placed in the center. The fresh blood would require a quick stop by the animal shelter. As for the talisman... he knew just the place to find that.

As Ralph Means sat in the back of the cruiser staring out the window, a nearly imperceptible shadow withdrew from his body and flitted away into the bustle of the city. He looked around at his surroundings and wondered at the handcuffs that secured his arms behind his back. *What the hell did I do? What was I thinking?* His chin dropped to his chest as he vaguely recalled the guy running into him and then feeling completely out of control and attacking him. Sure the guy was a dick, wasn't he? So he deserved something. But what the hell possessed him to punch the guy? Means had often made derogatory comments to someone like that, but never went 'hands-on'. Something was different today, something had made him *want* to lash out violently, to put the guy in his place.

He would wonder about the events leading up to the altercation on the ride to the precinct. The whole time he sat in the temporary holding cell he'd think about it, and other events in his life that ultimately led him to be sitting in jail, alone, with no one to worry about him when he didn't come home from work. Once he made bail, he would walk into a church for the first time in nineteen years.

CHAPTER THIRTEEN

"The car was from the seventeenth precinct," Mitch said into the phone. He watched as New Yorkers walked the sidewalks, oblivious to the danger that enveloped their world in the form of a new anti-Christ waiting to be born. He found himself feeling very lonely just then.

"That moron," Benjamin answered back from the Cecidit Angelus Vigilum office deep under the city. "What'd he have to go calling the cops for? Is he a complete idiot?"

"Settle down, Ben," Mitch said. "He thought he was doing the right thing." Ben's raw nature and volatile temper made even Mitch cringe. But the man had a real gift and drive to fight evil in all its forms.

"Just because the law says it, doesn't make it right."

"Tell me something I don't know," Mitch replied. "Right now, we have to focus on getting him out of there."

"Why not let him just sit in there? You can do this alone or I could help you."

"No. I need you working on the software."

"He'd probably just get in the way. Let's take out this soul-sucking leach first, then let's get him out."

Though Benjamin couldn't see it, Mitch was shaking his head vigorously. After that last exorcism he did with Colin's help, he knew he'd need him again. "No. I need him out. I don't know why, but I really feel he needs to be with me when I encounter the soul-reaper. I don't know if I could have done the last one without him. I'm sure of it. We have to pull out all the stops to get him out. Our whole world might depend on it."

"This isn't going to be easy," Benjamin said. His breath huffed out through his nose. "Let me talk to Reginald and we'll see what we can come up with. I have an idea, but it'll be risky. I still think we should just let him sit."

"But you aren't running this show, Ben. Just work something up."

"Yeah," Ben huffed. "I'll call you back in a few."

Mitch pocketed his cellphone and took a deep, cleansing breath. Why did Colin have to call that detective? Now they were going to lose time trying to get him back, and time was running out. He hadn't told Colin, but he was deeply concerned about Julie's pains. It was very possible the dark forces would have the wherewithal to speed up the delivery date. As far as he knew, all bets were off as to when she was due.

Nowhere to go but forward.

He looked around until he found a businessman who didn't look to be in too much of a hurry. A quick inquiry for directions proved successful and Mitch thanked the man as he headed off in the direction of Precinct 17 Headquarters.

Julie climbed out of her car and doubled over before she'd taken two steps. The pain passed quickly but the fear of what was happening made her eyes tear up. Straightening as much as possible, she tottered over to the emergency room door and plodded inside to the intake desk. The clerk at the desk took a look at her belly and inclined his head, obviously suspecting that she was in labor. But after Julie explained, filled out some paperwork, and turned over her insurance card for photocopying, she was told to sit down, and they'd have someone take her to the examining room shortly. Despondent and alone, she sat down for what would most likely be close to an hour's wait.

But the clerk was true to his promise and she'd barely pulled out a book — one that she probably wouldn't have been able to read through tear-blurred vision anyway — when a hefty nurse in her late thirties, with a lilting voice, called her name. Julie was escorted through a sterile hallway with blue curtains that hung on beaded silver chains, obscuring the view into the rooms on both sides of the corridor. The nurse pulled one of the curtains aside and led her into a large room with two examining stations and smaller versions of the blue curtains suspended from tracks that encircled each table, providing at least some measure of privacy. An elderly, black woman was sitting on a chair next to one of the tables, waiting to be seen by a doctor. Though she appeared frail, her broad smile belied what must have been at least eight decades of aches and pains.

The nurse asked Julie to sit in a chair near the other examining table, then gently and politely took her vital signs. Her demeanor indicated that she found nothing outlandishly wrong with any of the readings, which was a comfort, small though it was. When she had finished typing data into the computer, she told Julie that a doctor would be with her in a minute. Julie slumped in the chair.

"When are you due?" The voice was kind and crackled. It reminded Julie of her long dead grandmother and her eyes drifted up to see the old woman leaning forward and smiling at her.

"The first week in November," she answered.

"Less than two weeks then," the woman said with delight. "Are you in labor?"

"No," Julie said glancing down to fight the tears. "I'm not sure what's going on."

The old woman stood up and shuffled over to Julie, dragging her chair behind. She sat down in front of Julie and took one of her hands between her own.

"I'm Mabel. And you are?"

"Julie."

"Where's your husband? I see your pretty ring there." She motioned to Julie's left hand.

Julie was momentarily stumped, not sure how to answer. Finally she said, "He's in New York on business. He wasn't able to come home."

"Must be some business. But sometimes it's up to us girls to trust our men to do what's right, no matter how dumb their reasoning might seem." She flashed Julie a conspiratorial smile. "Well, you have me instead. I used to work at this hospital years ago. In the delivery room and maternity ward. Do you want to tell me what you're feeling?"

Julie glanced around, uneasy. Ordinarily she would never open up to a total stranger. But something about Mabel felt very comforting. She could see the genuine concern in the old woman's eyes, and she *had* been a nurse.

"Pain. Not Braxton Hicks. Not cramps. It's like... someone is twisting my uterus, like they're wringing out a wet towel. It doesn't last long, only about five to ten seconds, then it's gone."

"Has your water broken? Any bleeding?" Mabel's eyes held the sharpness of a twenty-year-old, and the kindness of a loving mother.

"No. Nothing," Julie said. Her eyes watered up again.

"Is there something more?" Mabel stroked Julie's hand patiently.

Wiping a tear from her cheek, Julie nodded.

"Don't hold back, child. We have to know everything if we're going to give a proper diagnosis."

"I had a little mishap," Julie lied. "I slipped on our wet floor and landed on my side. My belly kinda hit the floor. Just a little bit."

Mabel's eyes narrowed. "Well, now don't you worry. They have some of the best imaging equipment available in this hospital. If they need to, they can measure the nails on your baby's toes. And the doctors here will really take good care of you. If they don't, they answer to Mabel." The old woman smiled and stood up so she could lean over and give Julie a comforting kiss on the forehead.

Julie strained through a laugh and did her best to smile up at Mabel, still wiping tears from her cheeks. As Mabel sat back down, Julie asked, "Why are you here, Mabel?"

Mabel waved her hand, shaking her head. "Ahh... My blood pressure was way up this morning. Doctor told me if it got too high, I had to come in. Not sure why it spiked like it did, but they want to check me out, maybe give me a magic pill or something."

"I'm sorry to hear that. I hope it's nothing serious."

"Even if it is, I've had a good life. Eighty-four years ain't bad."

"Do you have anyone here with you?"

Mabel laughed. "No. I drove myself here. I won't worry my family 'til there's something to worry about. I'll drive myself home again too." Mabel saw the concern on Julie's face. "Oh, it's okay, child. My kids and grandkids are scattered all over the country. One of my grandsons and his wife live down near Albany, but I don't need to bother him with this."

For a moment, Mabel looked thoughtful and then sad.

"Was a time when I never would have been able to come here on my own. No. Eddie, my hubby, he'd have driven me here and carried me in if I had an ingrown toenail. He couldn't provide a lot, but between us, we didn't want for anything. Especially love. That man didn't shy away from showing me how much he loved me." Now it was Mabel's time to wipe a tear from her cheek. "He waited on me like I was Queen of the Earth. Always taking care of me, protecting me, helping me, holding me. If I ever had any pain, I swear he would have cut off his own arm to make it stop."

Julie couldn't help seeing images of Colin fawning over herself and Claire. "He sounds like a wonderful husband. How long were you married?"

"Not long enough," Mabel answered. "We were wed for thirty-two years. Got married when we were twenty. When he was twenty-five, Eddie became a state trooper. One of the very first black troopers on the force. I was so proud of him. He liked order and keeping people safe. But, not everyone was overly fond of a black police officer. He got spit on and names called at him. Some of the criminals even refused to be handcuffed by a black man. If there was a white officer available, he'd let that officer take the guy into custody, just to keep things peaceful. I would get so mad at him for that kind of thing. 'You're the law!' I'd yell. 'Next time just wallop 'em on the head with your night-stick and handcuff 'em before they wake up.'" Mabel gazed at the floor and snickered. "But he wouldn't. It wasn't 'the right thing to do' he'd say. Now, there were times when he was the only officer there, and like it or not, the bad guy was going to get 'cuffed by a black police officer. Most of the time, Eddie was able to convince the guy. He was very well spoken. And it didn't hurt that he was six-foot-four, two-hundred and sixty pounds."

"Oh my," Julie said. A smile claimed her face. She enjoyed seeing Mabel reminisce about her "hubby", the little smiles, the way her eyes lit up at the memories. She wished Colin were here with her now, to share Mabel's story.

"When he died—the cancer got him—all of his fellow troopers came to the funeral and some of the men he'd arrested did too. They had served their time of course. One of the men told me that he'd been very disrespectful to Eddie when he was arrested, but Eddie treated him with more respect than the white officers did. The man reformed in prison, found Jesus or some such, and realized just how strong and righteous a man Eddie was. They met a couple of times for coffee when he got out of prison."

Julie was quiet for a moment, contemplative. "Did he give you that brooch?" Julie asked, pointing to what looked like a strange letter "T" pinned to the woman's upper chest. It appeared gold, though tarnished and dull. It looked older than Mabel.

Mabel glanced down and smiled. "My tau cross? No. I got this long before I met Eddie. I wear it every day." The old woman fell silent.

Not wanting to pry, Julie quietly found herself thinking of Colin, wondering if they'd found the demon. She shivered. And she realized she missed him. When she acknowledged to herself that she may never see him again, a hollowness opened up inside of her. Trying to steer clear of more pain, she addressed Mabel.

"You said you worked here in the maternity ward?"

Regaining her demeanor, Mabel smiled a grand smile, revealing her own slightly yellowed, but otherwise healthy, teeth.

"Yes. I don't know how many little ones we delivered here. Thousands. It was always so much fun, seeing the mother's eyes light up when we handed her that little flour-sack-sized bundle of heaven. It didn't matter how tired they were, or how hard the labor was, they always had a warm smile and loving arms for their new baby."

"That must have been wonderful," Julie said. She tried not to think about the dread she'd feel if her own child was born with the soul of a devil.

"Most of the time it was. But once in a while, we'd get a single mom in here who didn't have two dimes to rub together. She'd still smile at the babe, but it was a sad smile, a scared smile. You just knew she was wondering how she'd manage to take care of the little pumpkin on her own. There was naught that we could do but hold her hand and give her comfort. We'd send her on her way with all the diapers and formula that we could scrounge up. But it wasn't enough. Those were some sad situations." She shook off the melancholy and smiled at Julie, patting her hand again. "I'm glad to hear you have a good man to help you out."

Julie nodded as her breath quickened. She had a man, but for how long? Would he make it back from New York? And if he did, will he have been successful in killing the demon? Just then her insides knotted up again, buckling her in half with a squawk of pain. Mabel was there with one arm around her shoulder and the other roaming on Julie's swollen abdomen.

"Tell me when my hand is above the pain," she said as her hand slowly caressed Julie's belly.

When Mabel's hand was just below the

navel, Julie grunted, "Right there."

Mabel's mouth scrunched up and her brow furrowed above closed eyes. Then, just as soon as it had come, the pain was gone.

"That one almost felt a little like a contraction," Julie said. Tears trickled down her cheeks sporadically. "I'm afraid I'm going to lose this baby, or something terrible is going to happen." *Like the baby being born with a devil's soul.*

"Don't worry dear. Even back in the sixties and seventies we hardly ever lost one. If we did, it was almost always due to trauma, a car accident or fall down the stairs. I can see from looking at you that you are healthy and didn't have a major fall."

"Really?"

"Really. I can remember only one time in my thirty-seven years of nursing when we *almost* lost a baby when everything had seemed normal. And notice that I said 'almost'." Mabel closed her eyes as she spoke, a slight grin on her lips. "It was in the early eighties. Mom came in in labor. We zipped her into the delivery room and she was dilated to eight centimeters, almost ready. We didn't have to wait long. The doctor was right there and caught the little sucker when he came shooting out, like he was fired from a cannon." She giggled out loud at the memory. "Good thing too because he had no vitals when he came out. Doctor and I went to work on him immediately, we weren't going to let the little fella go. I never prayed so hard in the delivery room as I did that day. And the good Lord must have heard me because when I bent to kiss the little guy on the head—I guess I just wanted him to feel some love or something, I don't know—but when I kissed him on the head, his mouth popped open and he let out the most beautiful cry I think I ever heard."

"Wow," Julie said through her tears. "Sounds like you guys did a great job."

"Yeah, that was one of our best moments. I don't think anyone in the delivery room ever forgot little baby Hampton. 'Colin' they named him. I wonder how he's doing?"

CHAPTER FOURTEEN

Mitch had not yet made it to the police station when his phone rang. It was Benjamin.

"Got the results of the blood test. It was positive."

Mitch stopped and braced himself against the nearest building. "What? Are you sure?"

"Yep."

The priest's chin dropped to his chest. "The poor bastard." He found himself thinking of his own life and the challenges he'd lived through, the sacrifices he'd had to make, of having to deal with bad circumstances.

"Are you going to tell him?" Benjamin asked.

"I dunno."

"We can talk about it later. Meet me at the Romanian safe house in fifteen minutes. How tall are you?"

"Six feet, even," Mitch answered, curious.

"Great. I'll brief you when you get there."

Mitch stared at his phone after the line went dead. Things were progressing nicely until Colin got picked up. And now this. If he told Colin about the test, it would put an unnecessary burden on him when he was already in a highly stressed state. He couldn't risk it. There was too much at stake. But when all this was over, he would have to tell him. It was life changing.

Dedicating himself to the task at hand, he made his way to the safe house as quickly as he could. He wanted to be there ahead of Benjamin and Reginald so he could make sure everything was secure and countermeasures were in place. It amused him to think about how relatively easy traditional intelligence organizations had it. They were only competing with other men, not supernatural beings. Electronic bugs and physical surveillances could be discovered and countered by a skilled agent. Demons who could flit around unseen, who could disguise themselves as rodents to hear and see you... much tougher. And the evil ones would do everything in their power to foil Mitch and Colin's efforts to locate and exorcise the soul-stealing demon. They would even try possession of cops to see if they could glean any inside information. And of course, there were the rats. In fact, he suspected the reason Colin was in the mess he was in, was because of these types of devilry. The guy who'd attacked Colin had had a look about him, one far too familiar to the exorcist.

When he got to the building on West Fifty-Fifth, he stole a glance around and then slipped into the doorway that was sandwiched between two businesses. He keyed his way in and went to the stairway that led him up two floors to the sparsely furnished, nondescript apartment they referred to as the "Romanian safe house" for reasons long forgotten. After he unlocked the door and let himself in, the exorcist slapped it shut and locked it. He walked through the small, one-bedroom apartment and checked to see that all the blessed talismans were still stationed strategically around the place and that it was rat free. Satisfied that everything was in order, he collapsed on the couch.

Across the room was a small painting depicting Jesus wearing a crown of thorns and gazing heavenward, pain and sorrow in his eyes. Mitch didn't want to admit it, but he was feeling a little alone right now too, and scared. He knew they'd eventually be able to find this demon and exorcise it, but would they be too late to save Colin's son? And then a horrible thought penetrated his mind. If they were too late, would the Church suffer the child to live, knowing it was essentially an anti-Christ? Would anyone in their right mind have killed Hitler as a child, knowing what atrocities he would unleash on mankind? He was afraid of the answer.

In times like this he did the only thing he could think of; he prayed.

He was finally feeling comforted and determined again when he heard a key in the door's lock. Benjamin stepped through the door carrying a big black duffel-bag. He closed and locked the door behind him.

"Where's Reginald?"

"He's back at the office," Benjamin answered, tossing the bag onto the floor in the middle of the room. "He thinks we are almost done with the tracking algorithms and didn't want to lose his train of thought."

"Yeah. Hate to derail that train." Mitch gestured to the duffel-bag. "What's in there?"

Benjamin dropped onto the couch next to Mitch. "Let me explain."

Mitch listened with apt attention as Benjamin laid out the plan he and Reginald had hatched. He interrupted only twice. Once to get clarification and once to provide advice that would make the plan a bit less complicated. Being former military, Mitch was all about 'keep it simple stupid'.

Was the plan fool-proof? Not even remotely. Could they be arrested? Absolutely, though they'd make bail very quickly because of Mitch's financial connections in the Church. Would it work? Maybe with a little divine intervention, which is what prompted Mitch to nudge Benjamin, telling him to bow his head in prayer.

Then they changed their clothes and were off to save Colin. Maybe.

Detective Jake Keller and Sergeant Sean

O'Malley were already racing down I-87 on their way to New York. Keller had received the call about Colin Hampton being held on a misdemeanor 'disturbing the peace' charge which would most likely be dropped based on eye-witness accounts that said he'd been attacked. But NYPD knew he was wanted for questioning, so they were dragging out the process so that the time frame of investigative detention did not become overly long by the time Detective Keller arrived to question him. Both Keller and O'Malley were hoping for a confession but expecting him to lawyer up. Earlier, Keller told O'Malley that according to the coroner, the wounds on the remains of Tim Forth looked like they were most likely caused by some kind of animal, just not an animal with which she had any experience. Keller thought it had looked like the guy's arm had been cut off with a serrated knife, not gnawed off by an animal. In upstate New York, animal attacks were almost always about the teeth, not claws. So until a forensic expert familiar with those types of wounds could see the body parts, he was still investigating it as a probable homicide. Colin had made reference to a possible bear, so he may just make an outright denial, hoping to create a reasonable doubt. A confession would be so much easier. Keller pushed the squad car to ninety as they worked out an interview strategy. He figured in less than two hours they'd be face to face with a homicidal maniac.

Colin sat in a hard, plastic chair, leaning forward with his elbows resting on his knees. The police were holding onto his backpack that contained the antique knife and flint-lock pistol. He was enormously happy he and Mitch hadn't reloaded the pistol because the assistant district attorney was still mulling whether to charge him with carrying a concealed weapon. He'd explained that the two weapons were antiques and were just collector's items. He thanked God that Mitch had the powder and balls for the pistol, otherwise the investigators would see through his lies instantly.

After thoroughly searching him and confiscating the two weapons he did have, the police were nice enough to remove the handcuffs while they conferred with the district attorney's office about possible charges. They also advised him that regardless of the disposition of any criminal charges for the altercation downtown, he would be waiting for a detective from the Saratoga Sheriff's office who needed to talk to him about a little matter from up north. So he should make himself comfortable for the next couple of hours until the detective arrived. Which was pretty much impossible to do sitting on a crappy plastic chair.

He was at least happy to have time to come up with a plan on how to answer questions regarding Tim's death. But the longer he sat there, the less happy he was. What lies could he tell that sounded plausible? He'd mentioned having seen a bear. Great. A medical exam would rule out mauling by a bear as a cause of death. But he didn't kill Tim. Why should he be nervous? They had no evidence that he'd killed Tim because he *didn't* kill Tim. Of course, the truth would just get him involuntarily committed.

What would Mitch do? He'd pray. Colin was terrible at that kind of thing and was not sure it would be of any help. Then again, not too long ago he didn't think he'd ever be attacked by demons. Folding his hands he sent up an almost accurate rendition of the only prayer he remembered, the Lord's Prayer. Maybe God would give him an opportunity.

He looked toward the exit and quickly realized that he would not be able to sneak out the doors without being seen. There were cops walking in and out, and the officer sitting at what looked like a complaint desk between him and the door spent his free time watching Colin.

He could fake a medical emergency—oh, right. Sick prisoner. Done to death.

Nope. He was going to talk to this detective. Like it or not. The clock on the wall smiled evilly down at him as its minute hand moved with the fluid rapidity he thought was reserved for the second hand, which was either missing or moving so fast he couldn't see it. The detective would be here soon and he still had no idea what to tell him.

"Hampton," a stereotypical, burly officer shouted at him, despite being only ten feet away. "On yer feet. Yer going uptown. Guess this upstate detective don't wanna come any further into the city than he has to." The barrel-chested cop waved him over to where two officers waited for him, one holding out a set of handcuffs.

"Where are you taking me?" he asked the officer.

"They're gonna take you up to the Fiftieth, on the north side." He turned to the waiting officers. "Stay safe fellas."

"You too," the one holding the cuffs replied.

"Are handcuffs really necessary?" Colin asked.

"Yes," the older officer answered.

Colin cursed under his breath but held his hands out so the handcuffs could be snapped around his wrists. The older officer took Colin's backpack from the desk sergeant, then the two cops escorted him out the door, one in front, one behind. Colin scanned the area outside the police station, looking for a possible method of escape. They turned to their left and walked to an unmarked car that was backed up to the sidewalk. The younger of the two opened the back door and stuffed him into the seat, pulling the seatbelt down far enough for Colin to grab it and secure it in its clasp. The door slammed behind him and the cops climbed in, neither of them saying a word as they pulled out onto the narrow one-way street. The young officer, in the passenger seat, looked back over his shoulder and then turned to the driver.

"That wasn't a NYPD car that pulled into the space we just left. Looked like Saratoga County Sheriff."

"Then we'd better make ourselves scarce real quick," Mitch said. He peeked into the rear-view mirror. All three men released bottled tension with a relieved laugh.

"Hey. Doesn't that look kinda like our guy," O'Malley said from the passenger seat.

Keller watched as a handcuffed man who bore an uncanny resemblance to Colin Hampton was loaded into the back of an unmarked vehicle by two NYPD officers. The officers glanced around, climbed into the car and pulled away.

"That can't be a coincidence," Keller said. He pulled back into traffic to follow. "Where the hell are they taking him?"

Colin glanced over his shoulder to see the Saratoga squad car pull out behind them. Only two cars were between them and the squad car. "Aw, crap. They're coming after us."

Mitch glanced in the mirror and shook his head, letting out a huff. "Ben, keep an eye on them in your rear-view. Colin, eyes forward. I'm going to try losing them."

He increased his speed gradually, hampered by the city traffic. He zipped around a car that was trolling for a parking spot.

Colin stared ahead, desperately wanting to turn and see if they were putting any ground between them and their pursuers. He wanted Mitch to just floor it and fly around cars to escape, but that would draw too much attention.

Without warning Mitch made a hard left in front of an on-coming beer truck. The truck's horn blasted an angry protest as it pitched forward, slamming on its brakes. Colin saw the driver raise his middle finger, his mouth silently articulating various curses. He stole a look back and saw the Saratoga squad car waiting to make the left. "They're stuck at the intersection," he said.

"Good," Mitch replied, peeking into the mirror. He stomped on the accelerator, cruising to the end of the block where he was able to repeat the left turn maneuver with less risk of being broadsided. The uniformed demon hunter sped down the street, until he reached the next cross street and turned right, the wheels chirping on the pavement.

Colin looked through the rear window. He

shook his head. "I don't see them. Looks like you lost them."

"What the fuck is that all about?" Keller railed. "Can you see them?"

"They took another left at the next corner," O'Malley replied.

"Another left?"

"Maybe they're heading back to the station."

"What the hell? They just out taking him for a sight-seeing tour?"

"Someone probably got their signals crossed," O'Malley said. "That's where we're supposed to meet them. Why don't we head back there?"

Keller sighed. O'Malley was probably right. But he couldn't formulate any reasonable explanation as to why they were driving around with their subject. "Nothing else we can do," he said.

"Yep. They're gone," Colin said. He turned to face the front seat. "Police uniforms? Where did you guys get those?" He reached forward, holding his hands out so Benjamin could unlock the handcuffs.

"The Cavemen have resources that know no bounds," Mitch answered with a smile.

"We made arrangements for these about two years ago for a different project," Ben said. "We held on to them just in case. The badges are even real, though if anyone ran the numbers they'd end up running in circles trying to figure out what precinct we're from." He spoke with a proud demeanor, and actually seemed much nicer than the first time Colin had met him.

"Thanks. And I'm sorry," Colin said. He shook his head. "I don't know why that guy went off on me. I did run into him, but hardly enough to warrant a fight. I hate big cities."

"Don't worry about that guy," Mitch said. "He was possessed and trying to get you busted. The demon network is starting to show its teeth."

Colin shuddered. "That was a deliberate ploy to get me arrested? Why didn't they just make him kill me?"

Ben shook his head. "There are a lot of demons, but not a lot with the strength to possess a human. Of those, it would take a very powerful demon to make someone commit a homicidal act if the person didn't have a predisposition for it. Like any organization that is short staffed, they probably did what they could with the resources available at the time. But that's not to say you shouldn't be wary of the possibility that a possessed guy could kill you."

Colin scrubbed his forehead with his fingertips. "Oh, this is crazy. How do you not lose your mind?"

"Pray a lot," Mitch answered. "You want to get something to eat?"

"Absolutely," Ben answered.

"Not really," Colin said.

"We're going to go back to a safehouse and I'll have Ben go out and get us a pizza or something. You really need to eat. It's been a rough day already and we don't know when we'll get the chance again."

Colin bobbed his head in acquiescence, silently wondering how he was going to make it through this ordeal. Then a thought occurred to him: why had the possessed guy tried to get him arrested and not Mitch? Mitch presented more of a risk to the demons than he did. Or did he?

"What do you mean, he was taken up to the Fiftieth Precinct?" Detective Keller asked through clenched teeth. He was taking care to be politic and appreciative, despite feeling a growing sense of alarm and anger.

"Two officers came to get him. Said you wanted to meet with him up there," the desk sergeant answered. "They were real cops. Must just be a miscommunication. I'll call up there and make sure they don't send him back here." With that, the sergeant picked up the phone. After a brief discussion he hung up. "They'll be waiting for you up there. You know where it is?"

"We'll find it," Keller said. O'Malley was tight on his heels as they sped out the door.

Despite his churning gut, Colin bit hungrily into the rolled-up piece of pizza letting the cheese grease run down his chin. Ben was already on his second piece, apparently having inhaled the first.

"Where's Reginald?" Colin asked between bites.

"He's putting the final touches on our tracking algorithms. I hope," Ben answered before taking a swig of root beer.

"Did you guys figure it out?" Mitch asked.

Ben nodded and shrugged as he worked his jaws around a big bite of pizza. Finally he said, "I think we have the algorithm to trace the origin of the materialization nailed. If this idiot brings another demon here, we should be able to tell you, at least, the exact block where it landed. I'm not sure about tracking it though. We still haven't picked up anything on the one we're really interested in and I would have thought we could at least determine it's here on Earth."

Though this was good news, Colin couldn't help feeling hopeless. It really didn't help him to know where *new* demons came into our plane. He had to find the one that carried his son's soul. And it didn't sound like the Cavemen were any closer to figuring out how to track him.

"Colin, let's go over the ritual again," Mitch said. "I want you to be rock solid on it when we find this bastard."

Colin looked up, confused at first, then realizing what Mitch was asking of him. "Okay, should I recite the steps first?"

"Please do. Then go ahead with the dialog for each step."

Ben listened intently as Colin went through the ritual, appearing to take silent notes in his head. Mitch munched nonchalantly on his piece of pizza, listening to his pseudo-apprentice. Colin knew all the steps, he was fairly sure that part wouldn't confound him. Despite his progress he felt like a rickety wooden table, overloaded with books. But he would not collapse. Could not. His family was depending on him.

Each step of the rite had its own dialog associated with it. When Colin started to falter with the lines in the third step Mitch stopped him and corrected. He intimated that he didn't want Colin to recite, and hence learn, anything incorrectly. The priest held that the words had to be rote repetition if he had any chance of performing it correctly under pressure. Once Colin could repeat the dialog from the third step Mitch had him start over and put it all together. He made it most of the way through the fourth step before needing to be corrected again. For the next hour they went over the ritual, drumming it into Colin's head. Finally, Mitch called an end to the exercise.

"I'm heading back to see how Reginald is doing," Ben said picking up the duffel-bag containing the police uniforms. "I'll call you if we get a break-through." Quickly and quietly he slid out the door.

"What now?" Colin asked.

"Pick up where we left off. But more cautiously. We'll really have to be on the lookout if the netherworld is going to such lengths to mess us up. First thing we have to do is get to the book dealer I want to talk to. Horace reinforced my idea that whoever is doing this probably had to conduct a bit of research first."

Colin considered their course of action. Nothing sounded like it was going to do them any good. Time was starting to run out, Julie was having problems and going to the hospital. And he didn't feel like they were any closer to getting this damned demon than when they started. But he didn't have the first clue how to proceed. He looked Mitch in the eye. There was strength and determination in the penetrating green orbs. And something more, something Colin couldn't quite identify.

"Let's go," Colin said. "I've wasted enough of our time."

Mitch slung his bag on his shoulder and tossed Colin's backpack to him. Colin unzipped it and reached in to pull out the pistol. He held it up for examination.

"We should probably re-load this thing, huh?"

"Yeah, let me show you." Mitch demonstrated and then set it on half-cock to prevent an accidental discharge. Once the weapon was loaded, Colin placed it carefully into the pack.

The two demon hunters loaded themselves up. Colin dropped his cap low over his eyes and they left the security of the safe-house. Mitch made Colin wait in the vestibule of the building until he had secured a taxi and then they jumped in the backseat and sped away at the mercy of a wanna-be NASCAR driver.

As they zig-zagged through the city, Colin scanned the people walking the streets. Some were bundled up like it was mid-winter while others – usually young macho looking men – walked around in shirt sleeves or less. He saw faces that were happy, sad, in love, arrogant, down-trodden, kind, and some that seemed filled with hate. The latter caught his attention, causing him to recoil and be glad to pass out of sight. He wondered if any of them were working for the enemy without even knowing it. His unease growing, he slunk down low in the back seat and kept his face hidden.

He perused the advertisements posted on the back of the seat in front of him. Advertisements for gentlemen's clubs and rehab centers, liquor stores and cigarettes were prominently displayed. How depressing. He wondered how much worse things would become if they failed.

He didn't notice Mitch watching him as he silently fumbled through a desperate prayer.

The cab swung right and jerked to a sudden halt, apparently having arrived at their destination. Colin peeked out his window and saw a small storefront consisting of a door on the left and a picture-window on the right that revealed a dark interior of shelves filled with books. The siding was darkly stained wood and golden lettering above the door read "Bound Over Books".

Mitch paid the driver while Colin popped out of the car and strode to the book store and slipped inside. Mitch was close behind him and stepped past him once they were through the door. Mitch led him to the cramped checkout desk that was nestled on the left side of the store. A woman in her early forties sat behind the desk, black hair pulled back in a painfully tight ponytail that gave full view of the ornate silver earrings that weighted down her earlobes. A gray T-shirt strained against the woman's bust that served as a viewing platform for a large pentagram pendant which lay there comfortably, held in place by a black cord around her neck. An unbuttoned, black blouse covered her arms but failed to hide the multitude of pewter bracelets she wore. Her legs were crossed beneath a dark, gray skirt, the top leg swinging in time with the soft music playing on the radio behind her. She looked up from her book, her eyes narrowing upon seeing Mitch, and her leg ceased its rhythm.

"Father Mitch," she said. Lifting her chin, she put the book aside. "Come to try and save my soul from eternal damnation again?" Her eyes were as cool as the black ice they resembled.

"Would you like me to?" Mitch said.

"I don't believe in your Devil, Mitch. I'm fine." She turned to look at Colin who stared at her, wide-eyed. "Yes?"

"You're a witch," Colin said.

"And you're a prick." She glanced at Colin's hands then turned to Mitch. "Who's the married guy?"

"Colin, meet Celia. Celia, Colin."

Colin reached out his hand. "Nice to meet you."

"I don't believe you," she said. She looked away from Colin. "What brings you in today, Father?" She said it as though she spoke to the Pope himself.

"Looking for someone who may have stopped in here looking for a book."

"Most of my customers are."

Mitch ignored the jibe. "A book on demons, demonology."

Celia shrugged her shoulders and painted an innocent smile. "There are so many. Any one in particular?"

"Any books on conjuring or summoning

demons?"

The witch's eyes glared. "What business is it of yours if someone wants to play at summoning demons?"

"Because this guy has been successful. And he isn't doing it just in the spiritual world. He's bringing them into our physical plane."

Celia's countenance changed in an instant, looking both frightened and skeptical. "Resorting to scare tactics? Bullshit."

Mitch raised his chin and pointed to the red scratches Nephalen had left. Then he pulled open Colin's shirt and displayed the four big, pink and raw scars across his chest.

"Do any of these look fake? 'Cause I can tell you, getting them sure hurt like hell."

Colin nodded in agreement. Then he added, "I wouldn't have believed it myself if I hadn't been attacked by one."

Celia examined the scars from where she sat, then turned to Mitch. "I did have a guy come in here and buy a book. It was one I didn't even realize I had, been so long since I got it. It had some stuff on conjuring in it. Got a pretty penny for it too. Guy didn't even blink. Just slapped down the credit card."

"You get his name in your business ledger? That wonderful black, leather bound book of yours?"

Celia's lips peeled in a superior grin. "Of

course. I try to keep track of where the rare books go. Might have another buyer looking for it one day."

"What was his name?" Colin asked.

"Oh, no sir," Celia said. "Colin, was it? I don't go around giving my clients' names and information to whoever pops in here."

"Dammit! This is really impor—"

Mitch nudged him in the ribs. "How much do you want for the information, Celia?"

Now her face took on a gleeful and evil glow. "I don't want your money, Mitch. But I might accept another form of payment." One finger traced down her throat to circle a breast and her tongue slid across her smiling lips. Colin couldn't believe what he was seeing. She knew damn well that Mitch couldn't do that.

"Celia, you can't ask that of me."

"I'm just asking you to be a man, a human man. You aren't leaving your God, just taking a break to enjoy what you are. Besides, you are a very attractive man." Her eyes smoldered as her breath quickened.

Mitch turned to Colin, a pained and resolved look on his face, and exhaled a great breath. His mouth tightened and he pulled Colin aside. "I don't trust her," he whispered. "Her ledger has got to be in her desk somewhere. Get the name."

Colin's eyes sprung wide. "What? You can't do this," he said aloud. Then in a whisper, "I'm not a burglar. And you can't go have sex with her. Are you crazy?"

"For the greater good," Mitch whispered back, giving him a weak smile. Then he turned to Celia. "Okay. Let's go."

Celia squealed in delight and surprise as she grabbed his hand and pulled him toward the staircase that lead to her private quarters above the store. Horrified, Colin watched them leave.

Alone, Colin remembered that Mitch told him to look for the ledger. He ducked behind the desk and pulled out drawers, examining the contents of each before going to the next. All the while he couldn't believe that Mitch had given in so easily. Was this really the only way to get the name? Quietly, he hoped God would forgive Mitch, not knowing how all that would work out.

He opened the last drawer. Nothing in it but incense, cards and witchy crap. *Shit.* Annoyed and desperate, he sat down to think, his butt slamming down on what he thought would be a cushy seat, but was decidedly not. Looking down, he saw that below the cushion of the chair was a strange, metallic frame that looked odd and out of place. Looking at it closer, he could see that there was the outline of a removable drawer, with a small indentation in the metal to allow one to hook a finger in and pull it out. With a quick glance toward the stairs, he opened the drawer and found the ledger within.

He flipped backward through the pages, starting at the last entry and looking at the titles of the books that were sold. All the titles sounded boring and benign.

"Excuse me," a male voice said.

Colin slammed the ledger closed and thrust it into a desk drawer. He hadn't heard the shop's front door open or noticed the towering, lean, man enter. The man was in his early fifties, broad shouldered, clean shaven and wearing a Fedora. Colin looked up at him, trying to pretend he belonged.

"Yes. Can I help you?" he asked.

The man looked around. "Celia's not in?"

"Not at the moment, no. I'm just helping out temporarily while she—" There was a clunk up above, and a woman's brief scream. "She's in a meeting. Is there something I can help you with?"

"She was trying to find a book for me. The Killer Angels, by Michael Shaara, first printing."

Colin looked around the desk, then had a thought. He dug the ledger out of the drawer and sat back, flipping through the pages again. More noise from upstairs, Mitch and Celia's voices, loud. "Uh, right. Killer Angels... let me see." He traced his finger down each transaction, still looking for the name of a book on demons. Alarmed, he looked up at the giant of a man who gazed down at him with unusual intensity. "What is that about again?"

"The Civil War."

He let out a breath. "Right. Civil War." He continued to peruse the entries. His eyes locked onto one of the titles. Sitting bolt upright he said, "Here it is." Then realizing the man was still waiting, he added, "But she doesn't have that in yet. Give her another week, hopefully."

Clearly disappointed, the man strode out of the store.

The door at the top of the stairs opened and he heard the heavy foot falls as Mitch made his way down, Celia screaming at him as she followed. Colin grabbed a small piece of paper and scribbled the name of the purchaser and the name of the book, stuffing the note in his pocket. He crammed the ledger back into its hiding spot and jumped over to one of the isles of books and grabbed a random tome from the shelf.

Mitch and Celia were clearly arguing and it looked as though Celia hadn't had time to throw the T-shirt back on under the unbuttoned blouse and her feet were bare. Mitch looked at Colin, inquiry on his face. Colin nodded slightly, indicating he'd found the name.

"So are you going to give me the name or what?" Mitch snapped over his shoulder.

"Not after that," Celia said.

Mitch spun around to face her. "You're so predictable. You know what? When there's a big, ugly, scaly demon knocking on your door, don't call me." He looked at Colin. "Come on. We'll get the name some other way." Then he looked at the book Colin was replacing on the shelf and his face screwed up. "Little Women? Really?"

"That's a good book," Celia shouted at their backs as they left the store.

The door slammed shut behind them and Mitch said, "Tell me you got the name."

"I got *a* name." He pulled the crumpled note out of his pocket and gave it to Mitch.

Mitch took the note and read the name aloud, "Seth Myska? Crap. Never heard of him."

The electronic tune of "Battle-hymn of the Republic" rose above the noise of the traffic. Mitch pulled his cellphone out of its holster and answered it. His eyes darted to Colin as he listened to the caller. His eyebrows creased and he said, "Can't read the signature? Hold on." He examined the paper once more, then asked, "Could it be 'Seth Myska'?" Then his head began to bob. "That's our guy, then. When was he there? Did you see a vehicle? Nuts. What was it he bought? Any idea why? Oh boy. Thanks a lot, Horace. Let me know if he shows up again. Thanks." He replaced the phone in its holster and looked at Colin, his visage grave.

"The antiquities guy?" Colin asked.

Mitch nodded, raising a hand to hail a cab. He punched a key on his phone and then he had his phone to his ear again.

"Reginald? Hey, find out where a guy named Seth Myska lives. He's probably early thirties or so. Call me back as soon as you know. I think he may be our sorcerer. And keep a close eye on the meta-rift tracking. He may be up to something soon."

A taxi stopped in front of them and they were aboard and rolling through traffic in seconds. Mitch gave the driver the address to Horace's antique store. Colin was watching him with questions plain on his face.

"What'd Horace say?"

"This guy, Myska, came into the store, looking pretty beat, and bought an ancient phallic statue. He was the same guy that had inquired about the Seal of Solomon."

Colin pulled his chin back in shock and confusion. Squinting at Mitch he said, "A phallus? What's significant about that?"

Mitch regarded his unschooled friend patiently. "Have you ever heard of Lilith?"

"Yeah. They have some sort of fair for her, right?"

"Yes. But that has nothing to do with what worries me." Mitch noticed the cab driver's eyes in the rear-view mirror so he leaned close to Colin and dropped his voice to a whisper. "Lilith was thought to have been one of the first females. One who believed she should be on even ground with, or even dominant over, Adam. Lilith's followers and underlings are very sexually open. A demon of significant power has taken the name, and the seductive nature of Lilith. This sculpture may be used to summon her or one of her lesser beings."

Colin started to understand. "Great. So he may be getting ready to summon another demon?"

"Exactly," Mitch answered. "And this may mean Myska is getting more sophisticated at his craft, being able to target specific demons, *if* he wasn't able to it before."

Colin's weary eyes drooped nearly closed, a by-product of despair. Once again they'd end up chasing the wrong demon, just to try and stay ahead of the damned idiot bringing them into this world. He clawed for some twig of hope. "Do you think we'll get an accurate pinpoint of where it comes into our plane?" he asked.

Mitch shrugged. "Ben seemed to think so. I gotta think the boys are getting close to having that algorithm nailed. I certainly hope so. But even if we do get a good reading, we have to get there quick before it leaves the area looking for Myska."

Colin's mouth drew into a frown. "If we are going to have to get there fast, maybe we should go get the Jeep and head out to where we found that little guy. At least then we'll be fairly close. Theoretically."

Mitch smiled. "Good thinking. I'll do you one better. By the time we get to the hotel and get the Jeep, we should have Myska's address. We'll go out there and see if we can stop him altogether."

As Mitch leaned forward to tell the driver to change course for their hotel, Colin saw not only a twig of hope, he saw an entire tree. A big frigging oak tree of hope. If they got to Myska before their demon did, all they'd have to do is wait for it. And convince Myska that exorcising the damned being was the right thing to do. Which didn't seem like it should be that hard to do, given the alternative was ushering in a new anti-Christ.

"What do you mean he's not here?" Detective Keller asked, working to control his growing impatience.

"We didn't send anyone to get him and so," the sergeant from the Fiftieth Precinct said. He gestured around the room. "He's not here. Are you sure they told you the Fiftieth?"

Keller rubbed his forehead with his thumb and forefinger, trying to wring out the tension. "Yes. Could you please call down to the Seventeenth and see who it was that picked him up?"

"Yeah, yeah. Hold on."

It was clear the desk sergeant wasn't in the mood for this run-around, but Keller didn't care. He had to talk to Colin Hampton. The only thing that kept him from jumping down someone's throat was the fact that the NYPD had gone out of their way to help him in the first place. He turned to O'Malley.

"What the hell is going on? How could they lose him like this?"

"It's a big city and a big force. I imagine lines of communication just got crossed up a bit. The guy in the Seventeenth probably told us the wrong precinct."

"I hope you're right." He could hear the desk sergeant finishing his conversation, so Keller turned his attention that way.

"The guys who picked him up aren't in our precinct," he said. "Why don't you have a seat and I'll see if I can figure out which precinct they are from." He gestured to some hard, plastic chairs against the wall behind them. With a quick flip of his thumb, he drew their attention to a drip-coffee machine with a carafe brimming with jet-black liquid. "I dare you to have some coffee." His smile conveyed the challenge more than his words did.

Keller and O'Malley took seats, choosing to forgo ingesting the tar-like substance that simmered in the coffee pot. They waited impatiently for well over twenty minutes until the sergeant waved them over. He was shaking his head.

"I got nothing. The names are in our system, but no one can seem to agree on where they are stationed. Seems they get moved around a lot. Really weird. Why don't you leave me your number and I'll have someone call you when they turn up. I've already sent a notice to all the precincts so as soon as they check in, we'll get hold of you."

"Crap. Okay. Thanks for checking." Keller provided his number to the officer and he and O'Malley left the station.

"Now what?" O'Malley asked.

"Let's go find a cafe' right smack in the middle of this messed up city."

Mitch and Colin wasted no time at the hotel. Mitch demanded their car from the valet and gave him a ten-dollar bill to speed him along. The black Jeep jounced to the curb two minutes later, its headlights momentarily blinding Colin. Mitch rewarded the valet with another ten-spot as he climbed behind the wheel, the valet closing the door and wiping the gleaming black metal with a smooth cloth to eliminate any finger oils. Colin was already buckling up, their packs thrown without care into the back seat.

The Jeep launched into the flow of traffic like a serpent striking at its prey, drawing more than one angry horn blast. Mitch was energized. Colin could see it and feel it radiating outward. The man was acting as if he really was on a mission from God. The energy was contagious, filling Colin with a purpose he hadn't felt since graduating from college, when he thought he would conquer the world. Now he and Mitch were trying to save it.

"Do you know where you're going?" Colin

asked.

"Basically. Right now I'm just heading over toward Brownsville." Mitch's cellphone interrupted, and he dug it out of his pocket, trying not to crash in the process. "What do you have for me?" Mitch commanded into the phone. Then, "Colin, write this down."

Colin looked around for something to write on. When he came up empty, he pulled out his phone and opened the 'memo' application and nodded to Mitch. Mitch rattled off Myska's address while Colin recorded it into his cellphone.

"Excellent. Thanks. Keep an eye open for any summoning and call me immediately if you detect anything. I don't want to be surprised by a demon popping into our plane." He stuffed the phone back into his pocket. "Put that address into the GPS on your phone. Now we just have to get to his place before he starts the ritual." He gave Colin a huge, relieved smile. "This is it, man. We can just wait there until your soul-stealing demon arrives and then, wham! We'll have saved the world and hopefully put an end to this nightmare."

"I just hope we can take it down easier than that last little guy."

Mitch swallowed hard and raised his eyebrows. "You and me both. At least we know that this one is a fear-caster. But knowing that isn't going to make this less scary."

Colin sighed in agreement and then both

men fell into themselves, thinking and planning for the encounter that loomed over the horizon like an approaching invader. Colin stared out the window, watching the neighborhood become more deteriorated and foreboding. He glanced at Mitch and wondered at the man's courage and selfless attitude. How could anyone do this for a living? Never getting any acknowledgment or acclaim? And what kind of risk was Mitch taking? Could he somehow be possessed himself, or cast into Hell? Certainly, he could die. Yet here he was, striving to save Colin's unborn son, and the world. All this he did out of love and concern for a largely undeserving people. He was the protector of every single person he came across. He decided that Mitch would have made a very good father.

They arrived at Myska's house in what felt like an excruciatingly long time. They cruised by the front of the old two-story, verifying the house numbers that hung to one side of the slightly crooked door. Mitch pulled into the first parking spot he could find, and they climbed out onto the sidewalk, donning their strange leather jackets and slinging their weapon packs over shoulders.

A huge oak-tree buckled the sidewalk in front of Myska's house and cast dark, eerie shadows from the street lights, making the darkened upstairs windows and screened-in porch look like the eyes and mouth of a wailing skull. The homes on either side of Myska's were similarly quiet, commensurate with the late hour. The place looked lifeless.

They scaled the three, rickety wooden steps to an aluminum storm door that refused to close in its skewed frame. Mitch hammered on the door with authority, rattling it. They waited.

No answer.

Mitch pulled the door open and stepped onto the porch, so he could approach the main door which was worn wood with three, small, lead-glass windows aligned across the top at eye level. Colin stood back near the porch door, watching the curtained picture window to the right of the entrance. Mitch pounded on the door with his fist, then found a decrepit looking doorbell button and jammed that with his finger. The men could hear the classic ding-dong tone resound through the residence.

Still, no answer.

Mitch looked at Colin and shook his head. He tried the doorknob. Locked.

"Why don't you go around back and see if you can see a car in the alley or any lights on inside. Looks dark from here, but I don't want to assume he's not home. We gotta find him and do it soon."

Colin grunted his assent and quickly walked along the side of the house to the back yard. He couldn't see any cars that appeared to be attributed to Myska, just one parked at the home next door.

The other vehicles were all several residences away. He turned to examine the rear of Myska's home. Another door was situated in the middle of the back of the house – this one with a larger window taking up the top third of the door. Peeking through, he could see that the door opened onto the stairs descending into the basement. Just inside on the right, another closed door most likely opened into the kitchen area. Stepping back, he scanned all the windows he could see, from the basement to the attic. Not a light shone from the dark interior.

He heard a thump from inside the house, followed by a slow, rhythmic pounding. Someone was moving around in the house. His heart quickened as he crouched low and took cover next to the wall beneath the kitchen window. Fear tickled his senses as he wondered if the final confrontation was about to begin.

Footsteps. There was definitely someone walking around in there. He was just about to sneak around to the front to tell Mitch when he heard an interior door open, the one he'd seen through the back door. Unprepared and frightened, he flattened himself against the building and tried to come up with an excuse for why he was standing in Myska's back yard in the dark when the exterior door swung open.

Mitch's head popped out and he looked right at Colin.

"Just for the record, I could totally see you

through the kitchen window. Come on. Get in here," he said opening the door wider and waving Colin inside.

Once inside with the door closed, Colin whispered, "How did you get inside?"

"Don' worry about that."

"You broke in, didn't you? What kind of priest are you? You can't just go breaking and entering," Colin said.

"I'm the 'trying to save the world from a new anti-Christ' kind of priest. And besides, which Commandment says 'thou shalt not break and enter'?" Mitch raised his eyebrows waiting for an answer he knew would not come. "Right. Now we gotta look around. He should have a spot set up to summon the demons. Look for a big pentagram drawn on the floor or something like that. You check the basement and I'll start in the attic and we'll meet in the middle. And no lights. Don't want anyone to know we're here."

"The basement? No lights? Thanks," Colin said. He clicked on the flashlight application on his cellphone. He had finally calmed down and now he had to go into the light-less cellar of a demon-conjuring, madman's house. Mitch disappeared into the kitchen, closing the door behind him, leaving Colin at the top of the descending staircase.

He started down, forcing his feet to move with the precision and stealth a cat would envy. He'd taken only two steps when his stomach clenched and his breath shortened. He swung his pack around front and quickly snatched the loaded flint-lock pistol from within. As quietly as he could, he verified it was loaded and on half-cock. Once he had the pack firmly secured on his back once more, he proceeded down the stairs, one hand holding the flashlight phone high, the other pointing the antique pistol forward. He was sure that any minute he would see the metallic gleam of the demon's eyes shine out of the pitch black at the bottom of the stairs.

No eyes.

But it was not relief that washed over him but a sense of doom. His mouth dried out and he found it hard to swallow. Something about this basement was awful, dreadful, evil. He remembered what Mitch said about the demon casting fear, so he stood frozen on the stairs. Colin's ears ached with the strain of seeking out a predator in the dark, but no sound came but his own strained breath.

Summoning his courage he continued forward, working the light from left to right and back again. For the most part, it appeared to be a normal basement, though certainly a gloomy one. Junk was piled here and there, and about twelve feet to his front was a wall that blocked his path, with a doorway a little off to his right. The walls on either side of him looked to be about equal distance away, with boxes and shelves to the right and a furnace and water-heater to his left. The hairs on the back of his neck prickled when he realized, with growing horror, that there was space behind the stairs he'd just descended. Slowly he turned the light back towards the staircase and saw that there was no kick-board at the back of any of the steps, allowing him to see through them to what lay in the shadows beyond. Raising the pistol higher, he approached the darkness, the illumination of his flashlight sliced by the steps into ineffective planes of bluish light, like blinds pivoting to just the angle that prevented you from seeing past. As he neared the foot of the staircase, his breath caught in his chest. He pushed the diminutive light forward, angling it to shine between two of the worn, wooden steps. When he'd almost finished his scan, the light suddenly reflected back to him, catching something silvery and small in its rays. Crying out, he swung the light around to get full view to fire the gun.

The light settled on a chrome colored Bud Light can.

In the lightless basement behind him, he heard something move, claws scraping against concrete.

His head swirled as he turned around, bringing the light to bear in the direction of the sound. It had come from the corner, behind the furnace and water heater. He wanted to call out, scream for Mitch, but all sound stuck in his throat. He exhaled a weak puff of air. He'd been holding his breath. Fresh air filled his lungs again as he sucked it in like a drowning man's desperate last act. Something thumped against the water heater and Colin focused his aim in that direction. He envisioned the black monster hunkered behind it, waiting to pounce on him. A movement near the floor, just under the lower edge of the flashlight's beam, caught his attention. A rat stuck its nose out as it sniffed around. Before Colin could find something to swat it, it hustled away into the shadows. Colin felt the after effects of adrenaline as his limbs trembled. He waited there for a minute, getting his breathing back to a normal rhythm.

Taking a deep breath, he turned back to his original direction and walked to the doorway into the next room. Shining the light through it, he peeked around the door frame and wrinkled his forehead in curiosity. A smallish room lay before him, with a cozy round table surrounded by three chairs. All the furniture was black, as were the three half used candles that sat on the table, one before each seat. Strung to the ceiling with thick, dark cords were six gleaming metal symbols, none of which Colin had ever seen before. A tall floor-lamp was situated in the far-right corner of the room, but within easy reach of one of the chairs. A half-empty bookcase was against the left wall and a black trunk against the right. No windows or other doors were evident.

He wasn't sure what he'd found but it was definitely worth telling Mitch about.

"That's interesting."

Colin let out a chopped scream and bobbled his phone, nearly dropping it. Mitch's voice sounded like the boom of thunder in Colin's ear. He hadn't heard the exorcist approach.

"Son-of-a—! You scared the hell out of me."

"Sorry. Keep it down a bit, huh," Mitch said walking forward to examine the table with his own flashlight, a big four D-cell battery type that could double as a club and threw off enough light to cook a hot-dog. "This isn't where he's summoning from, but he does commune with demons here." He sniffed the candles and shined a light on the silvery ornaments hanging from the ceiling, fingering two of them curiously. Then he turned his light on the book case and grunted as he read some of the books' titles. "The Black Arts, The History of Demonology and Witchcraft, Malleus Maleficarum... This guy definitely does his research." Mitch looked up at Colin and shook his head. "But I'm afraid to say, he isn't using his house to bring the demons through. I think we should head out to the Jeep and wait for him to come home. Wherever he is, the demon will try to get to him to complete the ritual. If we get him, we'll get the demon."

Colin grunted. "Nothing upstairs then?"

"Nah. Just his porn collection."

"Could have sent me upstairs," Colin said. Both men laughed out loud, glad to ease the tension. Then Mitch led them up and out the front door, pulling it tight behind them. It was time to start the stake-out.

"Who was that?" Reginald asked. An amused smile played across his lips as he sat watching Benjamin hanging up the telephone.

"I had to call the Fiftieth Precinct. Buy the boys some time. Plus, I didn't want the NYPD worrying about the two officers who were transporting Colin," he answered, a wicked grin shining.

"Very nice," Reginald said in his English accent. "Very nice, indeed."

The days were getting shorter. As if the gray overcast hadn't made things dark all day to begin with, the setting sun—which Sergeant O'Malley surmised may actually still exist—dropped below the horizon, precipitating the emergence of an electric glow on the city streets. He and Keller were disgusted with how the NYPD had managed to lose their suspect after having him in custody and were about to resign themselves to having some brews at a local pub when Keller's phone rang.

O'Malley called for their check so they could get out of what was beginning to feel like a prison cafe. As he waited for the waitress to bring the bill, he watched Keller's expression go from positive and expectant, to surprise, to utter disappointment. Keller's head was shaking like a bobble-head doll when he stuffed his phone into his coat pocket.

"That doesn't look good," O'Malley said as he took the check from the waitress.

"Go figure," Keller replied. "Apparently the guys who were transporting Hampton were broadsided in an intersection. They were both dazed pretty good." Taking notice of O'Malley's concerned face he said, "They are going to be okay. Just bumps and bruises, I guess. Anyway, in the confusion, Hampton disappeared. They have no idea where he went. He unlocked his cuffs using one of the officer's keys."

"Wasn't he locked in the back of the car?" O'Malley asked, incredulous. He slapped some money down on the table before sidling out of the vinyl booth bench.

Keller just shrugged and stood up. "Who the hell knows? He's in the wind again. Let's go get a drink. We've got two nights of hotel stay if we need them. I suggest we make use of at least one."

Colin was asleep in the passenger seat of the Jeep, his snores rattling the windows. He was roused from his slumber a little past midnight when Mitch's phone went off. It was Reginald calling to let them know that Myska had successfully summoned another demon.

"Do you know where?" Mitch asked.

Colin could hear Reginald's tinny voice emanating from the ear-piece of Mitch's phone. "I can give you the exact block, but not an address. You'll have to be on your game to locate it, particularly if they are starting to look more human like that last one." He provided an address which Mitch hastily scribbled on a scrap of paper he had grabbed from his glove compartment. As he was thanking Reginald for the information, he handed the paper to Colin who understood to put the address into his phone's GPS. As soon as Mitch hung up, the Jeep was running, its tires chirping on the pavement as he tromped on the accelerator.

"Crap," Colin said. "He brought another one across, huh?"

Mitch just pursed his lips and nodded his head. "You have the pistol loaded, right?" His hands danced along the steering wheel as he complied with the female voice dictating directions from Colin's phone.

"Yep. Why can't this son-of-a-bitch just leave it alone? Why does he keep bringing these damned things here?"

Mitch glanced at Colin. "I think we're going to find out soon enough. This one is going to require both of us. I doubt it's going to be weaker than the last one. Hopefully it won't be too much stronger."

Colin felt his insides collapse on themselves, leaving his entire torso hollow as a kettle-drum. If they could just exorcise the frigging demon that stole his son, he could stop this nonsense and go home. This wasn't his job. He was a computer salesman, dad, husband, Casper Milquetoast, nobody. Yet here he was, chasing after honest-to-God demons from Hell. The only solace he took was from knowing that for some reason the scratches he received from these damned creatures wouldn't ultimately kill him. Unless of course the scratch went so deep as to pull his innards out completely. Something he hoped his crazy linoleum-covered, leather jacket would prevent.

"Half mile to destination," the female voice with Australian accent said.

"Keep your eyes open," Mitch ordered. "Look for anyone creepy looking."

"Could be anyone in this neighborhood."

Mitch shrugged. Then, as his eyes sought out and found the block he was targeting, he said, "Oh shit."

Colin looked out in the direction that Mitch was staring. Already he could see at least three big warehouses, two of them two stories tall. "Is that the block we want?"

"Yep." Mitch drove slowly, scanning each of the warehouses, the vehicles parked in front of each, and the numerous garage doors that fed into each of the buildings. "Shit," he said again.

"You sure swear a lot for a priest," Colin said.

"That's the exorcist in me. I'll try to watch my language if it bothers you."

"No problem. I was just saying."

They examined the buildings and cars, looking for anything that could tip them as to where the demon was.

"Call up Ben and Reginald and ask them to find any information on whether Myska has a vehicle," Mitch said. He rattled off the number to Colin who punched it into his phone and was talking almost before it rang on the other end. Colin relayed their predicament and was assured he'd get a call back, posthaste.

"See anything that stands out?" Mitch asked.

"No. I haven't even seen anyone walking around. Why don't you circle the block?"

Mitch drove down all four streets that encapsulated the block. They counted five warehouses altogether. Two of them had bay doors open which allowed them to see workers bustling within. That reduced their selection to three big warehouses. Two with two levels, one with a single level.

Colin's phone rang and he answered. Reginald provided him with a vehicle description and a license plate number which he repeated back for Mitch's benefit. He rolled his eyes as he disconnected.

"What is it?" Mitch asked.

"We hardly need the license plate number. The car is a gold, nineteen-eighty-five, Chevy Citation. Can you believe that? There are probably about—hmmm, let me see—three still on the road. And he has one of them."

"Didn't see it on our drive-around. Crap." Mitch pulled into an empty parking space in front of one of the presumably empty warehouses. The window on the second floor was dark and there was a loading bay and door just to the left of where they parked. The other two quiet warehouses were on the opposite side of the block. They could see the lights from the two busy warehouses just down the street they were on. Their Jeep could easily be mistaken as belonging to someone working at one of the busy buildings. Mitch pulled a set of lock-picks from his inside pocket and smiled deviously at Colin who just shook his head and sighed. "We'll have to check inside each of these warehouses. Be ready." The sodium-vapor lamp on the corner to their right shed a dim, pink glow that just barely reached the door in front of them. It was enough to see the lock in the door-knob, but also enough to let anyone within eyesight see they were up to something. They'd have to work fast to break in.

They exited the Jeep and closed the doors as quietly as they could before stepping over to the door. With deft fingers Mitch jammed the tension tool into the lock and then began trying to manipulate the pins with the rake. Colin, shivering and twitching, kept a look-out, his head swiveling back and forth. He found that as nervous and frightened as he was, he kind of got a little kick out of doing something that was technically illegal. But they weren't doing it to steal, just to save the world. And as long as he didn't think about what might be behind the door, he was okay. He heard the lock pop as Mitch worked the tension tool around, unlocking the door. The demon-hunter twisted the knob and quickly slipped inside, Colin close behind.

Mitch closed and re-locked the door before turning his attention to the warehouse interior. The only light was what street-light filtered through the windows spaced evenly around the top level of the exterior walls. In the faded glow they could see the place looked abandoned and empty. Above them and extending to their right was what had obviously served as the office area, the stairs just to their front and right. The offices only took up the last third of the street-facing wall, the rest of the warehouse was constructed to use the extended height of the second story roof, allowing tall equipment to move around inside.

Mitch flipped the switch on his club-like flashlight and a beam of light seared through the dusty air. Colin glanced at the exorcist long enough to see him shaking his head, his lips pursed in a frown.

"Doesn't look like it. Follow me," he said.

Without waiting, he strode through the center of the building. He worked the light back and forth, scanning the floor and walls. Before he'd reached the other side, he spun around and headed toward the stairs. He mounted these two at a time, his eyes always fixed forward. At the top, they found a balcony style hallway with three doors that opened off of it. Mitch made quick work of checking each of the rooms. In the last one he took a peek out the window and his face contorted into a snarl.

"Damn it," he said.

Colin stepped to the window and looked out. A security car was stopped in the street directly behind their Jeep. They stepped back from the window to remain out of sight, but where they could still see out. The door to the cruiser opened and a rent-a-cop got out, drawing his flashlight with one hand, his other hand rearranging his privates. He shined the flashlight around the doorway and around the Jeep. Flipping the light off, he started for the door to the warehouse.

CHAPTER FIFTEEN

Seth Myska had never actually seen a demon coming into our world before, though he'd performed the ritual four times. With the previous four demons, they all came over at some location far from where he was conducting the summoning. This one though, came through right where he wanted her. As he crumpled to his knees from exhaustion—the ritual was very physically and psychologically taxing—he raised his head to look at the center of the pentagram painted on the floor.

What he saw was the most awesome and terrifying spectacle he had ever witnessed. He had seen chairs levitate with three-hundred-pound women sitting in them. Faces had distorted beyond the physical capabilities of any human, with jaws spreading until the mouth took the appearance of a sea lamprey's parasitic maw. Bodies scaled the walls and clung to the ceiling in arachnid mimicry. Voices had boomed at near infrasonic frequencies causing nausea and dizziness then at the next moment shattered glass at ultrasonic pitches too high to hear. None of that prepared him to get a glimpse of Hell itself.

As he was finishing the ritual, a black, reflective, pool, about the size of a hotel hot-tub, formed and hovered directly over the center of the pentagram. Slowly it started to rotate about its horizontal axis so Myska was facing the entire surface of ebon evil. Within its shiny surface, he could see his own naked, prostrate form, his face lifted in awe and gazing at the unbelievable. Outside, thunder rolled and crashed, rattling the walls and doors that enclosed him. A searing flash of red lightning smashed through the metal of the building's roof and penetrated the oily liquid that floated before him. The smell of ozone penetrated his nostrils, followed instantly by an acrid stench as the black pool bubbled and steamed, sending tendrils of putrid, purple smoke snaking through the air.

As he watched, the bubbles took on greater size and viscosity, reminding Myska of scenes he'd watch on television about boiling tar pits. Each time one of the tarry balloons burst, he saw a flash of color behind it. It seemed to Myska that the longer the boiling went on, the longer the flashes endured. And they were no longer just sparks of color, but more like viewing a scene through the lens of a camera, visible when the shutter opened to let him see beyond his world, only to snap shut again. Each time the aperture opened, he saw more of what was beyond: a slender leg; a finely crafted arm; a delicate hand with painted nails; a firm breast; red, wet, pouting lips covering glistening white teeth. Behind it all was a world of red, orange, yellow and brown. There were no flames, as Hell was often portrayed, but rather the burning of an internal flame, much like the red-hot appearance of the heating element of an electric stove.

Finally, in one gigantic explosion of darkness that momentarily sucked the light and vision from him, everything was gone, and left standing at the center of his demonic diagram was the most sensuous, arousing, lustful woman he'd ever seen. She was not naked, but her seductive outfit forced the mind into fits of creative sexuality. Her hair was black as night and her skin golden and smooth. Glossy lips of deep burgundy parted in a devilish grin beneath intelligent eyes so dark one might say the cornea and pupil were one. Myska's stare slid down her perfectly proportioned body, stalling on the firm breasts that strained against the V-shaped, red, satin negligee that extended down to pass between her legs only to emerge as a g-string on her back-side. Red stiletto heels rounded out her hellish apparel. Kylova had arrived.

"Geez. This is great," Colin whispered.

Mitch motioned for him to be quiet and to step back even farther from the window. They stood in the dark shadows of the little office, waiting. A powerful thumping on the door resonated through the whole warehouse, followed by the guard's voice announcing "Police. Is there anyone in there?" It was followed by more pounding. Mitch frowned at Colin and mouthed the question, *police?* Colin could only shrug.

They were just about to peek out the window again when the guard's light flashed through, illuminating the ceiling. Mitch pulled Colin back and made a show of wiping his brow and letting out a relieved breath. When the light disappeared, they took a quick glance out the window. The guy, wearing a neatly-pressed but overly large uniform, pulled a notepad out of his pocket and peered at the license plate of Mitch's Jeep, quickly jotting down the number before climbing back into his car.

"Looks like he's leaving. Let's give him a minute and then get out of here. We'll slip around the corner and check out the other two locations."

Colin looked at him with eyes wide. "Are you crazy? You want to break into another warehouse with that security guy already cruising around suspecting something?"

"We don't have a choice. One of these warehouses is most likely where Myska is and we have to find him as fast as we can."

Colin didn't like it, but he knew that Mitch was right. Time was not on their side. And as long as they were able to get into the warehouses unseen, there shouldn't be a problem. But they had no idea where the security cruiser was going or when it would be back. It would be just as problematic if they emerged from one of the warehouses right into his line of sight. He resolved himself to the fact that they really didn't have any other options and nodded his compliance.

"Follow me," Mitch ordered.

Together they descended the stairs and stood near the exit door. Mitch opened it slowly and peered out, looking both ways. When he bolted through, Colin was tight behind him, carefully pushing the door shut behind them, quietly as he could. Once on the roadside, they proceeded at a businesslike, but not rushed, pace up to the corner and around where they fell into the shadows between street lights.

"At this next warehouse, you so much as see the hint of a headlight, give me a nudge and we are walking again. Got it?"

"Don't have to tell me twice," Colin said.

As they turned the corner that would take them to the second warehouse they could see headlights coming down the street.

"Walk like we belong here," Mitch said.

His heart hammering, Colin stood up a little straighter while turning his chin down to use the brim of his cap to shield his eyes from the vehicle's headlights, while at the same time obscuring his face. He could hear the tires throwing up a fine mist from the rain dampened street. Though his face was turned slightly away, his eyes followed the car and he could see that it was not the security cruiser. He heard Mitch's relieved exhalation when the car passed. The car was out of site by the time they made it to the door to the next warehouse. Like the first door, this one was bathed in pink glow from the sodium-vapor street lamps.

Mitch prepared his tools, glanced in all directions, and seeing no activity, marched over to the door and knelt to begin his burglary arts. Had anyone seen the two men just then, they would have no problem realizing they were breaking in. Colin's head was raised up as high as his spine would allow and constantly swiveling, like a protective goose watching over the rest of his flock, while Mitch was huddled over, eyes nearly on the same level as the doorknob. Colin heard a 'thunk' and the door was being drawn outward. It seemed Mitch was trying to set a record time for breaking-and-entering. The two men slipped inside before Colin could even consider the consequences if a demon waited within.

Inside the darkness of the warehouse, Colin heard Mitch's and his own heavy breathing. The staleness of the air convinced him that this warehouse hadn't been opened in a long time. Unlike the first site, this warehouse had plenty of windows up high that let in the glow of the streets. Also unlike the first, there was no office or visible second story within, just an iron-grate, cat-walk that lined the outer walls, with the exception of over the tall, bay garage door. In one of the back corners of the open interior, a small room was set apart by ramshackle, wooden walls. In the middle of the floor, on a rugged, six-wheeled, steel trailer was a massive yacht, bow aligned with the huge garage door.

Mitch flipped on his flashlight and swept it around in a slow arc. Even in the subtle light Colin could see his disappointment. Nonetheless, the demon-hunting priest started pacing around inside the building, scanning the floor and walls for any signs of conjuring. Colin followed closely, none too surprised at Mitch's rapid pace. Colin watched as Mitch clambered up the stern of the yacht to check it out. In less than a minute, Mitch was climbing right back down, shaking his head. They covered the little, one-room office and the whole warehouse, corner to corner without finding anything.

Finally, Mitch turned to Colin and said, "If it isn't the next one, we have a serious problem."

"If it *is* the next one, we still have a serious problem."

The copulation, which in this case served as the sealing contact for the conjuring, lasted a remarkable three minutes. Myska was exhausted and sexually no match for one of Lilith's ranking succubi. Kylova's mastery of the carnal arts enabled her to bring her subjects to climax with little effort on her part. And their mental subjugation afterward was always uncontested. But this was a new experience for her, being here in body and spirit, able to feel and be wholly felt. However, she was limited in her ability to do as she pleased, due to her spiritual subjugation to her summoner. A fact that she had to make Myska forget so she could control him. Though she didn't have to obey him, per se, neither could she do him harm. And if she was in this plane long enough, she would have to re-establish herself periodically through physical contact.

She could do whatever she wished to others.

If only Myska were dead, she could come and go as she pleased, answering to no one of this plane. Physical contact with any human of this world would suffice to maintain her ability to remain, but she could not kill Myska, nor unduly influence another to kill him. It was one of those immutable *laws* put into place by the hated Creator. They had some latitude, but it was not unbridled.

If Myska were dead, as she wished, Apophis, who carried the stolen soul of an unborn child, could hide safely until the anti-Christ was delivered, instead of being drawn inexorably to this man, his earthly anchor. But Apophis had not yet completed the ritual, as she had.

She looked down at Myska who lay between her knees on the floor, eyes closed, his glistening chest rising and falling slowly with his slumber. Gently she leaned down, letting her breast brush lightly against him, and whispered in his ear.

"Lover, it's time to awaken." Her breath, the scent of lightly fragrant flowers, tickled his nose.

Myska's eyes fluttered and his head turned toward her. When his weary eyes focused on her beautiful face, they came immediately open and he sucked in a breath.

"Hello," she cooed. "I was afraid I'd killed you. I'm so glad you are still with me."

She stood up, rising above him, letting his eyes see her full nakedness as she turned and walked away. With a subtle hand-gesture, she was fully dressed in skin tight jeans and an equally tight, white, waffle-shirt. With delicate grace she sat on the corner of Myska's desk, pulling one leg up to her chest while the other remained planted on the concrete floor. Myska rolled onto his side, reaching out to snag his clothes. As he slipped them on, Kylova said, "Where's Apophis?"

Myska looked at her, his eyes full of question and incomprehension. He stood up, hiking his jeans around his waist. "Who's Apophis?"

"He is the... being you summoned but which has not been cast back into the Abyss." Her eyes were cool yet smoldering with incredible intelligence.

"I don't know," Myska answered, not particularly distressed about the missing demon. "I imagine he'll show up eventually."

"Lover, we need to make sure he completes the ritual. He has to touch you." She gestured with one languid finger, summoning Myska to her side. He walked over as he pulled on his shirt.

"What difference does it make? He's not who we want anyway. And now that I know how to bring your kind right where I want you, as soon as I'm rested up I can summon Belphegor."

The succubus recoiled at mention of Belphegor and raised her other leg off the floor, so she was sitting completely on the desk. Once so, she spread her legs allowing Myska to come to rest tightly against her as he stood between her thighs. "Belphegor. Why Belphegor? He is a despicable creature with nothing to offer. Now you have me," she said. She raised her dreamy eyes to his. "You don't need anyone else. But we need to complete Apophis or I fear for your safety."

Myska wrapped his arms around the lustful demon and pulled his head back to look at her down his nose. "Fear for me? Why? If we don't complete the ritual, he'll revert back to Hell where he's from."

Kylova put one side of her head against his chest so he could not see the smirk on her face. These humans were so easy to deceive. "You've felt the pain of one of your subjects being exorcised, yes? If one reverts to Hell without the rite of exorcism, you will not be able to bear the pain. Your heart will burst in your chest."

That got Myska's attention. It was plain in the frown on his face. "So how do we find him?"

"He will come to where the ritual was performed and find you. He will hasten to this place. But it will still be some time, I think, before he reaches us. Until then, I need you to take me to meet someone."

"What if he gets here while we're gone?"

"He will wait for us to return here."

"But I don't want my heart—"

"He will wait," Kylova said, meeting Myska's eyes.

Embarrassed by his chastisement, Myska backed down. "Who could you possibly need to meet?"

She pulled his head down and whispered to him, her lips brushing wet against his ear. When she released his head, she could see the wicked smile on his lips.

"That sounds delightful. Completely delightful."

CHAPTER SIXTEEN

Once again, Mitch cautiously peered out of the warehouse door, and, once again, the coast was clear. They slipped into the night shadows and headed toward the third warehouse, this last being a single-story, windowless building with one garage door and one door for foot-traffic. Unlike the first two, this one was completely engulfed in shadows, making it look not only abandoned, but decrepit and poisonous. Despite its inhospitable appearance, both men were thankful they wouldn't be breaking into it in clear view of anyone who happened to be traveling the quiet city street. As they approached the door, Colin's limbs trembled slightly and his mouth turned stone dry. Within the confines of this final warehouse they would most likely be stumbling into a demon and its master. There was no telling what was going to happen.

Standing next to the door, Mitch pulled out his blessed dagger and set it on the ground within easy reach. He turned to Colin. "I gotta think this is going to be it. Get the pistol out and be ready. Try to keep it concealed until you are right up next to it. I'd like you as close to this thing as possible before firing."

With that, he went to work on the lock. He didn't have to tell Colin to keep an eye out so they didn't get busted. It seemed like hours that Colin scanned for incoming traffic or foot security or demons lurking in the dark. Even so, he heard the click of the lock far earlier than he was expecting. As a matter of fact, part of him secretly wished this lock would prove too difficult for the exorcist/warrior/burglar. Their lives may end in the next few minutes, making this an appointment Colin wouldn't mind delaying. He watched as Mitch bagged his lock picks and grabbed the knife, then he turned to look at Colin and gave a nod. Without a word he slunk through the door into the darkness beyond.

Colin followed.

After a couple of steps he noticed there was a light on. Not one of the big ceiling lights, but a small desk lamp about halfway through the warehouse directly in line with the door they had entered. Nothing moved and there was no one in sight. At least not within the feeble halo of light.

Mitch froze and slowly raised the dagger out in front of him in an underhand grip. Colin stopped immediately, moving only his eyes, trying to pierce the dark corners of the building. He kept the pistol pointed in a safe direction, tight to his body. He wasn't sure if Mitch saw something, heard something, or both. So he remained as still as possible, waiting to act on Mitch's lead. His heart thundered in his chest and his legs and arms trembled. For a moment he was back in the forest, seeing his first buck with his dad's borrowed rifle in hand, adrenaline pumping through his veins, afraid to move, but afraid he'd miss the opportunity for a kill if he didn't. But what he hunted now was much more dangerous, capable of killing him easier than he could kill it. Here, he was equal parts prey and predator and the stakes were much higher than a freezer full of meat or not. He heard a click as Mitch flipped on his flashlight, casting the white beam into the shadows to their left where it illuminated the nearest wall and no more. Then it scanned to their right, piercing the darkness in their immediate vicinity but fading to near uselessness as it tried to reach the farthest corner of the building.

Mitch began to walk right, away from the desk and lamp, his own light penetrating deeper into the black, unexplored areas. The man made no sound, walking as if there was a cushion of air between his feet and the concrete floor. Colin followed reluctantly, wishing rather to bathe in the glow of the lamp, the light being a safehaven in this vile, black pit. They reached the far, back corner without encountering anything other than a refrigerator and custodial closet. Between the desk lamp and the flashlight, both men could see there was no one anywhere to be found.

They walked over toward the desk, Colin's

breathing and heart-rate settling down to near normal as the disappointment and relief set in. As they neared the desk, Mitch shined his light on the floor a few feet from the desk, nearer the center of the warehouse. The beam revealed a smeared pentagram, painted in now blackened blood, with a variety of talismans scattered haphazardly around the design, some on their sides. Mitch wrinkled his nose.

"Smells like sex," he said.

"How would you know?" Colin asked.

Mitch glanced sideways at Colin. "Wasn't always a priest. Remember." Mitch scrunched up his face and shook his head, disgusted. He looked around at the site. "Probably copulated to complete the summoning ritual."

Colin pointed at the artifacts scattered around on the floor. "What is all this stuff?"

Mitch examined the talismans and the symbols that hadn't been obliterated. He found the phallus and showed it to Colin.

"The sculpture Horace told us about. Apparently this Myska guy used it in his ritual. He did it right here, and judging by the mess, this is where the demon came through."

"So where are they?"

"Hmmm," Mitch said. He gazed around and shined his flashlight over near the garage door where two wet car tracks could be seen on the concrete. "Don't know where they are now, but it looks like Myska pulled his car right in here. No wonder we didn't see it." He turned serious eyes on Colin. "They've left. And whatever they are up to, I'm sure it's not good."

Colin rubbed his eyebrows with the heels of both hands. "Dammit. We missed him. What if my demon made it here already and Myska is driving all over town with it and the new arrival? How are we going to find them?" He slumped in the sole chair, despondent.

Mitch walked over to the center of the pentagram, whipped out his phone and poked at its screen. Finally, he punched a button and held the phone out in front of him.

Ben's voice sounded from the speaker. "Hello?"

"Ben? It's Mitch. I just sent you some GPS coordinates from the center of the pentagram that Seth Myska used to summon that last demon."

"Great! We can use those to help us zero in our software. Uh, I take it you are there by yourselves?"

"Yep. They're gone. Left in his car."

"That's not good. I do have some good news for you though. Or maybe not. When he did his summoning this time, it was followed shortly after by a pretty significant spiritual resonant disturbance. I'm guessing it was the consummation of the physical conjuring. But it did give us some great data that we can use to help with the tracking algorithms. We're testing it now, but we're getting a lot of hits around the city, so I'm guessing it still needs some tuning."

"Let me know as soon as you have anything remotely promising. If we can't find that demon from up-state, the Pope isn't going to like me much."

"As soon as we have something, I'll let you know."

"Oh, one other thing. We're inside a warehouse that Myska was evidently using. If I give you the address, can you track down the owner? Maybe they have more contact information that could help us find him. We'll check his house again, but from the look of things here," he eyed the cot and rumpled blankets, "he probably hasn't been there in a while."

Mitch proceeded to give Ben the address of the warehouse and disconnected. Then he walked over and slapped Colin's arm like a sergeant rousing his soldiers to resume a march.

"Come on. Let's go check Myska's house. Hopefully by the time we get that done, Ben and Reginald will have found out whose warehouse this is and have contact information for us."

"I'm exhausted," Colin said. "Do you even think it's worth going over there?"

Mitch looked at Colin, his own eyes red and glassy, a wan smile on his lips. "If we don't find anyone at Myska's, we'll head to the hotel and get some rest. May be the last sleep we get."

They arrived at Myska's residence a short time later and parked the Jeep directly in front. Mitch knocked on the front door and when there was no response or sound from inside, the two demon hunters slunk around to the back door. They saw no evidence of Myska's car in front, or in the alley behind the house. Mitch banged on the rear door as well, his lack of enthusiasm evident. Again, no response. Mitch pursed his lips.

"I guess we go get some sleep."

Colin followed Mitch to the Jeep and they headed back to the hotel. Each man was tired and lacked desire for conversation, so Colin stared out the window at the city streets. He wondered how Julie and Claire were doing. He was sick with worry about his pregnant wife, but he had not even had time to think of them with all that he was doing. He wished he could just wrap his arms around both of them, kissing each one on the cheek. Hopefully they were getting over the trauma of what happened at their house. He worried about Claire. Though she hadn't seen the demon, she was a smart kid and had known there was some sort of monster coming for all of them. He could feel the tears well up, thinking about how he almost failed them. But there was still a child he could fail. He didn't even want to consider what would happen to his family if he and

Mitch didn't exorcise that demon, so he once again forced himself into distraction. Quietly, in his mind, he went over the exorcism Rite.

He was jolted out of his recitation by Mitch's phone going off. Mitch fumbled to retrieve it and jostled his head, as if he were clearing it of fog.

"Hello. Really? Wow, that's fortunate. Thanks." He stuffed the phone back into his pocket.

Colin stared at him waiting for an explanation.

"The warehouse is one of Adon Negaré's. We'll get with him in the morning. I'm sure he'll get us whatever information we need on who's leasing it."

"Huh," Colin said. He was simply too tired to display emotion. "Hopefully Myska gave him some good contact information."

Mitch only nodded.

When they finally arrived back at the hotel, it was nearly three in the morning. Getting up to their room was done through a gray veil of semi-consciousness. Colin collapsed on his bed, electing to leave his clothes on so as not to expend the energy of removing them. As his eyes fluttered between opened and closed, he thought he saw Mitch staring at his palm, examining something. Curiosity beat out slumber just long enough for him to see Mitch return the item to his pants pocket. It looked like a photo. A photo of a woman with jet black hair.

CHAPTER SEVENTEEN

"What the hell? Who could that be?" Robert Jones asked his wife as he turned on the bedside lamp and threw the blankets aside. Leslie lay in bed next to him, her blond hair splayed across her pillow. She kept her eyes tightly closed against the unwanted intrusion of light. Robert glanced at the clock; 1:33 a.m. Annoyed, but concerned, he pulled on the sweat-pants that lay on the floor, stepped into a pair of slippers and determined that his t-shirt was good enough for someone calling at this hour.

The doorbell rang again.

"I'm coming already," he mumbled. He turned on the light at the top of the stairs and descended, the muscles of his chest bouncing briefly with each step. He crossed the family room to the front door and flipped the switch to turn on the porch light. The light flashed and with a loud 'pop', went dark.

"Dammit."

He opened the heavy oak door and found himself looking into the terrified blue eyes of a blond woman who looked much like his wife. In a heartbeat he realized she was completely naked.

"Whoa! Come in. Are you okay? What's going on?" the questions rattled out of him one on top of the other.

The woman cast nervous glances around and crossed the threshold, on the verge of tears. As far as Robert could tell, she was not hurt, just unclothed and obviously upset. His eyes couldn't help but to flash over her perfect form, but he quickly turned away to yell for his wife to call 911. But before he could shout, the woman was upon him. Her once well-manicured nails were now long, wicked claws. Her perfect white teeth, now yellow, pointed fangs. She tore into Robert's throat with those fangs and ripped his chest open with her claws, rending a lung and rupturing his heart. He was dead before he hit the floor.

"Honey? Is everything all right?" Leslie peered down the staircase, a concerned frown distorting her lips.

The first thing she saw were the rage filled eyes glaring up at her. When the woman moved to the stairs, she noticed her blood spattered, naked body. Leslie shrieked hysterically and fled back toward her bedroom. The killer bolted up the stairs with incredible speed, catching Leslie as she ducked into her room. Leslie missed the opportunity to close the bedroom door before the blood-soaked woman's clawed hand burst through the secretary's chest from behind. With hardly a sound, Leslie crumpled to the floor.

Kylova stared down at her handy-work, then at her own body. With a grunt of disapproval, she stepped into the Jones' shower and cleaned herself off. With more work to do, she left the house. A more important prize waited.

"Yeah. Come in," Adon Negaré shouted at whoever was knocking on his office door. *Why is someone knocking? Is Leslie not in?*

A beautiful blond woman stepped into the room, only one step, and stopped, her hand on the door. She was dressed professionally but looked very uncomfortable, wearing an insincere smile that dwindled when Negaré looked at her. When he saw how pretty the young thing was, he tried to put her at ease by softening his own features. He even tried one of his charming smiles on her with little success.

Nervous green eyes tried in vain to meet Negaré's. "Mr. Negaré, sir, I'm afraid I have some bad news." The young lady looked at one of the most powerful men in the world, waiting for some form of acknowledgment.

In short order, Negaré raised his eyebrows in anticipation and splayed his palms wide. "Yes, dear. What is it?"

"I'm sorry, sir," she said. She took an additional step into the office. Then, seeming to remember some word of advice, she stood up straighter, held her head a little higher and said, "I'm afraid that your secretary, Leslie, and her husband were murdered sometime last night. I've been sent up to fill in temporarily until a suitable replacement secretary can be found."

Negaré slumped down in his chair. *Leslie? Murdered?* He could hardly believe what he was hearing.

"Mr. Negaré? Are you alright?"

"Yes," he said. He shook his head in disbelief. "Are you sure? *My* Leslie? Who would want to hurt her?"

The woman just shrugged.

"Have they found the murderer?" He asked the question as suspicion poisoned his stomach.

"No sir. And you should be prepared because the police will be contacting you."

"I'll be reaching out for them," he stated. "Please notify me when they arrive. Will you..." He looked at her expectantly.

"Kelly," she said, completing his sentence. "But I'm just up here temporarily. Human resources is already screening for your new secretary."

Negaré liked this woman. She seemed pleasant enough, and more importantly, impressionable. "I want you to call down there and tell them that you will be my new permanent secretary. I have to personally train whoever they send up here anyway. May as well be you." He threw her one of his patented smiles.

"Yes, Mr. Negaré. And thank you. I will do my best."

"I'm sure you will," he said taking in her whole body in a glance. Very much like Leslie, but younger. "First thing I need you to do is to pack up Leslie's personal belongings so that... does she have family?"

"Yes, sir. A sister lives here in town."

"Pack up her things so we can give them to her sister. And then see that her survivors get a check for fifteen—no, her husband died too—thirty thousand dollars to offset funeral costs. I understand those things are getting pricey."

"Yes, Mr. Negaré." She turned to start out the door, giving Negaré a delightful view of her firm backside.

"Oh. And... ah," he said. Why was he struggling to remember the woman's name? "Kelly. You'll have questions. When you do, just call my number in here."

Kelly gave him an ingratiating smile. "I will. Thank you." Then she walked out and closed the door behind her.

Negaré felt his heart beating a touch quicker than usual, a result of being in the presence of the gorgeous secretary he'd just promoted.

The memory of Leslie crashed through his

thoughts of Kelly like a jealous lover, swamping him with guilt that crushed him back down into his chair. *How could Leslie and her husband be dead?* he wondered. *Murdered, no less. What in the world did she get into? Or was it her husband?* Leslie had been a great secretary for the last five years. She was smart, attractive, with a great body which, in Negaré's world, was a must. Leslie was everything he could hope for and seemed to have her own situation squared away. She learned quickly what Negaré needed and was soon able to anticipate his demands, there with a phone number before he asked, the car readied before being requested. In short, she was great. But now she was gone. And violently. Despite not having time to mourn—busy men like him did not have that luxury—he could not shake a growing sense of angst deep within his subconscious.

He picked up the phone and punched in a number. A voice on the other end of the line answered, "Commissioner Brown's office."

"This is Adon Negaré. Get me the Commissioner please."

After being asked to wait, there was a short pause before Gary Brown, NYPD Commissioner answered the phone. "Mr. Negaré. I assume you've heard the bad news?"

"Yes. What happened?"

The Commissioner explained how they had found the Jones' bodies and the gruesome nature of the attack. It was all Negaré needed to hear.

It was a long time since he'd had a day start out this bad.

And it was going to get worse.

Keller and O'Malley were grabbing their breakfast at one of the local diners, sipping scalding hot coffee that was actually quite good. Neither man was in good humor, having received news the previous day that Colin Hampton had escaped custody from the NYPD. Now they were relegated to waiting around for another call telling them the NYPD had him again. Keller would have loved to actively start trying to find Colin but being out of his jurisdiction and not familiar enough with the city, they decided to wait. Impatiently.

Keller was cutting into a giant stack of pancakes done up with berries, whipped cream and syrup when his phone rang. He threw a hopeful glance at O'Malley and dug the phone out of his pocket, its ring-tone amplifying when he brought it out.

"Hello."

"Detective Keller?"

"Yes. Who is this?"

"Lieutenant Dan Humphries, NYPD, seventeenth precinct." Keller started nodding and smiling at O'Malley who quickly started to wolf down his own pancakes. "We got a call here with some interesting information. Anonymous caller indicated that your boy Colin Hampton is going around with a guy named Mitch Stackwell. We got a vehicle description and license plate for you if you are ready to copy."

Keller pulled a pen out of his pocket and snatched O'Malley's napkin. "Yeah, go ahead."

Humphries then described Mitch's black Jeep and provided the license plate number. Keller scribbled down a number and repeated, "A black Jeep. Got it."

"We've issued a BOLO for the vehicle," Humphries said. "If we find it, we'll let you know."

"Likewise. Thanks," Keller said.

O'Malley slowed his consumption to that of a normal forty-year-old man and not a teen-aged boy. "They don't have him?"

"Naw. But they did get a tip." Keller related all he'd just learned to O'Malley. "So when we're done with breakfast, I say we head down toward the seventeenth precinct and keep our eyes open."

"Beats sitting around getting fat," O'Malley said around a mouth full of flap-jack.

With NYPD in receipt of this new information, Keller was sure that they'd pick up Hampton again soon. It was just a matter of time. It was *always* just a matter of time.

Solomon's Seal

CHAPTER EIGHTEEN

The drive to Adon Negaré's office tower the next morning was one of both despair and hope. Despair that Seth Myska had taken off with a demon in tow, hope that Negaré would have some records that would lead them to finding Myska again before the demon did. Colin was filled with a growing sense of dread as each day slipped by. An early call that morning told him that Julie was still in the hospital, under observation. The doctors did not know what was causing her cramping and pain, a fact that only served to amplify his and Julie's fears about their unborn baby boy. He knew he could not fail but felt nearly helpless in his hunt for the devil. He looked at Mitch, the man in whom he'd put his faith. Mitch appeared unflappable, determined, and single-minded of purpose. Where Colin felt he was not allowed to fail, Mitch appeared to believe with certainty that they would not.

Mitch grumbled at the lack of parking as they neared the office tower. After a ten-minute search that took them on a circuitous cruise around the building, he finally found a lot that had space.

They hoofed the three blocks to Negaré's building, their breath visible in the unusually frigid autumn air. The sky hadn't lightened appreciably since daybreak, a thick gray overcast making it impossible to locate the sun.

"Feels like it could snow," Colin said.

"Be pretty early, end of October like this." Mitch held the tall glass door open for Colin who then returned the favor with the next door.

The attendant sitting at the front desk was the same one they'd encountered the other day. He looked up at them and smiled pleasantly, now under the impression that they were very important men who had a relationship with his boss-of-bosses.

"Good morning. Here to see Mr. Negaré?" he asked, his perfect white smile no doubt missing from the cover of a men's health and style magazine.

"Yes," Mitch replied. "Mitch Stackwell."

"Yes, of course, Mr. Stackwell. Just a moment." He dialed his magical telephone, connecting directly with Negaré's office secretary. After a brief, pleasant exchange on the phone and then a short wait, he said, "Okay, I'll send them up." He gestured toward the private elevator where Carmine was already waiting, elevator door opened.

They made the ascent to the top of the office building, each man still too tired to make much in the way of conversation. The elevator stopped and they stepped into the secretary's office. The woman sitting there was not the secretary they'd seen on their previous visit, though she was even more astounding in appearance and younger. An enticing smile formed on her lips as she rose to greet them.

"Hello. You must be Mr. Stackwell," she said. She extended her hand as she came out from behind her desk. "I'm Kelly. It's a pleasure to meet you." Mitch took her warm and firm handshake, smiling. Her eyes flowed to Colin. "I'm sorry. You are?" Again, she reached out her hand.

Gripping her hand, Colin supplied his name.

The secretary gasped slightly when he did, the smile faltering barely long enough to notice.

"Don't worry," Mitch interjected quickly. "The news reports are very misleading. I was with Colin and he is not even remotely guilty of what happened up state."

"Of course. I'm sorry." She turned to lead them into Negaré's office, a seductive sway to her hips. Both men struggled to keep their eyes above waist level. She opened Negaré's door, announced their arrival, then withdrew.

Adon Negaré was already striding across the floor, his hand extended, a wide smile parting his lips.

"Hello, Father Mitch," he said, grasping Mitch's hand firmly. He greeted Colin in kind.

"Please. Just Mitch." Mitch motioned to the door with his jaw. "New secretary?"

Negaré frowned and gestured for them to

take seats in his alcove. "Yes. New secretary." His voice was grim. "Leslie, the woman you met, and her husband were murdered last night."

That got Mitch and Colin's attention. "Murdered!" Mitch said. "How?"

"It sounded pretty heinous. Torn apart." He looked at both men, discomfort and apprehension in his eyes. "NYPD will be looking for leads. I suspect one of their officers will be around to question me soon."

We better be gone by then, Colin thought.

Mitch caressed his jaw between his thumb and forefinger. "That's terrible..." He was lost in his own thoughts. Colin stared at both men, feeling Negaré's sense of loss, but hoping the subject quickly came around to the task at hand. The task of saving the world. "What will you tell them?"

"Not what I suspect. Probably just what I know, nothing."

Mitch nodded.

"I hope you have some good news for me," Negaré said. "Did you get your demon? Or should I expect more of what happened to Leslie?"

Mitch shook his head, eyes diving to the marble floor. "I'm afraid not. We got the identity of the conjurer, a Seth Myska." Negaré shrugged, unfamiliar with the name. "Last night he conjured another demon."

Negaré's eyes jumped to meet Mitch's. "Another one? Last night? So there are two here now. Or were you able to find it and exorcise it?"

Mitch's mouth wrinkled up. "Not exactly. We were able to find where it was summoned. It seems Myska has mastered bringing demons through exactly where he wants them."

"That's crazy," Negaré said. His brow tightened. "But it's still out there?"

"Yes. We found the warehouse where he conducted the ceremony, but they had already left by the time we arrived. That's where we hoped you might be able to help."

"Of course. What do you need?" Negaré said.

"The warehouse belongs to you."

Negaré jolted back. "One of mine? What's the address? I'll get my property manager on the phone."

"We were hoping you might be able to do that," Mitch said. He handed the address over to Negaré who stood and marched over to his desk, Mitch and Colin in tow.

Negaré picked up the telephone receiver and punched a number. He barked the address into the phone and ordered all information about the renter. He stood with chin raised in annoyed impatience as he waited for answers, his eyes casting about the office without focus. Finally, he scribbled frantically on a pad on his desk. With a sharp 'thank you', he hung up. He held the paper out to Mitch.

"Seth Myska. He is using the same name.

He paid for it with cash, up front. Here is an address and telephone number."

Mitch looked at the address, then at Colin. "Not his home address," he said. "We'll have to check this out."

Colin felt a bolt of hope. They had something to go on. Today they might find Myska, and then, hopefully, their demon. He turned to move toward the door.

"Hold on," Negaré said. "I've got an idea. How long do you have to find this guy?"

"We need to find him yesterday," Mitch answered. "We need to be with him when the demon who carries the soul reaches him, so we can banish it back to Hell."

Negaré's face crumpled with pain and concern. "Absolutely. Let me call this guy. I'll tell him I have a deal for him that he cannot pass up, but I need him to meet with one of my people face to face to discuss the particulars and explain why he could benefit from it. Then, once we have the meeting scheduled, I'll let you know the time and place and you can be waiting for him."

Mitch raised his eyebrows and looked to Colin. "It could work."

"It's worth a shot," Colin agreed.

Negaré took the number back and went to his desk phone and punched in the number. After a moment he shook his head, lips pursed. Then he said, "Mr. Myska, this is Adon Negaré. I understand that you are renting one of my warehouses. I'd like one of my people to meet with you to discuss an opportunity I'm sure you won't want to miss. But this needs to happen today, so please call me back at this number." He went on to leave his direct office line number, then shrugged as he hung up. "No answer. If he calls back, I'll let you know immediately."

"Thanks for trying," Mitch said. "In the meantime, we'll go check out this address."

"Good luck." Negaré looked at Colin, sympathy in his eyes. "I sincerely hope you get that son-of-a-bitch that has your son's soul."

"Me too." Colin said. His gaze lingered on Negaré a moment before he turned his back on the man, leading Mitch out of the office.

They stepped into the elevator and turned around, taking in one more glimpse of Negaré's angelic new secretary. Colin couldn't hide his scowl, even from her.

"I don't like him," Colin said. He motioned with his head in Negaré's direction.

"Why? He's being very helpful."

"I dunno. Just something about the way he acts. I don't think he really gives a shit about my situation. Probably because it doesn't affect him or his bottom line."

Mitch let out a sigh. "He's provided us a ton of money to research how to deal with demons and possessions. He's probably just so used to having to appear sincere, that even when he is, it looks fake."

Colin thought for a minute. "Wasn't he the guy who told those protesters, 'Sometimes the few have to suffer for the good of the many' when he bought that wildlife preserve for a new power plant?"

Mitch gave a conciliatory nod. "Yeah. He's a tough businessman, no doubt. But he is also very philanthropic. And if he can help us, and is willing to help us, I'll take it. Maybe he's just trying to score points with God. I don't care as long as we get our job done."

Colin shrugged and said nothing.

As they descended, Mitch gave Colin Myska's new address to program into his phone's GPS, so they'd be ready to go when they got back to the Jeep. Hopefully soon they would be lying in wait for the evil creature that had stolen his son's soul. His initial trepidation at having a rematch with the demon he had fought in his house was quickly eroding, dissolving into his hunter's instinct. He was seeing the demon less as an adversary and more like prey.

As if he read Colin's thoughts, Mitch said, "We still have to be cautious. Whichever demon we catch up with first will be a formidable foe. And I'm going to want you to recite the rite with me when we get into it. It may help us to overpower it, but at the very least, it will give you practice under pressure."

The last couple of times Mitch quizzed him on the rite, Colin had nailed it. But that was without a clawed, fanged, thrashing, creature from the depths of Hell slashing at him.

They arrived in the lobby and were heading out the doors when Colin's phone rang. It came up as an 'unidentified caller'.

"Hello."

"Mr. Hampton? Detective Keller."

Colin's mouth pulled into an exaggerated frown. "Uh, hi." He looked at Mitch and shrugged.

"I understand that you were taken into custody by New York's Finest."

"Yeah. That was a bit of a misunderstanding. I was attacked by this weirdo on the street and had to fight back. But once they figured everything out, they let me go." He plugged one ear so he could hear Keller over the sounds of the street as they continued toward the car. Mitch was looking at him, shaking his head.

"That's not what I heard," Keller said. Colin pinched his eyes closed tightly like someone about to witness a head-on collision. "I heard that when the vehicle you were being transported in was broadsided, you took one of the officer's keys, unlocked your handcuffs, and fled."

Colin's eyes popped open below a deeply furrowed brow. He stared at Mitch, who upon seeing Colin's expression, inexplicably seemed to relax. "Oh. Ah, well that's um..."

"Look, why don't you just come in to the nearest precinct and we'll talk? That's all I'm asking."

"You're in town?"

"Yeah. Let's get together at one of the stations and talk about what happened. It was your next-door neighbor. Don't you want to see him get justice? Help me find out who murdered him."

Colin was tempted to comply, not wanting to antagonize the police. By declining, he'd only create more trouble for himself later. But as Mitch had said, he *didn't* kill Tim and there was no evidence that said he did. He'd deal with the cops later. "Listen, I told you, I think it was an animal. And I do want to help. I just can't right now. I'll call you in a day or two."

"Wait. Where – " Colin disconnected the call and looked at Mitch suspiciously.

"The detective?"

Colin nodded.

"How'd he get your number?"

"He's a cop," Colin stated. "He thinks I escaped from a squad car when it got into an accident." He threw his hands up. "What the hell?"

Mitch just shrugged. "I dunno. Doesn't matter anyway. We have work to do. Try not to answer it again if he calls."

"That goes without saying." He looked sideways at Mitch and thought he detected the hint of a smug grin but decided to let it be.

Something cold and wet hit Colin's right cheek. He looked up and saw thousands of tiny, bluish-white flakes drifting in downward spirals, being tossed around by the turbulent city drafts.

"Great. Here comes the snow."

"Good. Demons hate snow," Mitch said.

"Do they?"

"I hope so." Mitch flashed a smile at Colin as he opened the driver side door to the Jeep.

As Colin climbed in the passenger side he said, "Boy, Negaré sure knows how to pick nice looking secretaries."

"That's a fact," Mitch conceded.

"I really like that Scandinavian look."

Mitch paused as he reached to crank the engine. "Scandinavian?"

"Yeah. You know, blond hair, blue eyes..."

"Oh, you're talking about the secretary that was murdered. Uh, Leslie."

Colin's face crunched up in disbelief. "No. Not the old one, the one we just met. Kelly."

Mitch licked his lips and the color slid off his face. He fixed Colin with an intense stare. "Describe Kelly to me."

Colin thought Mitch was losing his senses or was completely confused about whom they were speaking. "Kinda tall, slender, long, blond hair, blue eyes..."

"Shit!"

"What?"

"I saw Kelly with long *black* hair and *brown* eyes." Colin was totally confused. "Succubus. She appears to each person as their most desirous form."

"Those things are real too?" Colin asked. "What is she doing working for Negaré?"

Mitch fired up the Jeep and jammed it into gear. "I dunno. But I'm guessing Negaré has no idea, and she's obviously after him."

"Myska must be near-by then too, if he's controlling her."

The Jeep bounced and slid as Mitch raced to get to the Negaré Tower courtyard. "*If* he has the *real* Seal of Solomon. Otherwise, she may be acting all on her own. Here," Mitch said. He handed Colin his cellphone. "Call Negaré and let him know what's going on. But tell him to act natural until we get back there and we'll deal with her."

Colin took the phone, hit Negaré's number and waited. Finally he said, "It went right into his voicemail."

"Crap. We'll just have to get up there right away." Mitch hauled on the steering wheel as he zigged and zagged through traffic well enough to put the New York City cabbies to shame. As they approached Negaré's office building the demon-hunter laid on his horn and bounced over the curb, leaving jagged tire tracks in the dusting of white snow that had started to accumulate, and drove onto the Negaré Tower courtyard and right up to the front door.

They had hardly gotten their protective leather coats on and out of the vehicle when they were met by Carmine and one other guard. Both men looked ready to fight to the death, though Carmine seemed to relax minutely when he saw who it was.

"Sorry, sorry," Mitch exclaimed, strapping on his backpack. "This is an emergency. We need to talk to Mr. Negaré right away."

"What is this about?" Carmine asked in his stereotypical New York accent.

"He's in danger."

"I don't think he's even here. His secretary called down to have his personal car readied. Follow me." Carmine hastily led the two men into the building, the other guard taking a position of advantage behind them. In a line, the four men trotted past the reception desk where the dapper young clerk stared at them with wide eyes. They approached another, more fortified looking area where a uniformed guard stood watching them, phone at the ready. "Has Negaré left yet?" Carmine asked the guard.

The guard looked at a bank of monitors arrayed before him. "He's pulling out now."

"Is he alone?" Mitch blurted.

Carmine nodded at the guard, confirming the question. "No, he had his secretary with him."

"Can you get hold of his driver?" Mitch asked.

"He doesn't have one. He wanted to drive himself."

"Dammit! Call his cellphone, I need to speak to him immediately."

Carmine was already making the call. Then he shook his head. "Voicemail."

"What's he driving?" Mitch yelled as he and Colin ran for the door, Carmine and his partner on their heels.

"Copper colored, Bentley Continental Supersport," Carmine hollered back.

"Where does he come out of the garage?"

"Middle of the block on Fifty fifth," Carmine answered as he held Mitch's car door open for him. "Should we call the cops?"

"No," Mitch snapped. "That'd get him killed for sure. We've been trained for this." With that, he slammed the door and started the Jeep. Colin was still pulling his door closed when Mitch spun the vehicle around, laid on the horn, and punched the accelerator as he sped across the courtyard heading for the street.

"What kind of car?" Colin asked, pulling on his seatbelt, then helping Mitch do the same.

"An orange Bentley sedan."

"That should be easy enough to see if we catch him." Then he looked upward out the side window. "Of course, the snow is picking up. That could make it tough to see anything."

Mitch whipped the black Jeep out onto the

street and then pulled a quick right at the first corner, onto fifty-fifth. Up ahead, they could see a bright, copper colored car in traffic.

"That's gotta be it," Mitch said.

Colin agreed but scanned the sidewalks, disconcerted. "Where's Myska? He wasn't with them, was he?"

Mitch slumped. "He might be now. But you're right. I didn't see him anywhere, and I think from his description, we'd know him if we saw him."

A scowl darkened Colin's face. "I know we have to take out this succubus, but shouldn't our priority be to take out the one that has my son's soul? We gotta find Myska."

"Colin, this succubus is the strongest link to Myska that we have. He obviously summoned her. And if he really did find the Seal of Solomon, then she's acting on his behalf and she'll lead us right to him. If she isn't acting on his behalf, then we'll make her tell us where he is while we exorcise her."

"What if she killed him?"

"A demon can't kill its summoner. One of those immutable laws of God. They can do all they can to ensure the damnation of the warlock, which doesn't take much. But they cannot directly kill him."

"Could she have someone else kill him?"

Mitch thought about that. "No, she couldn't manipulate someone else to kill him, but if someone else did, she would be free of his bonds."

That seemed to convince Colin that they were following the only course of action. He was still aggravated that they didn't know where their principle target was, but Mitch knew what he was talking about. Hopefully nothing would go wrong when they confronted the succubus.

"Colin, call up the Cavemen and tell them we are following the succubus. Maybe it'll help them with their tech stuff."

Colin got on the phone as Mitch swung a hard left against a red light. The exorcist was struggling to keep sight of the copper Bentley through the increasingly heavy snow.

Reginald answered.

"Reginald. We are following a succubus who is with Adon Negaré."

"You're kidding. That's incredible!" Colin could hear the frantic banging on a desk and then fingers hammering on a keyboard. "Tell us exactly where you are and we can use that to fine tune our tracking software."

"We're uh..." Colin realized that he had no idea where they were. He looked at Mitch, suddenly at a loss for words and feeling like a complete idiot.

Mitch blurted out, "Southbound on Lexington, just turned off of Fifty-fifth."

"I heard," Reginald said into Colin's ear. "Just call out the streets as you pass them."

They managed like that for several blocks,

then the Bentley was headed across the Queensboro Bridge and got out in front of them a good distance, far enough to become one of the other colorless sedans that were a part of New York traffic. Colin was amazed how even the yellow of the taxis became a drab gray in the dead light of an autumn snow-storm.

"Can you see him?" Mitch asked, desperately bobbing his head side to side, trying to catch a glimpse of Negaré's car.

Colin mashed his head against the side window, then against the roof, doing all he could to see past the vehicles in front of them, with no luck. "No. Where'd he go?" For several tense moments they could not re-locate the Bentley. Colin's stomach knotted up, squeezing the acid into his throat where it burned like brimstone.

Then he saw the side of the luxury sedan as it turned at the next corner.

"He just turned right," Colin shouted. They had closed the distance more than he could believe and Mitch stomped on the brakes, sending the Jeep into a skid, the back end sliding wide left in the accumulating snow.

"Hold on," Mitch commanded. Colin dropped the phone into his lap and grabbed onto the handle above the door-frame. He heard the engine roar as Mitch jumped off the brake and re-engaged the accelerator. The vehicle slid around the corner like a low-riding street-racer in a Tokyo-drift contest. Colin could hear Reginald shouting from the speaker of the cellphone in his lap. He put the phone to his ear, then decided to activate the speaker phone and stuffed it into one of the cup-holders in the center console.

"Are you guys alright?" Reginald asked.

"Yeah. We're good," Colin answered. Then he updated the Cavemen on their location.

"Oh boy," Mitch said. "Look where they're headed."

Colin scanned the neighborhood around them and realized things were looking industrialized. "The warehouse?"

"I can't imagine they are going anywhere else. Shit." Mitch's lips pursed tightly and air gushed out his nostrils.

They watched as the Bentley turned down the street they had traveled just the previous evening. Mitch held back, not wanting to be detected and not needing to see every move the luxury car made. The road was quickly becoming covered in wet, heavy snow and Negaré's tracks were easily seen. They turned onto the road in front of the warehouse in time to see the back end of the copper-colored car disappear into the open garage door. The door wasted no time in dropping back into place.

"Myska is in there," Mitch said. "And so is the succubus. And Negaré."

"We gotta get in there before they kill him,

or worse," Colin said. He pulled the flint-lock pistol out of his backpack and concealed it in his inside coat pocket before pulling out the Palo Santo dagger and sticking that in an outside pocket.

"Hold on," Mitch said. "If you had one of the most powerful, richest, men in the free world under your control, would you just kill him? I doubt it. They are up to something else. Nothing good to be sure, but I think we can be a little cautious on our approach. Reginald," he said at the phone. "The succubus is in the warehouse now. Get whatever readings you can. We're going in to exorcise it."

"Will do. Be safe." Reginald disconnected and Mitch stowed the phone back in his pocket.

Mitch pulled out his own blessed dagger and made sure his linoleum-reinforced, leather jacket was zipped as high as it went. He checked Colin's coat and suggested they both don a hockey helmet as well.

"This is going to be a fight. We don't know what Myska is going to do, so try not to lose track of him either. Let's try to sneak our way in and see how close we can get to the demon before you shoot. As soon as you shoot, pull out your dagger and we'll rush her."

Colin's chest tightened and his mouth became papery. His nostrils swelled to accommodate his lung's increased demand for air. Despite the cold, a fine film of sweat coated the palms of his hand. *Here we go again,* he thought.

"Okay. I'm ready."

"Don't forget, when I start reciting the rite, join in." They climbed out of the Jeep. The slam of the car doors was muffled by the heavy wet flakes that were swirling in rising winds. Colin walked through a surreal world of white spirits that assailed him from every angle. The tread of their feet made no sound as they approached the door of Negaré's warehouse.

The black door loomed larger and larger in his sight as they approached. Beyond it was his hope of finding the demon that had seized his unborn son's soul. The demon that sought to bring another anti-Christ into existence. But also behind that door was a sly, evil being that would try to rip his heart out. Its master also waited, intentions unknown. And he and Mitch approached with daggers and a flint-lock pistol that would afford him one shot.

He drew the pistol as he watched Mitch's hand grasp the doorknob and turn it slowly. It was unlocked. Mitch's eyes met his as the passage of time slowed, and he saw the demon-hunter nod. A dark line appeared between the edge of the door and the door-frame that widened into a gaping, black breach that radiated hope and despair.

Colin raised the pistol before him and stepped into the shadows.

CHAPTER NINETEEN

"Hello? Julie?"

Julie half-opened her eyes and turned her head toward the door, pulling the hospital sheet and blanket up over her swollen breasts. "Oh, hello, Stacy." A tired smile warmed her worried face as she greeted the nurse.

"How are you feeling?"

Julie shifted uncomfortably and her bloodshot gaze dropped to her hands. "Uh, not much different. Still having those pains."

Stacy, a robust woman of about forty-five, with fading blond hair, dark eyes and a cherubic smile reached down to take Julie's pulse, staring at her watch. "Your pulse is fine. That's good." She flashed a big smile that was meant to put Julie at ease, but it fell far short. "The ultrasound showed the baby moving around a lot, and his vitals were looking good too."

"But why am I still having these weird pains?"

Stacy took Julie's hand in her own. "We're still working on that. But as long as the little trooper is still kicking and has a strong heart-beat, you can keep your chin up. You'll forget all about this little pain when you're going through delivery."

Julie blew out a laugh. "That's true. This will be number two so I know there's a lot more where this came from." She clamped her hands on her abdomen and let out a wail, crunching herself up around her belly.

"Is it another one of those pains?" Stacy asked, leaning over and wrapping an arm around Julie's shoulders.

Julie shook her head vigorously, blowing out through puckered lips. Between breaths she said, "Oh no. This feels like a contraction. Oh boy."

"Let me know when it stops," Stacy said. The nurse peered at the clock. "I'll time you. It may be getting close to delivery time."

"No! Not yet. My husband isn't here." *I don't know that our baby is safe,* Julie thought.

Stacy was taken aback by the vehemence with which Julie spoke. "Don't worry, Julie. We deliver babies all the time without the husband or boyfriend around. You'll do fine."

"That's not it," Julie said through clenched teeth. "We have to wait. To make sure the baby is safe."

Stacy looked Julie in the eyes, the confusion clearly displayed on her face. "Julie, the baby is looking fine. Still contracting?"

Julie let out a whoosh of air. "It's over."

"Close to a minute. I'll wait here for a little

bit and see if you are going into real labor. You'd be a little premature, but we can handle a week early."

Not with this baby you couldn't, Julie thought. *The whole world couldn't handle it if this baby was premature.*

As Negaré pulled up to the big garage door of the warehouse, he could not help but notice that Kelly's skirt had hiked up to a dangerously provocative level on her thighs. Through the plunging neckline of her coat he saw that her blouse seemed to have opened one more button, revealing more than a hint of lacy bra straining to contain her voluptuous bosom.

He pulled a remote door opener out of the center console and tried the button. A sly smile spread across his lips as the door started to raise. Within the building he could see another vehicle parked.

"Looks like we might give Mr. Myska a bit of a start, huh Kelly?" he said as he pulled in and parked next to the car, activating the door once again to close it against the blowing snow.

His secretary shrugged and climbed out of the car, letting Negaré stare at her form as she did. Negaré followed suit and stood looking around the dimly lit warehouse. A dark figure slowly emerged out of the shadows not far from where Kelly was standing.

"Mr. Negaré," Myska said. "I'm glad you could come. What do you think of Kylova?" He wrapped one arm around Kelly and gave her a deep, open-mouthed kiss.

Negaré stared for a moment at the woman, then let out a huff. "Kylova. A succubus. No wonder you're a perfect ten. Well done, Seth. I hear you were able to conjure her right here in the warehouse?"

Myska smiled as he parted from Kylova and approached the billionaire. "Yeah. I finally figured this shit out."

"And where is the other demon you summoned?" Negaré said. His eyes shifted between Myska and Kylova.

"Oh. Apophis?" Myska looked at Kylova. "That's his name, isn't it?" Kylova nodded, seduction pooling in her eyes. "I don't know. He isn't here yet. What difference does that make? You don't want him anyway."

Negaré's eyes narrowed and his face clenched. "Kylova, tell me where Apophis is."

"If you really need to know, he's almost here. It will probably take him only an hour. Maybe two."

"Why isn't he here already?" Negaré continued speaking directly to the demon, Kylova.

"He could not travel by day; the sunlight weakens him too much. But I sense he is approaching. This dark day and heavy snow seem to afford him enough protection to continue." She shed her jacket, her breasts straining against the already tight fabric of her silken blouse. Negaré forced his eyes back to Myska, though he could feel his pulse quicken in his loins.

"Why do you care so much about this Apophis?" Myska demanded.

"That's my business. Why didn't you tell me about Kylova?" he said to Myska.

"I thought it'd be so much more fun having her bring you here herself, so you could see. Isn't she exquisite? Did you take her in your office? On your desk?"

"No," Negaré snapped. "What about Belphegor?"

"What's with this Belphegor? Don't you like Kylova a whole lot more?"

Negaré cast a conciliatory glance at the succubus. He took a deep breath and continued, "I have a pact with Belphegor. I have to command *him* to release me from it." He twisted the ring on the finger of his right hand. "And I can only do that if he's here." Negaré hated explaining anything to subordinates.

Myska looked at Negaré, not bothering to hide his contempt. "Looks to me like Belphegor kept up his part of the bargain. Wealth. Power. Just like a billionaire to try and change the rules once he has what he wants." His eyes danced over Kylova's body once again.

"I could fire you now and you won't get paid. But if you want your money in short order, hurry up and get Belphegor here so I can finish this."

Myska seemed to consider that. "Seeing as how you like to back out of deals, I think you should pay me first. Then I'll summon Belphegor."

Negaré fumed for a moment and then said, "Fine." He pulled out his cellphone and started thumping away on it with his thumbs. He looked up at Myska. "What's your account number?"

Myska trotted over to his desk, grabbed a small note and brought it over to Negaré. Negaré snatched it away and finished the transaction over his phone.

"There. You got half. You'll get the remaining seven-hundred-fifty-thousand when you finish. Now bring me Belphegor."

Myska smiled. Then his eyes brushed Kylova with white-hot lust and she responded by dropping her skirt, exposing the racy panties that hugged her hips. She spun slowly to let Myska drink in her tightly formed butt and thighs. "But first, as an up-front bonus, I want another shot at this one. Command her to do me," Myska said through a devilish grin.

Annoyed, Negaré glanced at his watch. "Fine. Just don't wear yourself out. I want this done and finished before Apophis gets here."

Kylova stole a smoldering glance at Negaré

before turning her attention to Myska.

Myska rolled his eyes at Negaré and buried his face between Kylova's breasts as she peeled back her blouse. Soon they were both naked and writhing around on the concrete floor, partaking of each other in ways Negaré had never imagined. The billionaire soon found himself aroused well beyond comfort, Kylova throwing sultry looks in his direction. When she took a dominant position on top of Myska, the succubus locked eyes with Negaré and seductively invited him over with one slender finger. Negaré couldn't resist and slowly walked to her, his heart thundering. Kylova drew his right hand to her mouth and started to suck and nibble each of his fingers one by one, her tongue dancing down the lengths of the old man's digits. He closed his eyes, trying to catch his fleeting breath. A gasp escaped as the demon gently scraped the skin of one finger with her teeth from base to tip. She withdrew and smiled up at the powerless old man.

Suddenly she stood up and put on her clothes, a look of contempt and superiority on her beautiful face.

A dim glow emanated from the center of the warehouse where they had found the desk and pentagram. To Colin's immediate right loomed the dark shapes of the Bentley and Citation. In a crouch, flint-lock pistol held before him, Colin made his way to the side of Myska's car, Mitch right behind him, dagger at the ready. Someone was moaning at the edge of the shadows, about twenty-five feet away, on the other side of the vehicles. Groans mixed with the sounds of voracious sex echoed around them. Determined, sea-green, eyes stared out from behind the plastic face-mask of Mitch's battered hockey helmet. Colin tightened the chin-strap on his own and waited. The exorcist nodded.

A shout echoed across the floor of the warehouse. "Negaré, look out! She's a demon!"

Negaré and Myska looked up to see Colin rushing forward, a gun pointed at Kylova. Myska leapt to his feet, screamed "No," and threw himself on top of the demon as a thunderous roar and brilliant flash shattered the shadowy interior of the building.

Stacy looked at her watch. "Oh yeah, dear. You're definitely in labor," the nurse said. She snapped on a latex glove. "Let me check the dilation."

Julie grimaced as the nurse completed the task.

"Almost two centimeters. It may be a little

while yet. Can I get you some more ice or anything?"

Julie could feel the tears well up in her eyes. She didn't trust herself to speak so she nodded. As soon as Stacy stepped out of the room, she croaked out a sob and the tears sprang free. "Colin. You have to kill it," she whispered. "Kill it now. I can't have this baby if it's possessed."

"What did you say, dear?"

She snapped her head to the left to see old Mabel shuffling into the room, a hospital robe cinched tightly around her soft middle. Julie stifled the crying and forced a smile. "Mabel. Hi. Nothing. I was just... I'm just so worried about this baby. What are you doing here? Are you okay?"

Mabel shuffled to Julie's bedside, her smile revealing the extreme contrast between her ivory teeth and ebony skin. "I'm fine dear. The doctor just found some," she paused, "issues that made him want to keep me around for a day or two for observation. The question is, how are you?"

"In labor," she grunted. "And scared. I'm terribly afraid of this birth. Something isn't right." She felt awful not telling Mabel everything, but the truth was too unbelievable.

"Don't you worry your heart none, dear," Mabel said. The gentle old woman wiped the sweat from Julie's forehead with a small towel. "We didn't let nothing bad happen to your husband when he was born. We ain't about to let something bad happen to his son. When this is all done, you're gonna have a happy, healthy, sweet little bundle-of-joy. You just need some faith."

Colin burst around the front of Myska's vehicle and shouted a warning to the billionaire. Negaré was staring at 'Kelly', the succubus who was glaring back at him. Sitting naked on the floor looking distraught was Myska, one knee raised, propping himself up-right with both arms locked out behind him. Colin glanced at him and couldn't help but notice the silver stud in the side of the warlock's nose and the dread of realization that sparked in the man's eyes. As he surged forward, he re-focused on the incredibly sensuous woman in front of him. For a moment he was assailed by doubt. How could this beautiful woman be a demon? But then he thought of his wife, suffering with a possessed child inside her, and his focus returned.

His feet skidded to a halt on the concrete floor and the gun came up level with his right eye. The flat surface of the pistol's barrel superimposed itself on the center of Kylova's body. As he felt the trigger tighten, Kylova's eyes widened in confusion and her head snapped back.

The flash of fire and smoke, coupled with the resonating clap of the pistol's report in the echoic warehouse temporarily dazed Colin. He regained them only to see slashing claws and yellow fangs beneath rage filled eyes as Kylova slammed into him, knocking the pistol free of his grip. Grabbing her with both hands, Colin was able to thrust her back just enough to keep her teeth from tearing into the side of his neck, but one of her clawed hands was able to tear the strap from his helmet and knock it flying to skitter across the floor.

Then she was spinning away, a feral scream erupting from her throat as one arm lashed out at Mitch who struggled unsuccessfully to maintain control of the dagger he'd buried in her right shoulder-blade. In an instant she was on the exorcist, clawing at his protective coat. As Mitch went over backwards, Colin pulled the Palo Santo dagger from his pocket and launched himself at Kylova's back, sinking the knife to its hilt in her left shoulder, dropping his entire weight on top of her. The wail she emitted nearly shattered his ear-drums and she thrashed about, a bronco trying to throw its rider. Desperate to maintain control, he reached for Mitch's dagger that still protruded from the demon's other shoulder. He could hear a strained voice then.

Even pinned beneath both the succubus and Colin, Mitch was beginning the Rite. For an instant, Colin couldn't remember what to say. Then it came back in a rush, by rote. He matched the exorcist, word for word, and he felt the demon's fight slacken. Scrambling, Mitch pulled himself from beneath the wounded creature from hell, sliding her onto the floor and took firm hold of his dagger. Through the fog on Mitch's visor, Colin could see the man's frightened but determined eyes. Together they held the demon, pinned face down on the concrete, reciting the Rite. Mitch pitched forward slightly but caught himself by placing his palm on the back of Kylova's head.

Over and over they said the words, feeling the demon's resistance die. Colin felt confident in his mastery of the Rite. He was actually helping Mitch send a demon back to hell.

"No!"

The word rang through the warehouse. Distracted, Colin looked in the direction of Negaré. The old man stood staring at his hands, a look of genuine terror disfiguring his face. Mitch's words chanted on.

He felt the last twitching movements of Kylova's physical body as she entered the final submission to the Rite. Keying again on the words of the Rite, Colin took up the recitation, his voice joining with the exorcist's.

"No! Stop," Negaré screamed. His voice a desperate wail. "She has it. She has..."

A wave of darkness erupted, obliterating all the light in the warehouse. A hideous, screeching, hiss reverberated off the walls for several seconds, before abruptly falling into silence. Colin and Mitch were thrown in heaps to the concrete floor. Slowly the light returned, like the sun rising above a tranquil sea.

Where Kylova had lain, there was now only a smoldering black stain. A few feet away, Myska lay in a huge pool of blood, a quarter sized hole in his chest, his lifeless eyes staring at his own departed ghost. With a grief laden sob, Negaré dropped to his knees, burying his face in his hands. Colin stared at the billionaire, puzzled. Mitch flopped over onto his back, breathing heavily, and pulled his steamy helmet off. He lay there with his hands folded over his eyes, clearly exhausted.

"Mr. Negaré. Are you hurt?" Colin asked from where he sat on the floor.

Negaré's hands dropped from his face and he looked years older and utterly hopeless. "No. She had the ring. She swallowed it. Sucked it off my finger, the Seal of Solomon."

Mitch raised his head, squinting at Negaré. "Wait a minute. It actually was real and you had it this whole time? You are responsible for this? Why didn't you tell us?" The anger in his voice gave power to his words.

Negaré caressed his forehead. "Until you told me, I didn't know the significance of what had happened to Colin's son. I was going to order Apophis to release the kid's soul as soon as he got here. But I had to get out of... get out of this stupid pact I'm in. I didn't even really think it was true. I didn't think it was possible. But when I was younger, I was dabbling and encountered Belphegor and we made a deal, I guess. Then, about fourteen years ago, I had a visit from one of my business associates. He was possessed, by Belphegor, and he told me in no uncertain terms that he was looking forward to visiting hell upon me when I died. That's when I decided I needed a way out. I invested a lot of money in your unit's demon research. I wanted to know how to counteract the pact. Then I learned about the Seal of Solomon and its power. It cost me plenty, but I finally found it."

"Apophis? Of course," Mitch said.

Colin surged to his feet and dragged Negaré to his feet by the collar. "You son-of-a-bitch," he screamed in Negaré's face. "My son's soul has been stolen because you were trying to back out of a deal with the Devil?" He spun a slow circle, seething. "I've been kicked around by self-serving, arrogant, a-holes like you my whole life. All the while I've let it happen, wanting to be a good little trooper, coasting along hoping something good would happen to me. But you know what? If I want something good to happen, I gotta make it happen. I'm not waiting around to get smacked in the teeth again." His hands clenched into fists.

By this time Mitch was on his feet, moving to intercede. But when his eyes fell on Myska's lifeless body, he stopped cold, crest-fallen. "Oh shit, Colin."

Colin turned to his friend, the exorcist. "What? What's the matter?"

Mitch pointed at the dead warlock laying on the floor. "Apophis isn't going to come here now. He can't complete the ritual. He's free to go wherever he wants."

Colin stared at the corpse in disbelief. "You mean he's free? But if he can't complete the ritual, won't he go back to Hell?"

Mitch wobbled on his feet. "Not for a month or two. His time is limited, but he can hide until Julie gives birth."

Colin's head dropped, his chin practically bouncing off his chest. How would they ever find a single demon in New York City? If they had four months, they probably couldn't do it. They probably had less than four days.

Mitch grunted and dropped to his seat on the floor. Perhaps the priest was struck by the same hopelessness as he was feeling. Colin went to him.

"Mitch? You okay?"

Mitch shook his head, defeated eyes finding Colin's. Together they looked down at Mitch's shredded leather coat and saw the blood trickling up through one of the lacerations. Mitch pursed his lips and seized Colin's eyes with his own. His head bobbed from side to side, and he sighed deeply.

"This is bad, Colin. She got me."

"No. No. We have to be able to do something," Colin cried, smashing his hand over the wound to staunch the flow of blood.

The exorcist groaned, gritting his teeth. A

sulfurous stench rose from the deep gash in his chest. "I won't survive this one. I'm not like you."

"Dammit, Mitch! I can't do this alone." Tears broke free of Colin's blinking eyes, flowing down his cheeks. "I can't even find the damned thing."

"Colin, listen. You have to finish this. You know the Rite, I heard you helping me with the succubus. You can do it. Pray and find Apophis, then finish him. Heaven is counting on you."

Colin stared at his friend and mentor, a man he'd only met a few days prior, and wondered how he could do anything without him. But having seen Mitch's determination and faith, he knew he must promise to continue the hunt until its end. He nodded.

Mitch let out a groan of pain and settled back onto the cold, concrete floor. His right hand dug feverishly in the pocket of his pants and withdrew a photo. He held it up for Colin to see. It was Lily, the waitress from the Irish pub. Colin stared at it, confused.

"Please, Colin. Tell her that I've always loved her. I would have been there for her, but her mother had moved on and never told her about me. I didn't want to confuse her."

Colin scrubbed his hand on his pant-leg, cleaning it of Mitch's blood, and took the photo. He turned it over and saw her name, Lily Founder, written in ink, with a birthday. His face crunched into a sad, confused scowl.

"How could this be? I thought you were a priest."

"I wasn't always a priest. I had actually planned on being a dad." Mitch's eyes became distant, wandering aimlessly.

Colin grabbed the exorcist by the coat front and jostled him. "Then stay with me and be her dad," Colin said. He blinked away a tear. "Mitch. I can't do this alone. I don't know what I'm doing. It's impossible."

Mitch's face snapped to regard Colin, his piercing green eyes drawing Colin's undivided attention. "Everything is possible, with God." Colin trembled as he watched the shine fade in the exorcist's eyes.

He was gone.

"Detective Keller," Jake Keller said, answering his phone. He listened for a moment then signaled to O'Malley to give him a pen and something to write on. Frantically, he scribbled down an address. "Great. Good news. I'll get there as soon as I can." He disconnected the call. O'Malley stared at him expectantly. "They found the Jeep. Some security guy at an industrial park called it in. Saw it last night too."

"Great. They pick him up?"

"They're dealing with a ton of traffic

problems, but they're responding," Keller said popping the locks on his patrol car. "Let's head out there, just in case."

As they climbed in the cruiser, Keller tossed the pad of paper containing the address to O'Malley who punched it into their GPS unit as Keller started the engine.

"Shit," Keller said as he grabbed the combination ice-scraper and snow brush. He jumped out of the car and cleared all the windows of several inches of wet, heavy snow that had accumulated on them. Once clear, he hopped in the car and they were off, on their way to question Colin Hampton and hopefully solve a murder.

Through the fog of grief and tears, Colin heard a sound softly playing in the silence of the dark warehouse. Finally he realized that it was his telephone and he half-heartedly pulled it from his pocket. It was Julie. For a heart-beat he considered not answering. How could he tell her that their champion, their one hope for killing the demon, was lying dead on the floor of a warehouse in New York?

"Hello." His voice was dull and lackluster.

"Colin," Julie screeched. "Colin, I'm in labor! Did you do it?"

A linebacker wielding a sledge-hammer couldn't have hit him in the gut any harder. He didn't know what to say. "I'll be home as soon as I can," he said. Then he hung up.

He raised his eyes to the rich, arrogant bastard who had caused all this, who was standing there surveying the scene of death in his warehouse as if he himself had somehow been wronged. Breath came in faster gasps of air, his nostrils swelling to accommodate. An unfamiliar emotion seized control of his body, driving his heartbeat, tensing his muscles, honing his senses to clear his vision in the darkness, tuning his ears to the sound of Negaré's breathing, and filling his nose with the smell of blood and death and hellfire. Long, purposeful strides carried him to within arm's reach of Negaré. He spun the man around to face him.

"Still trying to figure out how to save your worthless ass?" he asked the billionaire. "You don't give a shit about anyone but yourself, do you? You don't care that the next anti-Christ is about to be born in upstate New York, do you?" He started shoving the older man as he spoke. "No, why would you? You'll be dead and buried by the time my son is old enough to wreak hell-on-earth. What do you care? Everyone else can go to hell, as long as you don't. Right?"

Negaré blinked at him, his eyes glassy and full of fear. "You don't understand. That's exactly where I'm going to go," he sobbed.

Just before Colin's fist came rocketing forward, he uttered, "Sometimes the few have to suffer for the good of the many."

CHAPTER TWENTY

The sirens rang clearly, singing down the streets and alleys of the warehouse district. Colin glanced at the two dead men and one unconscious billionaire and decided that this was *not* where he wanted to be when the police arrived. He scrounged through the pockets of Mitch's coat snatching the keys to the Jeep. As he stood up from Mitch's side, he grabbed the daggers and pistol from the floor and secreted them in his own jacket. Finally, he snatched the two backpacks up in one fist. Then, taking one last look at his dead, selfless friend, he fled into the deep gray daylight, which was further obscured by the driving, heavy flakes of snow that were being battered around by tempest-like winds. The Jeep's engine snarled to life and he jammed it into gear, spinning tires on the sloppy, snow-covered road. As he slid around the corner, he noticed the red, flashing lights enter the other end of the street. With any luck, they would not have seen him. Not that he had any luck.

The NYPD squad car slid to a halt in front

of Negaré's warehouse, two officers springing out, drawing their weapons. In an instant, they were at the door of the building and executed a two-man entry. As soon as they saw three bodies lying on the floor, one officer got on his shoulder mic, calling it in. He also reported that the Jeep they thought they would find here was nowhere to be seen. Quickly, the two officers cleared the building, a simple task given its wide-open interior. Then they rushed to the victims sprawled on the concrete, checking for signs of life. When his partner yelled that he had "a live one", a call for an ambulance went out immediately. The two officers tended to Negaré, finally recognizing him after they saw the pricey Bentley parked a few feet away.

When he'd finally regained full control of his senses, Negaré related the story of what happened:

He had discovered that someone had been using his warehouse for some wretched, satanic, cult-like rituals. When he did, he was so disgusted by this news, that he decided to go out and throw the bum out himself. But because he did not get to where he was in this life by being completely stupid, he brought some muscle, the man in the unsightly leather coat with the linoleum strips sewn to it. "That was in case he was attacked by a knife-wielding drug-addict, which the other guy turned out to be." Negaré further went on to explain that when they got here and confronted Mr. Seth Myska, the man with the hole in his chest, Myska became very agitated, almost as if he was possessed. Myska went berserk and pulled a knife and attacked Mitch Stackwell, the man in the unsightly leather coat. Negaré tried to pull Myska off Mitch, but he swung back with an elbow and hit Negaré in the face, knocking him out. What happened after that, he didn't know. But he was very upset that his bodyguard, Mitch Stackwell, a strong and righteous man who will be sorely missed, was killed in the ensuing melee. He wasn't so sorry about that unhinged weirdo, Myska.

"Was there anyone else here?" they asked.

"No. Like who?" he answered.

They asked him about a black Jeep.

"Black Jeep? What are you talking about? The only cars here were my Bentley and Myska's piece of junk."

By this time, another squad car arrived, and two more officers came in surveying the scene. One of those officers asked, "Where's the gun?"

"Gun? What gun?" Negaré replied.

"That's one big fuckin' whole in this guy's chest over here," the officer stated. "He was obviously shot. Where's the friggin' gun?"

Negaré looked around, frowning. "I didn't think anyone had a gun. Maybe my bodyguard had one, but he was a master of three different martial arts and preferred not to carry. You can search me if you like. And the cars. If there is a gun here, it should be obvious."

Negaré silently said a prayer: *There, God. I tried to help Colin out. I'm not so bad, eh? Maybe you could talk to Belphegor for me?*

The four officers huddled up and looked at each other, each of them coming to the same conclusion: this was an f'ed up mess, better let the lieutenant handle it.

"You hear that? The Jeep isn't even there," O'Malley complained. He'd tuned the radio in the squad car to NYPD's frequencies and he and Keller had both heard the first responder's transmissions.

"Yeah. And two more dead bodies and a third down. Who do you suppose did that?" The detective scowled through his windshield at the blinding snow. "Hampton. That's who. This guy is a raving maniac. Now that he's killed someone in the city, they'll pull out the stops and they'll bring him in. But of course we won't get to question him until they make their own case. Dammit."

"Do you think we even need to go out there now?"

Keller thought a minute. "May as well. We're almost there now. And maybe we can talk to the witness."

O'Malley nodded in agreement.

As they both stared forward at the snow flying into their collective face, O'Malley said,

"Kinda like going to 'light speed' in Star Wars, huh?"

Keller was in mid-laugh when a black Jeep emerged from the blinding 'stars' and sped by in the opposite direction.

"That was him," Keller screamed. The car careened into a sideways skid as he stomped on the brake, cranking the wheel over to come around. Unfortunately, the road wasn't wide enough to just flip a U-turn, so Keller was forced to endure the time-consuming execution of a y-turn, the car stopping, then backing up, then going forward, then backing up, finally taking off in the other direction as O'Malley flipped on the lights and siren.

"Want me to radio for back-up?"

"Naw. They'll see us soon enough."

Colin knew as soon as he passed the squad car that it was a Saratoga County vehicle. Which meant that it was the intrepid Detective Keller, the last guy he wanted to see. The flashing emergency lights lit up in his rear-view mirror.

"Dammit! Really?" He glanced skyward and felt his eyes burn, the desperate tears straining to escape. "Come on, God. One little break? You can't give me even one little break? Mitch! Mitch, you're up there right? You should be. Talk to him will ya? Ask him to..."

He was interrupted by the ringing of his

phone. Sure that it was Keller calling to tell him to pull over, he snapped as he answered, "What?"

"Colin? Colin, it's Ben. Let me talk to Mitch, his phone went right to voicemail."

"Mitch is dead," Colin said. The words caught in his throat. "What do you need?"

There was a moment of silence, then in a tentative voice Ben said, "We got him. We can track the demon. That data you gave us allowed us to—"

"F that. Where is he?"

"Shit! Where is he?" Keller cried. The snow was limiting visibility to about one hundred yards, and it showed no signs of slowing.

"I can't see any better than you," O'Malley said. "Speed up a bit."

"I'm afraid to. I can't see squat and I don't know this town. I'll hit something if I go any faster. Dammit. Keep your eyes peeled in case he turns right, maybe you'll see him."

"Shit. I can't even see any tracks on the road. You sure we didn't pass him already?"

"How the hell should I know?"

"Whoa! Oh, this is a big one," Julie wailed as she gritted her teeth and squeezed Mabel's hand until the old nurse winced. "Oh geez, oh geez, oh geez," she grunted between breaths. Her feet were up in the stirrups, a light hospital blanket draped over her privates. Mabel wiped Julie's forehead with a cool, damp cloth.

The doctor walked into the room. "How're we doing?" she said in a pleasant, yet authoritative voice.

Julie just looked at her with tears in her eyes.

"Hmm. Okay," the doctor said. With a gloved hand she reached to get a cervical measurement. "Five centimeters. Little while yet. Any unusual discomfort? I know you were having some strange pains."

All Julie could do was shake her head.

"Okay. The nurse will be back in a little bit to check on you. Hang in there."

I'll hang in there like this for the next three days if I can keep from giving birth to a demon, Julie thought.

"I'll call you when I get there," Colin said as he disconnected the call with Ben. Forgetting about the pursuing squad car, he applied the brakes until he was going a reasonable speed, so he could program the address into his GPS application on the phone. Once done, he stuck the phone in the center console, threw the Jeep into four-wheel drive and took off, letting the soothing Aussie woman's voice guide him.

"Those were brake lights," O'Malley said. "Punch it. It has to be him."

Keller accelerated as much as he dared in the thick, white snow. It was enough to catch a glimpse of the black Jeep slowing and making a left. "Turning left," both men exclaimed in unison. Slowly the gap between squad car and the Jeep shortened.

"Where the hell is NYPD? You'd think we would have passed one of their cars by now," Keller asked.

"I haven't seen one," O'Malley replied. "Want me to get on the radio?"

Keller considered that for a moment. Finally he said, "Not yet. Keep track of what streets we're on. If we lose him, then we'll call in with his last known position."

Colin saw the persistent flashing lights in his rear-view mirrors and could hear the muted sound of the siren. He was still several miles from where he needed to be. Apophis had almost reached the warehouse when that dumbass Myska jumped on top of the succubus to protect her, taking a fifty-caliber lead ball to the chest. Now, Apophis could come and go as he pleased, at least long enough to ensure Julie gave birth to a permanently possessed child. But Colin intended to stop Apophis, to exorcise him. He wasn't entirely sure he could do it, but he was tired of getting walked on, by his boss, his co-workers, the rich and powerful, now the police... it was all coming to an end, one way or another. Mitch was determined to succeed and was not going to stop, knowing he was fighting for what was right. And that motivation had rubbed off on Colin. If a priest could fight for what's right, couldn't he? Now he was not only fighting for his family, but against the worst evil the world could possibly encounter. The rules, even laws, were going out the window right now.

The Jeep accelerated as his foot drove the gas pedal closer to the floor. Traffic was light now, well after the morning rush-hour, but what traffic there was, was moving slow due to the limited visibility and slippery roads. He hadn't seen a single plow yet. The Jeep slipped and jolted as it raced through slushy piles of snow and the windshield wipers snapped away, fighting to keep the snow at bay.

Twice, the vehicle whipped around sharp corners, holding its track surprisingly well. Each turn resulted in an exasperated Aussie woman saying "recalculating", as she had to re-map a route to his destination. Colin hoped he would lose the pursuing squad car with the multiple turns, but thus far the detective proved very determined.

"Geez! Where is this guy going?" O'Malley said. He mashed up against the passenger door as they slid through another left turn.

"He doesn't know. He's just trying to lose us," Keller answered.

"Well, he might do it. He can corner a hell of a lot faster than us. Damn rear-wheel drive. He's taking the next right."

Keller found himself struggling to keep up with Colin, the black shadow growing fainter in the driving flakes of snow. They nearly slid completely sideways as they pulled hard right around the corner, the rear of the car whipping out to their left. But Keller was no stranger to winter driving and quickly regained control. Anyone who had seen the mishap would have thought it intentional, so expertly he recovered.

"I think he turned left up there, but I'm not sure," O'Malley said.

"Crap. He's getting too far out in front of us." Keller sped down the straight portion of the block and slowed for the left turn, but not enough. This time, the front end pushed straight at the parked car on the side street, the front tires failing to make purchase with the road. "Shit," Keller yelled.

The squad car, flashing lights and siren, slid to stop just as the front bumper made contact with the parked car.

"Whew," Keller said. "No significant

damage." He flipped his eyebrows at O'Malley. "On we go." He pulled in reverse, straightened the car out and took off in pursuit of Colin.

Both officers looked straight ahead, seeking their prey. All they could see was a wall of white, the snow now obscuring everything more than forty yards away. Keller pressed on, hoping against hope that they would see something, anything, that would reveal Colin's presence.

Finally he said, "Dammit. Looks like you better get on the radio. Did you see the name of the street we're on?"

Before he could answer, O'Malley started to laugh, pointing down the road in front of them.

Nothing was in the rear-view mirror after the last turn. If he could make one, maybe two, more turns without seeing the Saratoga County cruiser behind him, Colin might be able to relax a bit.

When his eyes returned to the street in front of him, he quickly slammed on the brakes. Both lanes of traffic had come to a complete stop on this one-way road. Panic blossomed in his stomach as he checked his mirrors again. Still nothing, but wait... there they were, the flashing lights, getting closer. He considered bailing out and running, but if he got away, he'd be exhausted by the time he found Apophis. *If* he could catch up to him. Desperately he scanned his surroundings; cars to the left, cars in front, now Keller cocking his squad car to block both lanes behind, a sidewalk bordered by a huge stone fence to his right. He was stuck. Despair launched its assault there in the snowy traffic jam, blasting Colin with both barrels. Julie was in labor, Apophis freed, and he was about to be taken into custody. He had failed, and his family and the world would suffer for it. He glanced around desperately as tears filled his eyes. Then he saw a camouflage banner with white lettering hanging above the porch of one of the houses to his left. It said "Welcome Home Daddy! Our Hero!"

"Now we got him," Keller said. With a smile, he climbed out of the car. O'Malley slid out of the passenger door and rested his hand on his sidearm as they marched toward the blocked Jeep.

Colin's eyes glazed as he stared at the sign, remembering the little boy and his mother that he'd seen at the rest-stop when this whole nightmare began. Heroes always found the one little thread of hope, the minuscule fraction of a chance, and they put all their chips on that chance. He looked back up the right side of the street, just where the sidewalk disappeared into a solid white mass, he saw what might be a ray of hope. A break in the stone fence? It was worth a shot, the sidewalk was wide here and behind that fence looked like some sort of open field, a park of sorts. A glance in the mirror showed Keller and another officer walking forward, weapons drawn.

He pulled the steering wheel to the right and trounced on the gas pedal. The Jeep bounced over the curb between a light-post and a tree and up the sidewalk he went. He quickly saw that the break in the stone wall was indeed the entrance to a park and he slid through it, driving up a small hill, leaving the squad car behind.

Expletives soured the air as both Keller and O'Malley dove back into the cruiser. The engine roared and the siren renewed its wail as Keller maneuvered the car to hit the sidewalk. The front tires had barely cleared the curb when the car came to a slow halt, the back end moving from side to side. The back tires, not yet replaced with snow tires, were spinning wildly on the slick road, unable to propel the car any farther.

Apophis couldn't believe his good fortune. He felt the death of his summoner, and his subsequent freedom as a result. Kylova's death drove him to his knees, just as Nephalen's banishing had done. But they didn't matter. Only he mattered, because he carried the soul. And he knew that he just had to find a deserted place to hide for a few hours and he would be hailed a hero in the underworld. When one of his demonic brethren was born in human form, they would raise Hell to this pathetic world. It didn't matter that he would eventually fade from this plane and return. When he did, he would be rewarded with so much more power than he had had before. And as fun as it could be wreaking havoc here, leaving it wouldn't be all bad. This physical existence was relatively exhausting, and the sunlight hurt. At least today, with the snow and the heavy clouds, he could move around with relatively little pain. Relatively little.

Nurse Stacy pulled off the latex glove and smiled. "Eight centimeters. Not long now. At ten, we can start pushing."

Julie checked her cellphone. No texts, no messages, nothing. Why had Colin hung up on her? They hadn't killed the demon, that's why. Her worried eyes lifted to the elderly black woman who had apparently taken it upon herself to be her coach. Mabel smiled down at her with a calm, warm smile, as if she'd done this all before. Which, of course, she had.

Colin sped down the sidewalk through the

park, the curves challenging his skill at the wheel. *This is a pretty big park,* he thought as he searched for the other side and a way out. When he had crested the first hill, he could see Keller and his partner standing outside their stuck squad car, watching him drive away. He descended the other side, hugging the curves and looking for an exit. At last he saw another gate out of the park. His Aussie chick navigator was terribly confused at this point, constantly telling him to turn around. He thought next she was going to tell him to stop and ask for directions. Before leaving the park, he hid the pistol away in his right-hand coat pocket and double checked to make sure the Palo Santo dagger was still in his left. Satisfied that he had his weapons, he drove back out onto the streets where Ms. Aussie relaxed and told him how to get to his location, approximately two miles away.

The snow hadn't slowed at all, giving Colin the feeling he was driving around in a giant 'snow globe'. He couldn't see street signs, and now even the stop lights sneaked up on him like springing snakes from a 'can of nuts'. He checked his mirrors. Nothing.

"Destination on your left in point two miles," Ms. Aussie said.

Colin grabbed the phone. He was close enough he'd have to call the Cavemen to find out where Apophis was hiding, or if he was on the move. He looked at the GPS map so he knew where he was, still unable to see any street signs.

"Colin? Is everything alright?" Reginald said as soon as he picked up.

"Yeah, I'm basically here." He related what street he was on, and approximately how far from the nearest cross street. "Where is he?"

"He's moved off a bit. You have to go two blocks north of your location. He seems to have holed up because he hasn't moved in about six minutes."

Some good news for a change.

Colin turned at the next intersection, leaving Reginald on speaker so he could call out his location. He found himself on a street of extremely tough looking, red, brick warehouses and gated parking lots. Like the district where Myska did his dirty work, some of these buildings looked used, while others looked dilapidated, abandoned, and dangerous. Reginald provided the address where it appeared Apophis was currently hiding. He slowed to a stop in front of one of the distressed buildings, this one with bright yellow numbers spray painted on the door.

He glanced around at the surrounding area, all of it seemingly devoid of life, and pulled over onto what little sidewalk there was. The road felt more like an alley, with the short, brick warehouses jammed together on both sides of the one-way street.

"This is it."

"Godspeed, Colin," Reginald said. Then the call disconnected.

He checked his weapons once again and realized he had to re-load the pistol. *That could have been bad,* he thought. He dug in one of the packs to find the wadding, powder and ball. As he loaded the gun, he rolled the ball around in his hand and saw a small word engraved on the bullet, "Hell". *I wonder what that's all about,* he thought. Silently, he hoped Hell was where the bullet would send this soul-stealing monstrosity. Once he was satisfied that he was "locked and loaded", he stuffed the gun in his coat pocket and climbed out of the car. In an abundance of caution, he pushed the door closed slowly, letting it click quietly, not wanting to alert Apophis with the sound of a slam. Without hesitating, he strode over to the spray-painted door and pulled the dagger, having had more luck with that in the past.

The door knob was icy, but very little accumulated snow was on it. It started to turn in Colin's hand, then it stopped. *Locked?* He hadn't learned the art of lock-picking, and it was too late now. Frustrated, he looked up into the gray and white sky. *Mitch.* If only the multi-talented demon hunter were here, they'd be in there in no time. Angry, he squeezed the knob and turned it again, this time it continued through the mechanical jam that had resisted his first twist and he pulled the door open. *Thanks Mitch,* he thought.

Unlike the previous warehouses they'd broken into, this door opened into a small office area, partitioned off from the rest of the building. The one frosted window allowed in enough light to illuminate four unused desks, a couple of chairs and some filing cabinets. A window in the far wall of the little office looked out into the open area of the warehouse. Slowly things became clearer as his eyes adjusted to the dim light. It was quiet, soundless in fact, except for his own breathing. The smell of dust and mold filled the frigid air and when he exhaled, tiny clouds of vapor wafted through the bluish-gray light.

Apophis was nowhere to be seen. Despite being the hunter, Colin grew uneasy, feeling more the prey. Apophis was here somewhere.

He moved silently over next to the warehouse window and peeked through. Windows spaced evenly around the perimeter of the exterior walls provided patchy illumination, leaving most of the warehouse in shadow. Through the glass, he saw no movement. The scars on his chest and cheek burned and itched. Still watching the empty warehouse interior, he reached out with his right hand and grasped the door knob. The door was light, as cheaply made as they come. The tinny knob turned smoothly, and Colin opened the door with little effort. He pulled it only wide enough to peer through the gap with one eye, ready to jump back if the demon attacked. Seeing nothing, he continued to draw the door open, pausing every so often to survey his new line of sight. But, like the other buildings, the darkness within was heavy and concealing, revealing nothing of what lay waiting. He almost had the door wide enough to walk through when the hinges groaned loudly, sounding like a dying man's whimper as it echoed off the distant brick walls.

To the right something moved and moved quickly. Through the weak light cast by one of the windows a black, scaly figure darted. Apophis. He was heading to the far-left corner of the building where Colin saw the glowing outline of another door in the back wall. Desperate, he rushed to intercept, dagger held at the ready.

"Apophis," he called as he ran.

Thirty feet away, the demon stopped and looked directly at him, chilling him more than the air. Dread swamped his spirit, driving his heart and lungs into a brutal rhythm. His hands wrung with clammy sweat and the leather jacket became stiflingly hot, sending perspiration in rivulets down between his shoulder-blades. The pain in his chest and cheek intensified. With a start, he realized he had left his helmet in Negaré's warehouse. His neck was exposed. Retreat seemed like a plausible, even good, idea.

Apophis laughed and the fear subsided.

The demon stood still, head turning from side to side, searching for what? Or whom? The demon realized that Colin was alone, and as much as a creature born of Hell can smile, it did.

"All alone, Colin?" it asked, its voice deep and menacing. "No exorcist?" Apophis cocked his head slightly as though someone were whispering in his ear. "Ah. Mitch, was it? He and Kylova are dancing together in Hell."

The comment hit Colin like a train. *In Hell? That can't be right.* Then he remembered what he was dealing with. "Don't bother lying to me." He held the Palo Santo dagger out in front of him, waiting for the moment to strike.

Apophis shrugged. "Is it a lie? How do you like this?" He glared at Colin and the shroud of terror and panic crashed into him again before dissipating like a retreating wave. "I'm sorry. I don't want you to flee. Once again, we have business." Then he added, "I should tell you that your son has been a terrible passenger. Whining and crying and terrified. But don't worry, he's got a first-class ticket to Hell where I'm sure we'll enjoy his company."

Colin fought the urge to launch himself at the demon, to stuff that dagger straight down his lying throat and send *him* to Hell, where he belonged. He knew Apophis was trying to goad him into doing something stupid, yet something checked his impulse. His knuckles cracked as he tightened the grip on his dagger.

Apophis fanned his fingers, the clawed tips slicing the dust-mites in the air. "And now, for some reason, you are trying to stand between me and the glory I deserve, and the scourge you deserve. I won't leave you alive this time. Today, your line ends."

It squared up with Colin and came forward, resolve and confidence in its stride as it closed the distance. Apophis's silvery eyes glanced at the Palo Santo dagger and quickly dismissed it as a fruitless, mortal, defense. Like a cougar, it sprang.

"It's time to push now, Julie," the doctor said.

"No. No. Not yet," Julie's tears slid down her sweaty face.

Mabel gripped her hand and caressed it. "You've done this before dear. It will be okay. The baby wants to come out now."

"Not like this. No." A contraction hit her and despite her protests, she clenched her muscles moving her baby boy down the birth canal.

Julie sobbed uncontrollably as she continued to work the child toward the doctor's waiting hands. Again and again she pushed as nature took control, not willing to be denied. Mabel held one of Julie's hands in her own while the other was around her shoulders, helping her to crunch up, thus pushing the baby on its way.

"You're cresting," the doctor said. Julie could hear her smile as she spoke behind the paper mask. On the next contraction the doctor said, "His head is out. Take a minute to breathe until the next contraction and we're almost home."

All Julie could think was, *does he have horns?*

Disengaged from the curb, Keller and O'Malley listened to the radio as one of the NYPD units called out the location of the black Jeep. O'Malley punched the address into the GPS and they were on their way to the location, only a few blocks from where they were presently cruising. In less than two minutes they were pulling in behind Mitch's Jeep, the NYPD car facing them on the other side of the road. The NYPD officers climbed out of their vehicle when they saw Keller and O'Malley arrive. As the four officers came together in the middle of the snow-covered road, Keller could hear the mobile radio of one of the officers put out a call requesting a specific unit respond to an armed robbery in progress. The officer held up one finger and keyed the microphone clipped to his shoulder, confirming receipt of the command and acquiescing.

The officer looked at Keller, shaking his head. "Well, you heard that. We gotta run. You okay here?"

Keller smiled inside. "Yeah. We're good. We just gotta find this guy and ask him some questions. Do you mind if we go ahead?"

"No problem, fella. Stay safe," the officer responded, directing his partner back to their car.

"You too," Keller said. He watched the NYPD officers leave, lights flashing. He turned to O'Malley who was examining the snow around the Jeep.

"He went into that warehouse," O'Malley said. Both men stared at the bland building, not knowing what waited inside.

"Let's take it easy," Keller said. He covered his holstered pistol with his hand. "If we can play this cool, I'm hoping he won't bolt."

O'Malley imitated his partner's posture and together the two deputies carefully opened the warehouse door and peeked inside. Seeing no one in the office area, they went in.

Colin's scream matched the demon's wail, the two voices blending in a dissonant harmony of good and evil. Apophis rode Colin to the floor. Devilish claws dug through the thick leather of the coat, slicing into the front of both of Colin's shoulders, the pain nearly causing him to relinquish control of the dagger he had driven into the center of Apophis's chest. But he felt the monster tremble and weaken, unprepared for the holy dagger. Without hesitation he began to recite the words that Mitch had taught him, the verses coming with little effort, like singing one of your favorite songs. His left hand wrapped around the dagger's handle, while his right worked to pull the hellish creature's claws from his shoulder.

The full weight of the demon atop him made his words breathy and chopped. Apophis jerked and thrashed, his claws digging and twisting in Colin's left shoulder. Apophis's left arm was locked in a stalemate battle with Colin's right, the dagger-like nails poised only centimeters from the wound they'd initially created. Heart hammering in his chest, Colin could feel himself tiring, the words harder and harder to say. It seemed the demon was getting stronger, or he was just failing. He had to get out from beneath the fiend, or he would die. Knowing more pain was to come, Apophis's wrist grasped in his hand, he yanked the demon's left arm hard to the left across Colin's chest and thrust up with his left hip. The movement sent the demon flipping over Colin's right shoulder where it landed on its back on the concrete.

Colin sprang to his unsteady feet, the wooden dagger still clutched in his left hand and now held out protectively in front of him as the black scaled creature rose onto its muscled legs, its chrome eyes locked on Colin. It was being cautious now, aware of the true nature of the weapon in Colin's grasp. The devilish eyes betrayed the monster's confidence and unwillingness to let the computer salesman best him. Combat and survival dominated Colin's thoughts, trying to anticipate his foe's next move. His breathing steadied and the fear dissipated completely, leaving only action and reaction.

Detective Keller and Sergeant O'Malley crashed through the flimsy office door into the warehouse, weapons drawn. For a moment, they trained their guns on Colin before realizing the black-scaled, and clawed creature, that was Apophis, presented a more serious threat. The metallic eyed demon scoffed as he charged the two officers, claws and fangs flashing.

"Run," Colin tried to scream, only to have it drowned out by the booming report of two nine-millimeter pistols. The guns did not silence as Apophis absorbed each round, quickly closing on the officers. As the vile creature threw himself on the two terrified men, Colin ran to intervene. He saw Apophis's clawed fingers bury themselves in each officer's chest as he slammed them back into the door frame where their heads collided with the solid brick wall. The men began to slump, dazed. Sliding to a halt, Colin thrust the ancient knife into Apophis's back. The pain of the attack forced the demon to yank his hands from the deputy's chests, letting them drop to the floor. Colin started reciting the exorcism, but Apophis kicked backward with one powerful leg, knocking the desperate father to the ground, somehow still clinging to his sacred dagger.

Instincts took over and Colin let himself continue to roll, bringing his feet underneath himself and springing up into an unsteady stance.

Apophis launched at him, dodging to the left as it swatted the dagger to the right across Colin's chest, leaving the blade slicing the floating, warehouse dust. The demon smashed into him and reached around Colin in a sort of hug, digging into the man's back with both sets of claws, putting them face to face. As they came together, Colin's left arm was pinned between his body and the black form of Apophis. If he tried to push the monster away, the claws in his back only dug deeper. With the limited movement of his left wrist, Colin was able to stick the tip of the dagger into the creature's neck. It weakened him, but not enough for Colin to take advantage.

Again Colin started the Rite, reciting the words in perfect order. He saw Apophis flag, but only slightly. His own strength was quickly draining away, the muscles in his shoulders becoming more and more useless tissue under the demon's claws.

O'Malley opened his eyes as he sucked in his missing breath, pain searing his chest. He continued to work his lungs as his mind try to comprehend the two figures locked in combat before him.

"You're too weak," the fiend said with a smile. "You cannot banish me. Your God has finally abandoned you."

Then Apophis thrust his face into Colin's. It wanted to watch his life drain from his eyes. He could see his own frightened reflection in those silvery orbs. He could see his blue, right eye start to twitch, so much like Claire, whose daddy vanquished the villains.

Don't let him take you out. Give 'im Hell.

Thomas Whitecloud's words echoed perfectly in Colin's mind, and he could still see the tiny inscription on the lead bullet. His mind came to life as his body was dying. *I can't get any closer than this,* he thought, reaching his right hand into his coat pocket. With one hand he drew the hammer back on the blessed, flintlock and angled it upward against Apophis's side.

"You're not strong enough to beat me," Apophis sneered.

"God is," Colin said as he pulled the trigger.

"Last push. And here he comes," the doctor exclaimed.

Solomon's Seal

CHAPTER TWENTY-ONE

There was the roar of thunder and a flash.
First, of Light.
Then of Darkness.

The flash was followed by an ear-piercing wail.
First, of a demon.
Then of a new-born child.

Crumpled against the wall, O'Malley turned to his right where he saw Keller staring with wide eyes at where Colin and a monster had been just a moment before.

Though he had finished the words of the Rite, Colin hadn't expected the pistol to finish it off in quite such an explosive manner. But there was no doubting it, Apophis was gone. The scent of burning tires filled his nostrils and there were small piles of charcoal-like dust on the floor. He'd done it, sent Apophis back to Hell. He pulled his phone out of his pocket, the screen cracked from his melee. A call to Julie went straight to voicemail, so he left a quick message that it was done. He followed that up with a text to her phone.

He stumbled over to Keller and O'Malley and looked at their shredded bullet proof vests. Seeing the confusion on their faces, he shrugged and shook his head. "You wouldn't have believed me."

Exhausted, he surveyed the floor around him and saw an alarming amount of blood pooling and smeared on the floor. His blood.

Colin dropped to his knees, his strength flying away like a frightened lamb. Then he fell over.

The delivery room erupted with a boom coupled with a wave of darkness that extinguished all light. The good doctor was knocked unconscious and fell over backward, the whimpering baby still in her grasp against her chest, the umbilical cord reaching over to where the placenta had dropped to the tile when it was ripped from Julie's body. The nurse was flung against the wall and lay crumpled on the floor, also unconscious. Julie was out cold, feet in the stirrups, head laying limp to one side.

Quietly, and with great purpose, Mabel shuffled over to the newborn and lifted him up into her arms and smiled down at the crying child.

Shaking her head slowly she said to him, "Uh uh uh. No sir, little fella. They couldn't take your daddy's soul and we sure ain't lettin' them have yours. I'll see you again in... eighty, ninety years or so." She bent and kissed the child's head and he immediately settled, his blue eyes searching without focus.

Mabel cut the cord, tied it off and cleaned the little boy off. Then she swaddled him up like she had his father and set him in the hospital bassinet. She found the certificate of live birth and filled in the important stuff, including the time of delivery: 1:23 P.M. Finally she lifted the child once more and carried him over to his mother. Carefully she shook Julie awake and laid the baby against her chest, also handing the young mother her cellphone and birth certificate.

"You have a happy, healthy little boy. Congratulations." Then she kissed Julie on the forehead and waddled from the room.

When she looked down at him, her eyes were grabbed by a brooch set into the child's swaddling blankets. A small, tarnished, tau cross clung to the baby's garment. Mabel's brooch. She quickly looked to the door to thank the woman, but she was gone.

Julie stared at her new baby boy, a lost look in her eyes, wondering if she held a monster. She still felt the natural love for him, that wasn't any different. But would she feel differently if he was...

Banishing the thought she glanced at the birth certificate for a moment and decided she didn't want to think about a name just yet. Then, hesitantly, Julie lifted her phone and noticed that there was an unread text from her husband. It read, "Got him! Pop that little sucker out!" It was time stamped 1:22 P.M.

Her laugh of joy roused the doctor and nurse from their slumber.

"Shit. What the hell happened to him?" The NYPD officer knelt beside Colin to check for a pulse. "Better call an ambulance," he said to his partner. "He's with us, but ain't gonna be for long." He looked at Keller and O'Malley, questioning.

"I think it was some sort of rabid primate," Keller said.

"I've never seen anything like that," O'Malley agreed.

"Where the hell is it?"

"We shot it," Keller said. "Couple of times and it took off. Never saw anything move that fast."

The officer quit his questioning and focused on administering first aid to Colin Hampton. To everyone's amazement, the ravaged man regained consciousness, sat up, and spoke. With the quantity of blood on the floor, they hadn't even expected him to live. All four officers were doubly awed when, after seeing the text from his wife on his cellphone,

Colin stood up and cried out in joy.

Colin's eyebrows arched and he held up one finger to Keller, indicating he needed a minute as he put his phone to his ear. "Hey Reginald. I'm good here. It's done. Everything is fine, though I have a rather angry Detective from Saratoga County staring at me. I gotta go." He disconnected the call.

When the first responding NYPD officers returned to their car to radio in a situation report, Colin went to the Saratoga County cops and started to explain what they'd just encountered. Keller and O'Malley shook their heads, nearly unable to process what they were hearing. If they hadn't witnessed it themselves, Colin was sure he'd be locked up in a psych-ward. Then he told them about his neighbor, Tim, and what had happened to Mitch. Keller finally said he could go, though he would want to talk to him more in the next couple of days, just to make sure everyone was still sane.

Colin thanked the detective who tried to return his smile. Then Colin climbed in the Jeep and started to drive, happy they hadn't checked his pockets where they would have found the gun that killed Myska. He wasn't sure why no one had asked him about that, but he wasn't going to look a gift horse in the mouth.

Even in his pain and exhaustion, he had to smile. He was alive and he'd saved their son's soul.

He couldn't have done it without Mitch. Mitch. The tears he hadn't been able to shed earlier came out in a gushing torrent. Though the mens' time together had been short, it had been invaluable. Mitch had been a brother, a father, a teacher, and a friend, all wrapped into one.

The thought reminded him that he had an errand to run before he left the city.

He found an open meter just half a block from the Irish pub where Lily Founder worked. He stared at the establishment a full two minutes before he walked up and grabbed the door handle. He felt the idiot for thinking that Mitch had been sexually attracted to Lily. In hindsight, it was so obvious. He pulled the door open and walked over to the bar.

At the bartender's summons, Lily came bouncing out of the kitchen, her dark hair and green eyes so clearly not her own. Colin asked her to sit with him in a booth and stared at his folded hands, wondering where to begin.

"Where's Father Mitch?" the young woman asked.

Colin turned his head sideways, still trying to imagine what to say. Finally, he said, "Lily, I'm sorry. Father Mitch was killed today." He felt the salt sting his eyes.

Lily gasped and put her hands over her mouth, sorrow shading her features. "That's awful. What happened?"

Colin looked up and massaged his forehead.

"He was murdered."

Eyes and mouth wide, the waitress exclaimed "Murdered?" The bartender looked over, concerned and obviously curious. "Who did it?"

"The most evil being we'll ever meet. But his killer is no longer with us." Colin's throat tightened and his nose burned. He couldn't imagine how painful it must have been for Mitch to hear his daughter call him 'Father', and not be able to reveal the true nature and depth of his love for her.

Lily wept, quietly brushing the tears from her pale face and green eyes. "I can't believe it. How could someone hurt him? He was so sweet."

Colin pulled the photo out and placed it face down on the table so she could see the birth date on its back. "Mitch gave me this and asked me to give it to you." He slid it across the table to the grieving young woman. She looked down at it, her eyebrows crunching together when she saw her name and recognized her birthday. She flipped it over and stared at it, confused.

"Where'd he get this? I was only eighteen in this picture."

"Your mother gave it to him."

She held her head in her hands, trying to make sense of the answer, but Colin saw she couldn't process it. "Your father loved you very much."

Waves of tears flooded from the young woman's eyes, her hands enveloping her nose and mouth to quiet her sobs. "Father? But he was a priest! How?"

A sad grin pulled at the corners of Colin's mouth. "He wasn't always a priest."

Before Colin could start the car to begin his long drive home, his phone rang. It was Reginald.

"Did Mitch happen to tell you anything about the blood test we did on you?"

"No. Why?" A moment of fear enveloped him as he recalled the Demon's Wrath. "Is everything okay?"

"Yes. No worries. But we do have the results back and..."

"What?" Colin nearly shouted. He just wanted to know that he and his family were safe, and this nightmare was over.

There was a pause on the other end of the line. "You have a very interesting lineage. Do you think you could come back to New York sometime next week and discuss it with the bishop?"

"No. I gotta be with my family, my new son. I'm done here."

"Maybe not."

Colin's heart fell. He wasn't about to risk going up against another demon. "There are more of them?"

"No. But we've been waiting to find you for... close to eight-hundred years."

That took Colin off guard, in spite of all the eye-opening experiences he'd had over the last several days. Still, an uneasy light of revelation was beginning to peek through the clouds. "What about my lineage? Tell me."

Reginald took a deep breath on the other end of the line. "You are a descendant of Saint Anthony."

Colin stared silently out the windshield of the Jeep, the phone still pressed to his ear.

"That's why you survived."

"How is that even possible?" Colin protested. "Wasn't Saint Anthony a priest when he was alive?"

He could hear a quiet chuckle before Reginald responded. "Perhaps he wasn't always a priest."

END